Unmasked

KELSEY CHAPMAN

Contents

To Isaac: Write your own story.

Chapter 1

Even the shades of green are different in Ireland, somehow deeper and more vibrant than any I've ever seen. I guess there is a reason it's called the Emerald Isle.

The forest around me encompasses a charming dirt road that leads to the cottage where I'll be staying for the next few months. The woods are alive with the sound of small woodland creatures: birds calling to one another, squirrels digging through the underbrush in search of food.

The crooked trees lining the path I meander along give a feeling of whimsy, but I suspect they could be equally as frightening at night with their spindly limbs reaching out overhead.

I emerge from the copse of trees to the sight of the little cottage. Settled neatly in the middle of a small cleared field, it looks every bit the fairytale home I had hoped it would. I imagine this stay will be nothing short of magical.

The home seems as if it's completely isolated from the outside world, but the small village it belongs to is only a few miles walk from the cottage.

I let myself in through the tiny wooden gate made into a low-lying stone fence surrounding the property. I've nearly made it to the green front door when it opens suddenly, revealing a kind-faced elderly woman, my host during this stay.

The flyer at my local library had been scant on the details about what sort of cultural exchange program this would be, but it was Ireland; I couldn't not apply for it. To my surprise and delight, the host selected me.

I've been ecstatic for months leading up to the trip, and now that I'm here, it feels surreal. I couldn't be more excited about not just visiting, but getting to stay for a few months in a place I have loved and dreamed about since I was a young girl.

Living in the same place all my life, I've never traveled very far, and I was ready for a change. Of course, it helps that I've always felt a strange pull toward this country, never quite knowing why. Maybe it's the history, or the slow-paced, old fashioned way of living in most of the smaller villages. Things like that seem to pull an old soul like myself in. Or maybe there's a little bit of me hoping something magical could happen, despite knowing their myths and legends are just that: stories.

But one can dream, right?

Either way, being here now just feels *right*, like I'm where I'm meant to be.

"Hello! Welcome, welcome! I'm so excited to meet ya'!" the elderly lady exclaims as she steps out to meet me. "I'm Mairead and I will be taking care of ya' while you're here." She greets me with a tight hug, the top of her head barely skimming my chin as I return the embrace. Reaching barely over five feet myself, I don't come across this occurrence often.

Mairead has a rounded jolly face with eyes that don't quite convey the years on her, and she seems just as sprightly in movement too. Her white hair is piled into a big, loose bun at the crown of her head and her dress and cardigan look like they're from many years past.

"I'm Carlin, it's wonderful to finally meet you. Your home is lovely," I answer her greeting.

She gives me a warm smile and ushers me through the front door, "I hope you will love it here."

The interior of the cottage is just as I had imagined it would be, leaving no doubt in my mind that I will, in fact, love it here. It's low white ceilings are crossed with natural wooden beams, giving the space a warm and cozy feeling. The mismatched living room furniture somehow looks like it all belongs together. On my left, the far wall is adorned by a stone fireplace and a wooden door that seems to lead to a bedroom. To my right is the dining area, filled by a large antique table set with lovely old dishes, and beyond it I catch a glimpse of the kitchen through another door.

Mairead leads me toward the staircase in front of us. "Your room will be up here, lass. Just up these stairs and to the left. You'll be right above me. I hope it's to your liking." She smiles up at me, turning to walk through the quaint wooden door to my room.

The bedroom is decorated with wallpaper printed with whimsical vines and dainty pink flowers and is much larger than I was expecting. Two doors on the right lead to a small closet and a private bathroom, Mairead explains to me. The sight of the wrought iron bed made up with crisp white linens make me realize just how jet lagged I actually am. My host, seeming to sense it, gives me a gentle pat on the back,

"Why don't you go have a little lie down before you unpack? You must be exhausted."

Being someone who doesn't like to draw attention or have a fuss made over me, no matter how small, I'm grateful she said so. I give her a smile that says as much. I wouldn't have dared to bring it up myself, at the risk of sounding rude.

She turns to leave the room, closing the door behind her as I make a beeline for the inviting bed. It isn't long before I start to drift off to sleep, apparently more fatigued than I had originally thought, because I think I see movement low in the corner of the room just as I begin to fall asleep.

I wake feeling quite rested after a deep sleep filled with odd dreams of tiny people whispering and inspecting me. Moving out of the bed and towards the window seat, I open the casement windows to peer out at the grounds of the cottage. Mairead has a surprisingly sizable yard, with what seems to be a small working farm.

The scent of something sweet and freshly baked fills my senses and I decide to head for its source. When I reach the bottom of the stairs, I can hear my host humming to herself in the kitchen. I cross the threshold into the small room as she's pulling a cake out from the oven. She looks up and beams when she notices me, "Oh good! I was hoping you'd be able to have a slice right out of the oven."

She takes a plate from a cupboard in the corner, cuts a generous slice and hands it over to me. "It's apple cake, a well-loved recipe, made with eggs fresh from my own chickens. I would've preferred the apples to be from my trees, but they're still a bit out of season."

"I'm sure it'll be delicious anyway," I smile shyly at her. "Thank you for this. You really didn't have to go through all of this trouble just for me." I've always hated to feel like someone was having to go out of their way for me, so having any sort of fuss made over me is a little torturous.

"It's really no trouble at all," she assures me. "I want to make sure you feel welcomed and comfortable here."

Her response helps to ease my guilt a little.

She ushers me to the dining room, following behind with her own plate. "So, tell me about yourself," she says, taking her seat across from me.

I laugh a little nervously. Talking about myself has always been a little difficult. "There isn't much to tell there," I shrug. "I'm quite the homebody, more of a loner really. I prefer living in between the pages of my books rather than going out and partying or getting into trouble."

She smiles warmly at me, nodding and listening intently to everything I tell her.

Aside from my family and oldest friend, Natalie, I've always been a little invisible and sometimes I wonder whether it's out of choice or circumstance. Back home, if you weren't part of the few 'small town celebrity' families, you were relegated to the sidelines. I never minded though. I much prefer it over fake friendships and face-value relationships.

Mairead and I sit together a long while, enjoying the taste of the cake while getting to know one another.

It's early evening by the time I finish unpacking and a knock on the door signals Mairead's smiling entrance. "Would you mind running back to town for me, dearie?" she asks, sticking her head into the room.

"Not at all. What do you need?" I answer cheerfully.

She smiles, satisfied at my agreement. "I need you to go to our local pub, The Lonely Crown, and find a young man for me by the name of Maddox O'Connall. I need him to come 'round the house and help with some things tomorrow, and I just don't think I have it in me to walk all that way." Her eyes gleam as she explains, but I can't quite figure out why.

I answer with a nod, "Yes ma'am, I can go for you. How will I know who to look for?"

"Just ask around, they'll point ya' to him." She gives me a playful wink as she turns to leave the room.

Since this will be my first proper impression on the town, I decide to change out of my comfortable travel clothes. With not much time to spare, I throw on a simple blue dress that managed to stay unwrinkled in my suitcase.

My phone rings as I'm pulling a light cardigan on over the sleeveless bodice to combat the evening's coming chill. "Well? How is it?" My best friend's voice comes through before I can even mutter a greeting.

I laugh, "Geez Nat, it's only been half a day at the most. You've got to give me more time than that."

"Excuse me," she says, "it's not every day your best friend gets to go on her literal dream trip. I'm excited for you, even if Ireland wouldn't be *my* cup of tea...too rural, not enough excitement."

I can't help but roll my eyes at my friend. Pulling the phone away from my ear, I glance at the time. "You know our versions of excitement are two completely different things. Shouldn't you be in bed anyway? Isn't it late there?"

"No, *grandma*," she chides. "My night's just getting started. I'm going to meet up with a few new friends I met at work for some drinks."

We'd always been two completely different people, but somehow still managed to stay friends for years despite it all.

I pull my bedroom door closed, heading down the stairs. "Well, you go have fun. I've got to run an errand for the lady hosting me, so I'm heading into the village."

"Alright, and don't *you* forget to have fun either. Crack open that shell of yours a bit. Flirt with some cute guys!" she teases.

I can't help but laugh at that. "You know that's not what I'm here for."

"You never know...aren't you the one always going on and on about those romances in your books? It'll never happen unless you get out there and try."

"Don't make fun of me, I'm not that delusional," I joke before saying my goodbyes.

Chapter 2

T he walk to town is pleasant and quick, though the growing
  darkness puts me a little on edge. I find my way easily to the
town square, straight out of a storybook with its cobblestone streets
and fountain bubbling in the center. The store fronts, nestled tightly
together, glow gold with lights from within. Looking around, I spot
The Lonely Crown and change my course to get there.

The big front windows are made with antique clouded glass, leaving
the interior a mystery from the outside. When I walk through the front
door, I'm greeted by a full house. People are lining the bar; the tables
and booths look to be just as packed. My ears are immediately greeted
with the din of patrons mingled with the sound of live traditional
music playing from somewhere deeper within the room.

I shyly make my way toward the bar, thinking the bartender will be the best person to direct me to the man I'm looking for. "Excuse me," my quiet voice is swallowed up by the noise of the crowd.

"You're gonna have to be louder than that if you want to be heard around here, lass," answers an older gentleman just beside me. He gives me a friendly smile, tipping his flat cap.

"Well, since you heard me, maybe you can help," I answer his smile with my own. "Do you know a man by the name of Maddox O'Connall? And where I can find him?"

"Aye, I do. He should be in the back of the house with the rest of his lads." He points toward a room behind me, partially divided from the rest, and gives me a bemused look.

Someone calls out a request for the band as I head for the room, something called the "Glasgow Reel."

This room is a little more intimate than the rest, with only a handful of round tables set inside, and the top half of the entrance wall covered in the same cloudy glass as the front of the pub. Dark wood panels partially line the other walls, the unpaneled parts covered in photographs from over the years. Only a couple of the tables are occupied, all by young men looking to be in different stages of their twenties.

As soon as I step over the threshold, they all stop their conversation to look towards me. Despite the nerves that I so suddenly feel, I smile.

"How's it going there?" One of them with short brown hair says, looking at me curiously.

"Would any of you happen to be Maddox O'Connall?" I answer with a question of my own, fighting past my nerves.

Another young man, a handsome dark haired one, looks to me lazily with a hint of a smile on his lips. "Whose askin'?" he says with a deep, Irish lilt.

"Ms. Mairead sent me to find him. I'm assuming that would be you?" I raise an eyebrow mockingly, letting him know I've already figured it out.

He stands and offers me his chair, pulling another one up for himself. "You would assume correctly," he says, that hint of a smile finally spreading across his face.

Up close it's hard to ignore how handsome he is. Brown hair so dark it's nearly black is cut short, but left long enough to see the beginnings of curls forming. A thick fan of black lashes frame blue eyes that look to hold more mystery than the sea. That slow smile fades into a soft pout as I catch myself staring, quickly shifting my gaze to look around at the others there. Wanting to break the awkward silence, I introduce myself, giving an awkward wave around the table, "I'm Carlin, I'll be living with Mairead for the next few months."

The one who spoke to me first speaks again, this time more animated. "Ah, you must be one of the exchanges we've been hearing about!"

"One of?" I'm caught off guard by that statement, I had thought I was the only one.

"Yeah, Mairead has been talking about taking in guests for *ages*, but she's finally gotten around to doing it. The whole village has been talking about it. We hardly ever get any actual visitors that *stay*," he explains, his excitement at having someone new in town palpable and comical.

Before I have a chance to reply, he's talking again. "So, what made you choose to come here?"

"It kind of chose me actually," I shrug sheepishly. "I was tired of seeing the same three stoplights every day, and I've always felt a longing to visit Ireland. After seeing Mairead's advertisement, I took a shot putting in the application, and the next thing I knew, I was on a plane headed here."

Maddox laughs a little beside me, shooting me a sidelong glance. "So instead you came to see *no* stoplights…"

I grin, returning his gaze. "What can I say? I've always been a small-town girl; I can't go having too much adventure all at once."

"I'm Theo by the way," the talkative one sticks his hand out for me to shake. Obviously the most outspoken of the group, Theo gestures around the table, introducing me to everyone there.

He points to one with sandy brown hair hanging to his brow, "This is Kellan." Then another with brown hair matching his own, only shoulder length, "This is my twin brother, Thomas. You already know Maddox, so that leaves Fin," he finishes, gesturing to a young man with long wheat blonde hair hanging around his shoulders. They all nod my way, murmuring their own polite greetings before we're interrupted.

"You aren't going to introduce me?" A snarky voice says from just behind us. It's one of the guys from the only other occupied table in the room, I realize. He gets up and makes his way over to me, giving off a sleazy air. Performing a mocking bow, his greasy blonde locks fall over his shoulder as he flourishes his hand, waiting for me to take it. "I'm Liam. It's not every day we get some new sights to see around here," he drawls.

I politely extend my hand, expecting another handshake, but instead he kisses it. I wouldn't usually mind, but it's overtly clear that he's making a mockery of the usually genteel act, and it makes me uncomfortable. I draw my hand back, placing it in my lap away from him. My discomfort must be apparent because Maddox unfolds himself from his chair, placing himself between Liam and me. Maddox is taller than I'd realized. He stands over Liam by a few inches, but dwarfs him just by presence alone. "Get out of here Liam, before you get yourself into trouble. I don't feel like dealing with you tonight."

"Fine, fine," Liam says, holding his hands up in mock surrender. "I can't have any fun." He backs away slowly and finally turns to leave, his two silent companions with him.

Maddox sits back down and studies me for a moment, seeming to make sure I'm not fazed. "So, can I ask *why* you were looking for me?"

"Oh, right!" Being so distracted by the last few moments, I had almost forgotten why I was here in the first place. "Mairead needs your help with some things around her home, but she didn't feel like walking all the way to town," I answer with a small shrug.

He nods at me. "Alright then. Come on, I'll take you back so you won't have to walk alone in the dark." Getting up from the table, he gestures with his head for me to follow. I say a quick goodbye to all his friends and follow him toward the front of the pub.

The sidelong glances being thrown at him from the other patrons are hard to ignore. They almost have me questioning whether I should be leaving alone with this man and it gives me pause.

He notices I've stopped and turns to look at me questioningly. "You coming?" he asks, brows raised.

The tension building in the room is palpable and puts me on edge. Confrontation, no matter how insignificant, has always made me horribly anxious, and judging by the way some of the men in the room are looking at Maddox, confrontation won't be far away if we aren't out of their sights soon.

I nod quickly, stifling my nerves as I follow him out the door. Mairead wouldn't have me come alone to find this man if he wasn't trustworthy. Would she?

Chapter 3

We walk out of the town square and make our way toward the small country road that leads to the cottage. "You really don't have to walk me all this way, I can get back on my own with no trouble," I look over to Maddox walking beside me, hands in his jeans pockets, surveying the dark fields around us.

He slides his eyes over to me, "Oh, I have no doubt you could do it; you just shouldn't be alone with the likes of Liam skulking about." He tosses me a playful grin, "That, and it gets a little scary out here at night."

"I do not scare that easily," I say with mock offense. But I do remember how haunting the woods are, even with the sun still low in the sky, and I'm secretly glad for the company. "So, tell me about yourself and your friends," I prompt, trying to break the awkward silence settling between the two of us.

"There's not much to tell," he shrugs. "We've all been friends for quite a long time, and considered the local outcasts by most. We do odd jobs for the ones that don't feel the need to look at us sideways, mostly farm work." His words are short and clipped. It's apparent he doesn't like talking about it.

So, I think, *I wasn't wrong about the looks he was getting as we left the pub*. He didn't seem to notice them though, apparently accustomed to it. I don't really understand the looks. I feel at ease around him, though there does seem to be a bit of a mysterious air hanging about him.

"Why are they like that toward you?" I push softly, not wanting to cause him to put up his guard.

He looks down at me, shrugging again. His nonchalance doesn't quite hide the hint of stiffness there, giving away his discomfort. "It's a small town. People talk, rumors grow, and with nothing better to do, they don't die down."

I breathe a laugh, "Trust me, I understand completely. My hometown isn't much bigger than this village and the people sound the same. If you aren't what they deem *somebody* then you kind of get shoved to the side. Then they turn their noses up, whispering about you for being different and not being part of their crowd. I don't mind it really; I seem to have a natural inclination towards being a loner. I mean, I have friends, some really close ones actually," I continue, "but, I'm quickly forgotten about when something more appealing comes along; always more of a wallflower, really." I realize I'm rambling now and shrug awkwardly, a little surprised by how easily I opened up to him. I'm usually anything but talkative.

He gives a sideways smile, "Somehow, I doubt that."

I can tell he's said everything about himself that he's going to say, so I direct the conversation elsewhere. "What's with that Liam guy anyway? Is he really so bad that I couldn't walk home alone?"

He doesn't even look at me to answer this time, his eyes scanning the night again. "Liam and his crew have always been untrustworthy. I've known them just as long as the lads and we've always run in different circles."

So many answers that aren't really answers at all with him; I decide to give up prying altogether. My phone pings in my sweater pocket, taking me off guard. I huff a laugh, rolling my eyes at sight of the message there.

"What is it?" he asks curiously.

I grin at him, "It's my best friend. She's sent me a reminder to have fun while I'm here." *And flirt*, I think, a blush warming my cheeks as I look at the handsome man beside me. "She's always pushing me to *'come out of my shell*,'" I explain at his inquisitive look.

He nods, understanding written on his features, "But you don't want to."

"Not really. It's safe in here," I say, laughing.

He returns my laugh and I shrug, "In all seriousness though, I think shells are good sometimes. They keep people out that don't need to be there."

"And show you the ones who are willing to work hard enough to be let in," he says.

"Exactly," I say, staring up at him, a little surprised. I've never had anyone understand me so easily. It's a breath of fresh air.

We come to the wooded area just before Mairead's cottage and my anxiety rises slightly at the sight of the spindly trees, like creeping hands, hanging over us in the dark. I was right when I assumed that they would be ominous during the night.

I bump into Maddox's side, not realizing that I had instinctually moved closer to him. He grins down at me with a dark eyebrow raised.

"Not scared are you, Mhuirnín?" he teases, the Irish word he uses pleasant to my ears.

I stare up at him defiantly, "Not at all, just a little cold."

Maybe.

"Well, I'd help you out if I had a jacket," he says, gesturing to his black t-shirt. For the first time tonight I notice the unique necklace he's wearing. The pendant is a model of a silver sword, an old and worn leather strap fastening it around his neck. Noticing my gaze, he tucks the necklace under his collar as the thatched cottage comes into view.

Walking up the path toward the front door, I can hear Mairead speaking to someone inside. Maybe another one of her guests has arrived? As we walk through the front door, we turn to find her, alone, coming out of the kitchen towards us.

"Weren't you just talking to someone?" I question, a bit incredulous.

"Oh no dear, sometimes I talk to myself," she giggles. "Must be a sign of my age." She notices Maddox, then, standing just inside the doorway. "Oh, Maddox! Thank you for bringing her back all this way. I trust she told you I needed some help tomorrow?"

"Yes, ma'am." He looks playfully suspicious when speaking to her, like there's an inside joke I'm oblivious to. "I'll be here in the morning to get started on whatever you need. Now, I should be off," he says, turning to leave.

I step toward the door to catch him. He seems to notice out of the corner of his eye and turns around. "Thank you again for walking me back. I'm sorry I interrupted your night with your friends."

He regards me coolly, and standing this close to him in the light, I notice a sliver of one of his blue eyes is brown; A flaw that somehow makes him even more striking.

"You are welcome to interrupt us any night," he smiles softly down at me.

An answering smile spreads across my face, butterflies running wild in my stomach as he turns again to leave.

"He's a lovely lad," Mairead breathes wistfully behind me. She seems to like him and doesn't appear to buy into whatever rumors he says circulate around him. I'm not sure I do either. There was such an ease between us on the walk back to the cottage.

Mairead starts, "Oh my, you must be hungry! Would you like some dinner? I ate earlier while you were gone."

"I'm actually not too hungry tonight. If you have something light, I'll take that and be fine," I assure her.

She walks to the kitchen, speaking to me over her shoulder, "I have soda bread I made just this morning, if you'd like, and some good old Irish cheddar."

I come into the kitchen behind her as she's pulling out a plate for me. "I can get it all myself, Mairead. No need to trouble yourself."

She gives me a friendly smile, "It doesn't trouble me at all. I enjoy helping people." With that, I let her prepare me a snack of bread, butter, and cheese while I stand, propped against the thick wooden counter. She hands me the plate on which she's slipped another sliver of her apple cake, and we go to sit together again at the dining table. Unable to resist, I start in on the cake first.

"So how did you like the village? Did you meet anyone interesting?" she asks me.

"It's a beautiful village, just what I'd hoped for," I answer genuinely. "And I did meet a few people, mostly Maddox's friends." Then I remember something Theo had said to me.

"There was talk of more exchange guests. Is that true?" I ask.

"Yes, dear. I've always wanted to host guests, lots of them if I could, but this year it will be just you and one other girl."

"I had no idea, I thought I was the only one." I'm surprised by her answer. "Why isn't the other girl here yet?"

She gives me a mischievous grin, "Because I decided to have you come a bit earlier. When I saw your information and photo, I knew I'd like you. Not that I won't like the other young lady, I'm quite sure we'll all get along famously, but there's just something about you. You're just what some of us in this town need, I think."

Her sentiments are sweet, but leave me wondering just what it was about me that led her to come to that conclusion. Pushing for that information would be a little rude, I think, so instead I lead the conversation elsewhere. "There was another guy, Liam, at the pub tonight, who was very..."

"Unpleasant?" she finishes for me.

"Yes," I look pointedly at her. "He's the reason Maddox walked back with me. He said I shouldn't be alone with him around."

"Aye, I'm glad Mr. O'Connall stepped up and did that. Liam is a lout who can't be trusted, especially with a young and pretty girl like you," she says matter-of-factly.

I guess he really is as bad as Maddox made him out to be. I nod my head in understanding as I finish up my bread and cheese. Taking the plate to the kitchen, I wash it before she has a chance, not wanting to make her do any more work for me tonight.

"I think I'm going to shower and get to bed; the jet-lag still hasn't quite worn off," I tell her as I dry the plate.

She pats me on the back and nods, "I understand, lass. I'll be seeing ya' in the morning."

"Thank you for everything," I tell her. "Goodnight, Mairead."

On my way up the stairs, I think I notice something darting quickly away near the fireplace out of the corner of my eye. Startled, I whip my head in the direction of the movement, but nothing is there.

"Everything alright?" Mairead questions, smiling up from the foot of the stairs, not seeming to notice anything.

I shrug it off as just being tired again. "I must be really sleepy; I keep thinking I'm seeing things."

She laughs softly at me, waving a dismissive hand, "Must be the jet-lag."

I make my way to my room, grab my pajamas, and head straight for the private bath. The bathroom is small, but has room enough for a claw-foot tub tucked into the corner, pedestal sink with a mirror, a skinny storage cabinet, and of course, a toilet. The tub has a shower head added and an iron bar around the top for a curtain. I turn the shower on as hot as I can stand it, thankful to finally be able to wash the grime of travel away.

Slipping into the cool sheets of the unfamiliar bed brings on a slight pang of homesickness. It's hard for a homebody like me to be away from everything comforting and familiar, even if it is a place I've longed for. But no one ever grows or changes if they don't push the boundaries of their comfort zone every now and then.

To combat the heaviness threatening to settle in my chest, I fill my thoughts with all the amazing things that could await me on this trip until eventually, I drift off to sleep.

Chapter 4

The smell of breakfast cooking pulls me from sleep. Pushing myself out of bed, I go to sit on the window seat until the fog of sleep has cleared from my head. I've never been a morning person, no matter how hard I try to be.

Leaning my head up against the cool windowpanes, I hear an engine running. A few moments later an old green truck comes to a stop alongside the cottage. Maddox steps out of the driver's side. He's dressed for work in worn jeans, a white t-shirt, and boots. I force myself to tamp down an unexpected feeling of butterflies in my stomach at the sight of him. Opening the windows, I lean out to greet him, but he sees me before I have a chance to speak.

"Good mornin'. I'm sorry if I woke you," he says, eyes squinted against the morning sun. A small grin tugs at the edges of his lips.

"Good morning," I answer, tilting my head to the side, "and you didn't wake me, what makes you think that?"

A bright smile spreads across his face. "No reason," he answers and heads toward the front door without another word.

Finally ready to start the day, I go to brush my teeth and I see it. To my horror, my brunette curls are wild in the mirror, looking very much like I had just rolled out of bed. That explains his roguish grin, much to my embarrassment.

I quickly freshen up before throwing on a pair of jeans and a thin sweater, then pull my hair back out of my face, leaving a few small curls to frame it. I slip on a pair of sneakers as I make my way downstairs.

Maddox is sitting at the table, enjoying breakfast, and Mairead is just coming from the kitchen with two plates in her hands. "Good mornin', dear! I hope you're hungry, I've made plenty of food," she greets me cheerfully, setting the plates down and sliding into her seat.

I slip into my own chair, immediately starting in on the eggs on my plate. Foregoing a normal dinner last night has left me feeling famished this morning. "Is there anything you need my help with this morning?" I ask, unsure of what daily work she tends to.

"No, lass," she answers, "but you could help Maddox this morning if you'd like."

"You really don't have to," he interjects. A little too quickly, I notice.

Mairead pats his hand gently across the table. "I'm sure she wouldn't mind. It'll give her something to pass the time."

"I do better on my own," he answers, barely looking up from his plate. The sting of rejection I feel at his attitude this morning catches me off guard.

"Nonsense lad, you can't do everything all on your own," Mairead urges.

I can only sit there silently, feeling like an intruder in some inside conversation I'm not yet privy too.

At no sign of objection from either of us she speaks again, "It's settled then! Carlin will help you. She needs someone close to her own age to spend time with. She shouldn't be cooped up with an old bird like me all day."

Looking back to my plate, I fight to hide my discomfort. It's not that I mind helping, I don't at all, but it's more than apparent that he doesn't welcome the company.

Mairead laughs, looking between us with a gleam in her eye as we finish our breakfast in silence. When Maddox finally makes his way toward the front door, he glances over his shoulder at me, "Are you comin'?"

I excuse myself from the table, leaving Mairead to her breakfast and follow him out the door. "What happened to, *'you're welcome to interrupt anytime*?" I parrot back to him, unable to hide the slight annoyance in my voice.

"That's not exactly what I said." That ghost of a smile plays at the edge of his lips at my attempt of an Irish accent, but he hides it quickly. He finally answers my question, pulling out a toolbox from the back of the old truck before starting for the small barn on the property. "Look, it's nothing personal. It's just that this isn't gonna go any quicker with you distracting me. Besides, I doubt you've ever done work like this a day in your life."

"Well, it kind of feels personal." I stop following him, crossing my arms in the process. "Even if I've never done it before, I happen to learn very quickly. At least give me a chance." I try to hide the surprising pang of hurt I feel at his different attitude toward me this morning, but I'm sure he can tell. I was unfortunately born with the curse of every tiny emotion I feel showing blatantly on my face.

He stops walking then and turns to face me completely, his eyes softening. "I'm sorry. I had a rough night last night and it's showing in my attitude today."

"Well that's not my fault, so don't take it out on me." I say as I shoulder past him, heading for the barn again.

He catches up to me as I'm opening the barn door, grabbing my arm and gently turning me to face him. "I am sorry, Carlin. I shouldn't treat ya' that way and there is no excuse for it. I don't realize how coarse I can come off sometimes."

He looks genuinely apologetic, but before I have time to consider how having him this close makes my stomach do back flips, I notice he has a busted lip along with a fresh bruise forming on his jawline. "Where did that come from? Those weren't there last night." Before I know it, I'm reaching out to touch his face, but I quickly stop myself. He rolls his eyes, but I can tell it's not at me.

"Liam and his ilk didn't take kindly to my running them off last night. They've never been a brave lot, only act that way when they get the jump on someone."

My eyebrows shoot up. "Liam did that to you? Just for running him out of the pub?"

"He's spiteful, and I'm sure my getting in the way of whatever he was trying with you didn't help. We should get to work," he says, putting an end to the conversation. I don't push any further, even though I can't help but feel there's more to the story.

"What kind of work are we doing exactly?" I ask him as we enter the barn. He points toward the back corner to an old cattle stall in disrepair.

"Mairead has finally gotten a few new cows and needs us to fix the old stalls for them. Other than that, just cleanup and minor repairs. It'll take more than just today for us to finish it all though."

"Oh, it's *us* now? Not just *you*?" I say, only half teasing.

He gives me a wry grin, shaking his head, "You're not going to let me off the hook easily are ya', Mhuirnín?" The foreign word slips effortlessly off his tongue.

"Nope, and don't try to soften me up with your sweet little Irish words," I protest, but he knows it's working judging by the gleam in his eye and the pleased smile on his face. It is working, but I'm determined not to let him off the hook so easily.

It surprises me just how easily I've taken to him. Talking, joking, flirting, things like that don't usually come effortlessly for me. But there's something about him that feels safe and familiar, and I like it.

He hands me a hammer, telling me to start pulling old nails from the stall while he brings in the pile of new lumber from his truck. I make quick work of the few nails left in the old wood, finishing up just as he's coming back through the door carrying the new wood over his shoulder. "What next?" I question.

He hands me a bag with new nails, "Put the old ones in with these and give me nails as I need them. Mairead likes to be quite frugal, so we'll reuse what we can." He moves the old wood out of the way and gets started on building a brand-new place for the animals, as I fight the rising annoyance at not being trusted to manage anything but the nails. He could at least give me a chance.

"I don't know Mairead, he doesn't seem like he wants the help or the company," I say to her over dinner a few days later.

"Ignore it," she says. "He's always been quiet and moody. But he needs someone, whether he wants to admit it or not. He's just used to being alone, been that way most of his life. But he'll come around. It takes time to chip away at the walls we build around ourselves. There's more to him than that aloof, detached facade he puts on."

"Are we still talking about fixing the barn or something else entirely?" I ask, giving her a pointed look. It's obvious she's trying to play matchmaker, and enjoying it immensely. Her answering mischievous grin is all the answer I need.

It takes a little over two weeks to completely finish the repairs on the barn. Of course, it could've passed a little quicker if it weren't for Mairead sending us on new and random errands together; always armed with a quick explanation of why she sent us instead of doing it herself. None of it was really a problem though. I'd rather enjoyed getting to see different parts of the area, and it seems with every little bit of time spent together, the pleasant ease of that first night settles between Maddox and I again.

It's hard to ignore the pull I feel toward him. There's a certain steadiness he holds that is so unlike anyone I've known. Something about him is so old-fashioned, like he's cut from a different cloth, and I find myself drawn to it.

He's been careful to keep up that stoic mask, but there are moments where I can see right through it. He'll smile while I sing and dance to music on my phone to pass the time and ease the load of work. He's even outright laughed a few times, a deep dulcet sound, and I can't ignore the way it makes my heart flutter. At first, he wouldn't let his guard slip for long, always snapping back to that stoic, stony facade. But over time he'd let that careful mask slip for longer and longer.

Mairead was right, he isn't anywhere near as callous as the picture he tries to paint of himself. There's a softness and gentleness there that I've been able to catch glimpses of.

"Why don't you let me take you to see the cliffs when we're done here?" After working in comfortable silence on the final touches of the barn, the sound of Maddox's voice catches me off guard, pulling me from my thoughts.

"What cliffs?"

"Ah, they're gorgeous. Just a few miles out from the other side of town. I think you'd enjoy them," he says, looking up at me as he spreads fresh hay, his striking eyes framed by unfairly thick eyelashes.

It's hard not to jump too eagerly at the chance to go anywhere with him, but my free hand finds its way to my hip, the other still holding a rake. "Is this a scheme to get back into my good graces?" I say with my best attempt at a flat expression. I'd been teasing him relentlessly about his attitude toward me that first day, drawing out any lightness from him that I could. It had seemed to work a bit; he'd started teasing back after a while.

He stands and walks over to me, so close that I need to turn my face up to see his. "I really do think you'd love them," he says softly, his accent beautiful and lilting. "But if it helps to cement my apology to you, I suppose it'll be two birds with one stone." He reaches his hand up to brush a stray curl out of my face, eyes intently on me.

Before I can gather my thoughts, he grins, takes a step backward and walks out of the barn, leaving me blushing and speechless. I pull myself together quickly and casually follow after him, not wanting to seem fazed in the slightest; two can play at this game.

He's loading his tools into the truck bed and watching me walk towards him. Trying to see if his little game worked, no doubt. I school my face back into a calm, almost bored expression, and make my way toward the passenger side of the truck.

"You should probably let Mairead know that I'm taking ya' to the cliffs so she won't be worried about where you've gone," he tells me. I breathe a small sigh and turn toward the cottage.

Mairead is reading in her armchair by the fireplace when I walk through the door. "Everything is finished with the barn, Mairead," I tell her kindly. "Maddox is taking me to see a few sights now that we're done."

"Thank you, dear. And thank Mr. O'Connall for me too," she smiles up from her book at me. "And have fun! You'll enjoy his company, no doubt!"

I can't help but laugh at her enthusiasm as I walk out the front door. Sometimes it's hard to tell if I'm the one falling for him, or if she is.

Chapter 5

Maddox is leaning casually against the passenger side door when I return to the truck. He doesn't say a word as he opens my door, only offering a hand to help me in. I pointedly ignore the out-stretched hand and climb in on my own. His lips purse in annoyance as he closes my door, making his way around the vehicle to get behind the wheel.

We ride in silence for a few minutes when he finally says, "So, are you gonna speak to me at all or are you gonna keep pretending you're mad because I didn't kiss ya' earlier?"

I scoff, looking at him in shock. "I am not pretending to be mad."

Only pretending to be unfazed by his little stunt.

He throws me a satisfied smirk; I'd walked right into his trap. "Then you really *are* mad because you didn't get a kiss? Is that what I'm hearing?"

Despite myself, a giggle escapes my lips and I answer his smile with one of my own. "You are insufferable."

"Insufferable maybe, but I got you to smile at me again," he says, taking his eyes off the road to fully look at me, the look sending the butterflies in my stomach flying into a frenzy. "Am I forgiven?"

"I suppose I can forgive you," I draw out the sentence, rolling my eyes playfully. "Maybe I already had. I just wanted to make you sweat a little." This time it's me giving the satisfied smirk.

"Good. I couldn't have you being angry with me for long," he says, moving his eyes back to the road.

We pass through town and are back on the small country road quickly. I'm lost in thought, watching the vibrant green landscape roll past my window when something catches my eye. Tucked neatly into a clearing between patches of woods, several rounded towers of grey stone stand in beautiful stark contrast to the emerald landscape around it.

"Is that a castle?" My voice pitches slightly higher with excitement.

Maddox laughs, but the smile doesn't quite reach his eyes. "It is. The same mysterious person has kept it up for as long as anyone remembers."

My shoulders slump the tiniest bit, "I guess that means we can't go see it?"

He takes me in coolly, "You can...at the ball this year."

I whip my head around to look at him, "What ball?"

"There's a masquerade every year," his voice is a little rigid when he finally answers, trying his best at nonchalance. "The entire village attends, as well as people from around the world now. I don't remember all the nuances, some silly local legend goes along with it. You'll have to ask Mairead to tell you more, I really don't care enough about it to know."

"Let me guess: magic spells, daring battles, a hidden prince and true love's kiss?" I say, grinning sidelong at him, paraphrasing one of my favorite childhood stories.

"Something like that..." his stricken expression stands in stark contrast to the casualness in his voice.

"Sorry," I shrug sheepishly, embarrassment washing over me now. "I might be a little bit of a fairytale nerd."

He takes his eyes off the road completely, taking me in for a moment. "I don't think that's a bad thing, but...you don't believe in all of that stuff, do you? Fairytales and true love?" he asks, shifting his eyes to me and sounding only halfway teasing.

"Maybe some part of me does," I answer thoughtfully while watching the landscape pass by my window. I shrug, "I'd like to. But nobody has ever given me any real reason to. Men are always running the other way when things get tough. No one has fought a dragon for me or come to my rescue...yet." A shy grin creeps across my face, trying to mask the fact that I'm not entirely joking. My heart has always ached for a romance like that; not just a romance, but love. Ached to know a love like I'd read about in all my favorite stories: fierce, selfless, and unwavering.

Embarrassment takes hold again, realizing his gaze has turned back to me. He probably thinks I'm a lunatic, and rightly so after I'd just spilled my deepest desires to him like that. But the thoughts behind his eyes are just as much a mystery as he is.

"Are we almost there?" The deflecting question comes from my mouth just as he slows the truck to a stop along the side of the road. "I'm guessing that's my answer," I say as he gets out of the truck.

He comes to my side, offering his hand again and this time I take it, much to his apparent satisfaction. Once I'm out of the truck he lets go of my hand, putting his into his pockets and motioning with his head for me to follow. "Not much further now."

We walk through a lush green field of grass, and after a few yards, come upon what feels like the edge of the world, and I lose my breath at the sight. As far as the eye can see in either direction, beautiful undulating cliffs frame a dark, tempestuous sea below. The strong wind rising from the sea blows my hair like a banner behind me.

"Oh, Maddox. This is stunning!" I say, but my words don't seem quite adequate.

"One of the most breathtaking sights I've ever seen." He's standing right beside me, his voice sounding almost reverent. Only, when I turn to look at him, he's not staring at the wondrous landscape around us. His stunning gaze is locked on me.

My breath hitches in my throat and I blink at him, trying to conceal my surprise. He seems to catch himself and quickly looks away toward the sea, putting his hands behind his back and fidgeting his fingers.

I feel his eyes on me again a few moments later as I chance a cautious step closer to the edge, craning my neck to see more of the view below.

"Afraid of heights?" he asks, noticing my obvious discomfort.

I look at him for a moment, shaking my head before turning back to look at the water below. "Not particularly. It's actually the water that scares me. I've always had an irrational fear of deep, dark water and, as crazy as it sounds, of what creatures might be lurking in it." I elaborate more at his questioning look, "Deep water and the dark are two of my worst fears, I think."

For a long moment he's pensively silent, indecipherable thoughts visibly swirling behind his eyes as he looks at me. He finally cracks a smile after noticing my curious gaze on him.

"Well, let's just stay on this side of the cliffs and we won't have to find out what could be down there."

I let out an obviously fake laugh, not entertained with his teasing. "Very funny. I don't plan on cliff jumping anytime soon."

Contented silence fills the space between us as we stand there a while longer, taking in the amazing landscape and watching gray clouds roll in from the distance, when a few heavy raindrops start to fall.

"We should get back to the truck before it starts pouring," Maddox says stiffly, that distance from before threatening to creep in again. Is it something I'm doing or something I've said?

As if on cue, the sporadic drops turn into a downpour as we turn back toward the truck. Both of us are unable to restrain our laughter as we run through the cool torrent of rain. Despite the rain soaking us through, he still opens my door for me. I quickly jump into the cab of the truck and he joins me only seconds later. We exchange looks, each taking in the other's near-drowned state, and laughter peals from our lips again. We finally manage to get ahold of ourselves, but the feeling of lightness lingers.

"How about we go into town and grab a bite to eat before I take you home?" Maddox questions as he starts up the truck. I nod silently at him, still breathless from our fit of laughter, and subconsciously rub my hands on my arms, only just realizing how cold I am. Maddox notices, reaching behind the seat to pull out a canvas jacket.

"Here, Mhuirnín, take this."

"Won't you be cold?" I ask as I take the jacket. "And what is it that you keep calling me?" The Irish word he uses never fails to catch my attention and my curiosity has peaked enough to finally ask.

He glances sideways at me, a relaxed smile on his handsome face as he says the Irish word again, "Mhuirnín. It means little darlin'."

A warmth spreads through my chest at his explanation, a slow smile creeping across my face to accompany it. Unsure of how to respond, I sit back against the seat and ride in pleased silence until we reach town.

Maddox parks the truck and we head for The Lonely Crown.

"I would assume the pub serves more than Guinness if we're here..." I trail off teasingly.

He gives me a crooked grin, "You would assume correctly."

He leads me to the back of the house with a gentle hand on the small of my back, the jacket he loaned me swallowing my small frame, and we enter the room he and his friends have seemed to claim.

Like a replay of that first night, they're all here again, seated at the same table. It would seem that the group of them are fairly regular here, and their not-so-great reputation with the townsfolk would explain their pick of this isolated room.

The talkative one, Theo, notices our entrance first and waves us over. "Well look who's decided to join us again!"

I wave, smiling broadly as we make our way to their table in the corner, the group of them situating their chairs to fit an extra person. I've seen them in passing a few times while out with Maddox, and it seems they've slowly started to get used to my presence.

Maddox doesn't sit, however. "I'll go get something to warm us up," he announces before heading to the front of the pub.

"Why are you both soaked to the bone?" asks the blond one, Fin, a small smile playing at his lips. This is the first time I've heard him say more than a 'hello' and I notice the remnants of an accent that I can't quite place.

"We were out at the cliffs and got caught in an absolute downpour." I can't help the giggle that escapes with my explanation and they all exchange bemused looks.

"He even gave you his jacket. Good on him. Maddox O'Connall, finally learning a thing or two," Theo teases.

I hear a deep laugh behind me and realize Maddox is back, bearing our food: two bowls of something steaming in his hands and a basket of bread balanced in the crook of his arm. He sets the bowls, full of stew, onto the table and places the basket of bread between us, taking his seat next to me.

"Watch it, Theo, or we'll have to start spilling your romantic short-falls," Maddox raises an eyebrow and grins to his friend. Theo puts his hand to his lips in a locking gesture and throws away an imaginary key.

I look around at their group, "Actually, I'd like to hear more about all of you, especially since I'm going to be here for a while. Maddox hasn't proven very easy to get information out of." They exchange glances, each looking for another to give me an answer. My eyebrows shoot up in question, waiting for someone to reply. I asked a simple question; how hard could it be to answer?

"Oh, we've known each other for what seems like *ages*," Kellan finally speaks up, the last word drawn out for effect. "There's too many stories to even tell, and frankly, some probably shouldn't be told in mixed company." The men all smile and nod, seemingly reminiscent, but there is a tightness in their gestures that aren't quite genuine. What is it with them? All so guarded and mysterious.

Theo interrupts the loaded silence with a change of subject, "I almost forgot, are you going to the céili in a few days?" He looks at me with hopeful eyes.

"Céili?" I'm caught off guard again. "Mairead never mentioned it. But I would love to go."

"Oh, it'll be grand. We'll all be there!" he answers enthusiastically.

"You guys don't strike me as the party type," I say to the whole table. Their guarded dispositions don't make it seem like a céili would be an event they'd be found attending.

Kellan shrugs, "Eh, not much else to do in this sleepy town."

I understand his sentiment all too well.

Everyone returns to their respective drinks and we finish our food in friendly casual conversation. They're clearly still not used to having someone different at the table with them. They were much more talkative with each other on that first night, before they'd noticed me in the room, which leaves me wondering what stories and secrets they hold between them.

I fight to stifle a yawn, not wanting to seem like I'm uninterested in their company, but my dark-haired companion notices. "I think it's time I take you back. You've had a full day." He touches the back of my arm gently as he stands from his seat.

I nod up at him in agreement, ready to just relax by the fire for a while. We make it to the exit just as Liam is coming through the door, alone this time. He tilts his head to the side, sneering at Maddox, "Well, well. Now I know why you jumped to her rescue so quickly. You'd already claimed her for yourself." Liam's eyes trail over me slowly, making me feel sick with disgust. "I have to say, I can't blame you."

Unconsciously I take a step back, positioning myself just behind Maddox's broad shoulder, making my unease apparent. Maddox's jaw is set, obviously trying to hold himself back as people start to notice their confrontation. Remembering the bruise on his jaw and not wanting this situation to escalate any further, I gently touch his taut arm. "Let's just go, Maddox. It's not worth it."

His arm relaxes at my touch and he gently takes my hand, leading me around Liam who is still leering at me. Just as we step out into the evening, Liam's voice carries over the crowd, "Remember your place, Maddox."

He doesn't let go of my hand until we reach his truck. When we're both settled inside, I take in his countenance. His hands are gripped tightly to the wheel, eyes far away, his jaw clenched. The silence between us is thick. I don't know what to say, but I want to comfort him.

It's apparent that Liam's comment struck a nerve, even though I don't understand what he could've possibly meant by it. Still unable to grasp the right words to say, I reach out to place a comforting hand on his arm, drawing his attention to me. His eyes are sad, but he paints on a weak smile, finally letting go of the wheel and starting the truck.

He steers us on our way to the cottage, surprising me by placing his hand on mine again; strong and calloused, but gentle against mine. We've barely made it out of the village when the truck jolts, accompanied by a loud pop. Maddox stops, getting out to inspect the source of the noise. I make my own way out of the truck when I hear him let out an irritated growl. I notice the source of his irritation as soon as I'm outside. One of the tires has blown completely, and from the sound of it, the rest of them are losing air rapidly.

"What happened?" I survey the damage, brows knitted.

"Liam."

I look up at him, wide-eyed, "Would he really do that?"

It isn't Maddox that answers my question, but a cold voice from behind us, "He would."

Liam steps from the shadows, clicking his tongue. "Maddox is just too stubborn. Warning after warning and he still won't listen."

"Get in the truck." Maddox pushes me behind him, glancing down at me quickly before flicking his eyes out toward the night around us; searching for what, I don't know.

"Get in the truck and lock the doors."

I almost question him, but the command in his voice is laced with urgency, so I make a move to do as he says. In the split second that Maddox is distracted by me, Liam lunges for him, his fist making contact.

"Know. Your. Place." he grits out through his teeth, grabbing Maddox by the collar and shoving him against the side of the truck. "We won't warn you again."

I whip around to face them completely, shock and adrenaline coursing through me. "Who do you think you are?"

Liam turns his head to me, still holding Maddox up against the truck. "Listen, why don't you just leave him behind and come with me? It'll make things easier on all of us."

What on earth is he talking about? The confusion in my thoughts is plainly written on my face, but defiance quickly takes hold. "What makes you think I'd ever go anywhere with you? I'll gladly choose Maddox a thousand times over." The fierceness in which I was ready to defend him shocks me, but I don't have time to dwell on it.

Maddox has made a move this time, loosing his arm from Liam's weight to land a powerful punch to his face. "She's not going anywhere," Maddox growls out.

Liam stumbles back a few feet, but isn't knocked out fully, recovering after a few breaths. He looks up at Maddox who is reaching a hand up to his collar, about to pull on the leather string hanging there. "You're really gonna do that in front of her?" Liam flicks his eyes over to me, then back to my companion.

Maddox takes me in for a breath, letting go of the strap around his neck and meeting Liam's eyes again. "If you don't leave *now*, I won't hesitate again."

"It's only her you're hurting," Liam shrugs. "Remember, she's an easy target." He flicks his eyes to me again before he turns to go. "Oh, and make sure you tell that old friend of yours to *stop meddling*."

I stand there in silence watching him walk back into the night, bewildered by everything I had just witnessed. If I thought I had questions before, it's nothing compared to now.

"Let's go." Maddox's rough voice pulls me out of my thoughts. "Looks like we'll be walking again."

I stop him with a hand on his arm as he shoulders past me, "Wait, you're bleeding."

"It's nothing." He doesn't even turn toward me, but I see his hand reach up to his lip, now split again, coming away with fresh blood.

I point toward a thicket of woods, starting towards the tree line. "I can hear a stream just over there. Let's at least wash it off. The cool water should help with the pain too."

I'm stopped short by his strong hand on my arm, turning me to face him, "Do not go near those woods."

"Why? It's just right there," I point over my shoulder.

"Just don't, okay?" His gaze is intense on me as he waits for my answer.

I nod, confusion twisting my features yet again, "Okay...I was just trying to help."

He turns and starts down the road again, "I can handle it on my own." His words are clipped. There's that distance again.

"Well excuse me for offering help when it is clearly needed." I stalk after him, trying to catch up with his swift gait, irritation clear in my voice.

He stops abruptly and I almost run into him as he spins to face me. "Why are you doing this?"

"I'm just trying to help. Why is that such a problem?" I shrug, looking up at him. Instead of giving him time to answer, I leave him standing there and start for the cottage by myself, feeling like I've annoyed him enough.

"Carlin, wait." His voice is soft, pulling my attention back to him. "It's not a problem," he mutters, looking deflated. He sighs, running a hand down his face before continuing, "Besides Fin and the others,

I've gotten used to being on my own, not out of choice but of circumstances. Always having to fend for myself has made it hard to accept help from anyone."

The confession, coupled with the haunted look behind his eyes causes my heart to ache. I walk back toward him, stopping just before his tall form. "Trust me, I get it. Aside from my family, I've spent most of my life alone too. In fact, I prefer it most times, especially over being surrounded by fake people," I admit to him. There's a certain kind of peace that comes along with learning to enjoy being alone.

"But that doesn't mean I don't need anyone or get lonely. Most times I *wish* for someone to come along that I can be truly close to," I continue, feeling vulnerable for even saying the words out loud.

He takes me in for a long moment, the sadness clearing from his eyes a bit. "I'll tell you what, let's get back to Mairead's and I'll let you patch me up," he says gently.

I breathe a laugh at his submission, smiling at him again before we start toward the cottage one more time.

Chapter 6

When we reach the cottage, a pensive silence has settled between us. Unable to bear it any longer, I turn to face him abruptly, brows knitted, "Why is he like that to you?" My thoughts had been swirling with all that had taken place tonight.

Maddox lets out a heavy sigh as he turns to me, his face serious. "There are things about Liam, about me, and this place that you don't understand; things I can't tell you, as much as I wish I could."

All of the worst-case scenarios run through my head, trying to piece together just what they could all be wrapped up in. Is it a gang? Drugs?

He huffs a quick laugh at the look on my face, "Whatever you're thinking, I can just about guarantee it's not that. Just know that Liam and his cohorts are much more dangerous than they may seem," he continues, "and you shouldn't be alone if they're around."

I nod silently, conveying my understanding. He's looking at me intently and it's impossible for me to ignore how much closer he's moved to me during our conversation.

I clear my throat, sudden nerves making me take a step back. "We should go and get you cleaned up. It looks like the bleeding has stopped already though."

"If you don't mind, I'll stay out here. I don't want to trouble Mairead with it all."

I nod, smiling softly at him, "I'll go get a cloth and some water then."

The cottage is quiet when I step inside, Mairead nowhere to be seen. Thinking she may be sleeping, I tiptoe through to the kitchen, quickly wetting a soft cloth and sneaking back out the door.

When I step back out into the night, Maddox is sitting patiently on the stone fence. Even sitting, he's still taller than me. His eyes stay steady on me as he lets me wash the blood from his face.

"Earlier, when you said you wished for someone to be close to," his voice breaks through the silence, thick with emotion, "what do you wish for?"

I'm thoughtfully silent for a moment, caught off guard by his question and how much it moves me. I finally answer, thankful for the task of cleaning his wound to distract me from how he's looking at me. "Someone who's true, and good, and steadfast. Someone who's there because they want to be, not because I was the only option, or the last choice. I'd want them to fight for me, to show me I'm something *worth* fighting for." Finished cleaning his wound, I look down quickly, toying with the cloth in my hand. I'd surprised myself with how much emotion answering that question made me feel, listing all the things I'd prayed for after being burned so many times. Suppressing the rise of embarrassment at my confession, I meet his eyes again, "What about you?"

It doesn't take him long to answer. It's obvious he's thought a lot about what he longs for. "I wish for someone to see through the facade, to understand all I've been through and not balk at it. Just, for someone to care enough to see beyond the mask, seeing *me* and not who I seem to be."

Something deeper than the ease between us was formed tonight, and I think we both feel it. Something snapping into place, like a soul tie that's always been there, just circling, waiting to be fastened.

I swallow the new emotion rising within me, shooting him a teasing smile, "That's real cryptic for somebody who just wants to be understood..."

The bright smile lighting his face, coupled with his deep laugh, makes my heart do back flips.

"You know, I still can't comprehend how anyone could speak to another person like that," I shake my head in frustration, unable to forget how horrible Liam was tonight.

Maddox reaches his hand up, placing it so sweetly on the side of my face. "Because you are good, Mo Chuisle." His eyes are locked on mine, the new Irish word he used so pleasant to my ears. "Everything that's wrong in the world, all the darkness...you're the direct opposite: innocence and light. The fact that you don't understand it is a good thing."

The way my heart beats being this close to him is unnerving, and the lilt of his voice completely enthralls me. For a moment I think he's going to kiss me, but instead he leans in, placing a soft peck on my forehead that sends a chill down my spine. I can only offer him a bright-eyed smile when he pulls back, his nearness rendering me speechless.

He finally stands, leading me to the front door with a hand on the small of my back. "Would you like to accompany me to the céili?" he asks when we reach the door, hands in his pockets.

I cast my eyes up toward the sky in jest, as if having to think about it. "I suppose I could grace you with my presence." I bring my eyes back toward him, smiling wide.

He laughs deeply, the timbre of the sound sending butterflies running rampant again. "It's settled then. I'll get the truck fixed and pick you up, so we won't have to walk yet again."

I give him a single nod, "I'll be waiting."

He turns to leave as I reach for the door handle. "Hey!" I call after him, suddenly remembering the pleasant sound of the new word he'd used, "That new name you called me...what does it mean?"

He turns back toward me, hands still in his pockets, and leans his head to the side. His eyes are alight with something I can't quite place. "I'll tell you one day," he says. And with that, he walks off into the clear night.

Mairead is coming down the stairs as I walk through the door. "Oh, hello lass! I was just getting the spare bedroom ready for the other young lady. She'll be arriving soon. Did you enjoy your evening?"

I smile brightly at her. "The cliffs were unbelievable," the memory of the sight leaving me just as breathless as the real thing. "And we joined Maddox's friends at the pub for a bit."

She nods, a satisfied smile on her lips as she listens.

"Maddox asked me to go to the céili with him," I add, barely able to restrain myself from acting like a giddy little girl.

She beams at me and clasps her hands together, conveying the giddiness for me, "How wonderful dear! You will enjoy that, no doubt."

"What should I wear? I've never been to anything like it and I'm not sure if I've brought anything appropriate."

She heads toward her bedroom door, holding her finger to her chin. "I might have just the thing. Wait here," she says, disappearing into her room.

I find a spot on the old, comfortable couch and wait for her to reappear. A few minutes later she comes through her door holding a bundle of blue fabric in her arms.

"Do you think this will do, dearie?" She holds it up, allowing me to see it fully. I move to examine the beautiful dress more closely. The sheer neckline covers a sweetheart bodice with a gauzy overlay of royal blue fabric extending down the whole of the knee length skirt.

"This will do perfectly; it was absolutely made for me." I hug her as she hands the dress over to me, a strange gleam in her eye akin to mischief.

"Go hang that up in your room and come back so I can hear all about your evening," she insists.

I do as she says, coming back down the stairs to find her waiting in her armchair by the fire.

"I got to see a glimpse of the castle on our way to the cliffs." I finally bring up the thing that's been in the back of my mind all day, carefully omitting anything about the problem with Liam as I return to my seat from earlier, "What's the story with the ball happening there soon? Maddox didn't seem too eager to talk about it."

"Well," her voice has taken on a reflective tone when she begins speaking again, "there is a legend surrounding that castle, not just local anymore. It's spread far throughout the years." She looks over to me, assuring I'm listening closely before beginning the tale. "According to the stories, centuries ago there lived a king in that very castle along with his wife and only son. The king was at odds with the Fair Folk, driving them from the land, with no care for if they were good or evil. The more benevolent ones, The Seelie Court they're called in some places, went mostly without trouble, but the Unseelie, creatures of your worst nightmares, didn't take very kindly to being run out. So, the Unseelie Queen visited the castle late one night and stole away the king's young son."

Her words have pulled me in completely, the skillful way she tells the story paints a clear picture, leaving me hungry for more.

She tells me of the king demanding an audience with the Unseelie Queen upon finding his only heir vanished, and how she burst into his throne room where he waited, placing a curse on the king and his family; causing the king to never have another heir, and his son to be bound to her service for as long as it took for the curse to be lifted.

"But she didn't stop there," Mairead continues, waving her finger for effect. "The dark queen made sure that the townsfolk never remembered the little prince, and assured the only way the spell could be broken was for someone to see past her deceiving magic and know him for who he really is."

"What exactly does the ball have to do with all of this?" I ask, my earlier question still unanswered.

"So," she continues her story with a pointed look, "a masquerade ball is held every year by the mysterious queen, to give the prince a chance to be seen. But no one has come along that knows him yet."

I stare at her, incredulous. "There's no way that prince would even still be alive after all these years. Why would people still come to try their hand at figuring it out?"

"Many have tried, but no one has ever succeeded." She adds, "People scramble to be the first to call out all manner of names, blinded by the greed, never caring for the man behind the curse, only seeing a chance at a crown."

I humor her, clearly seeing that she enjoys this story, "Why would the queen even allow him a chance to break the curse? She doesn't sound like she'd do anything out of kindness."

She's silent for a breath, thoughts clearly running through her head. "No, I don't think the queen allowed him this chance as a kindness. I quite think it was to torment the poor young man; always being looked at but never really *seen*." Her words are filled with a sadness that surprises me. "And as for the time, you'd be surprised. They say time works differently in the Otherworld. He was stolen away into the queen's service until such a time that the curse is broken; he would be bound to her service there, most likely."

I knit my brows together, noticing a certain look in her eyes. "You *believe* it, don't you?"

Mairead's eyes have a glow about them as she grins at me, "I've lived long enough to know that anything is possible, lass."

I give her a single laugh and smile, humoring her again. "So, what happens if this spell is broken?"

"The prince is released from his bondage of service and can take his place as king, not just in this land, but over the creatures of the Otherworld that inhabit this side too. And, if he so chooses, he will make the one who ends the curse his queen!" She gives a triumphant gesture at that, ending her story. "I am so excited that you'll get to go this year. Maybe we'll see some magic happen!" She clasps her hands together, excitement rolling off her at the thought. It's obvious she loves this tale and very much believes in it.

"Except, we have a problem," I abruptly remember that I was not aware of the masquerade before arriving here, and not at all prepared for an event of that scale. "I have nothing to wear to a ball. I didn't know to bring anything along."

She winks at me, "You leave that to me. I will make you a gown to rival them all."

"You've done so much for me already, Mairead. I can't accept another favor from you, especially something like an evening gown."

She holds her hand up to stop my opposing. "I won't hear another word. I love to help people, especially kind ones, and I am quite good at it. It is settled and I will not take 'no' for an answer."

"Thank you." My smile grows at her stubbornness and I nod my head in acceptance. "You have no idea how much I appreciate what you've done for me already, Mairead." I stand up and walk to her chair, wrapping her in a hug.

She hugs me back tightly, "Don't thank me, child. I'm only doing what I was made to do." She grabs both of my hands in hers as we let go, "Go on to bed now, I know you've had a full day."

I am grateful for her dismissal, ready to change out of my clothes which are stiff from being rained on. With that thought, I become acutely aware that I'm still wearing Maddox's jacket. Maybe it's knowing that he's had it on his skin and now it's wrapped around me, or maybe it's his lingering scent, like leather and petrichor, but it gives me a small thrill.

The morning of the céili has finally arrived and my excitement is brimming over before I've even opened my eyes. Trying to force time to pass more quickly, I'd spent the last few days keeping myself occupied by helping Mairead, much to her annoyance, with her daily tasks.

Opening my eyes to my small bedside table, I'm met with the sight of what looks like a tiny person sitting on the edge. And it's looking back at me.

I shoot straight up in bed, grabbing for my heart and gasping loudly. "Mairead!" I scream as the figure vanishes into thin air.

A minute later my host bursts into the room. "What is it, child? You look as if you've seen a ghost!"

"I think I might have," I say, a bit panicky. I search the room around me for any evidence of the apparition. "Did you happen to put a figurine or something on the table that I might not have noticed last night?" I question. That must be the most reasonable explanation for this, maybe I knocked it off in my panic.

Mairead's eyes light up with comprehension now, a warm reassuring smile spreading over her face. Putting her hands on her hips, she speaks into the otherwise empty room, "You may as well go on and show yourselves now. No reason in hiding any longer, she's already seen ya'!"

Confused, puzzled, bewildered...none of those words seem to be adequate for what I'm feeling as she looks expectantly around the empty room.

What on earth could she possibly be looking for, and who is she talking to?

As soon as the thought is formed, as if in answer, a group of tiny human-like creatures step shyly out from different places within the room, gathering next to my host. I blink rapidly. Stunned would be a terrible understatement.

The creatures are staring at me through downcast eyes, like they're children in trouble.

"What am I seeing right now?" I struggle to form a coherent thought, my eyes as big as saucers.

"They're Little Folk, dearie. Pixies, to be specific. I allow them to live on my land and in my house as long as they *behave,* and they've taken a liking to you." Mairead answers matter of factly; like she hasn't just told me that these tiny people in my room are mythical *faerie creatures.* "They only show themselves to people they like and trust, and you are one of those people. There's nothing to be afraid of, they're kind and helpful little things," she assures me.

I'm still not sure if I believe my own eyes, but there really is no other explanation for any of this.

"Are they the things I've been seeing darting around from the corner of my eye?" I question, finally putting two and two together.

She nods, grinning at me, "Yes, playful little creatures. They were probably seeing how much they could get away with before you caught them. Apparently, they decided you were someone they wanted to present themselves to. Which is why little Flynn here was sitting on your bedside table when you woke up." She looks pointedly over to a pixie in a little green hat. "Probably not the best way to go about it."

The one she called Flynn steps forward, tipping his cap to me and exposing a tuft of wiry red hair. "Hello miss. We didn't mean to give you a fright," he says. His voice is strangely normal sounding, only slightly higher in pitch; not at all what I was expecting from a six-inch-tall faerie.

He climbs his way back up to the bedside table and extends a tiny hand out to me. Using my thumb and index finger, I shake it gently. "It's nice to meet you. Although, I'm still not sure I'm not dreaming," I say, my mind still reeling. "Hello to all of you."

Before I can say anything else, a knock sounds at the front door. "That must be the other young lady! We'll explain everything a little more later. For now, you all need to hide!" Mairead looks around at all the pixies and the next moment they disappear.

Noticing that I still haven't been out of bed during the course of this morning's events, I get up to get ready for the day.

Mairead leaves the room, turning to me before slipping into the hallway, "I will go greet the newcomer, you come down whenever you're ready."

I get dressed quickly and casually, throwing on jeans and a comfy tee. Pulling my curls into a ponytail, I head downstairs to meet the new girl.

Mairead is just ushering her into the cottage as I make it to the bottom of the stairs. "Ah, there she is! Carlin, this is Claire," Mairead puts her arm around the girl's shoulders as best she can, given their height difference, and smiles.

"Hi, it's nice to meet you and to finally be here," she says shyly, brushing her jaw-length copper hair out of her face. Her sweet disposition is immediately apparent.

Mairead ushers her to the stairs, leading her to her bedroom and leaving me to myself for a moment.

"She is going to get settled in and unpack while I get breakfast ready. Would you like to help me, dear?" Mairead asks as she comes back down the stairs a few minutes later.

I smile down at her, nodding, and follow her into the kitchen.

After a nice breakfast spent getting acquainted with one another, Mairead tells Claire about the céili. "The dance will be tonight, and it'll be a wonderful first impression of the town for ya'!"

"What exactly does a céili entail?" asks Claire. "I don't think we have anything like it back in L.A."

Mairead clasps her hands together in delight, "Oh, it's just grand! Traditional music, singing, dancing and lots and lots of food and drink! You girls will love it, I look forward to it every year."

I can feel myself catching her excitement; this will be right up my alley. Plus, I get to be there with Maddox tonight, and that thrills me even more. "Why didn't you tell me you were going, Mairead?" I question her. "Do you need to ride with Maddox and me?"

"No child, I wouldn't dream of interfering with your night," she pats my hand across the table. "Claire and I will walk there together and catch a ride back to the cottage afterward. You just enjoy that handsome lad!" She gives me a conspiratorial wink.

Claire grins between the two of us, wagging her brows at me, "Ooh, who is Maddox?"

I can't stop the blush from creeping into my cheeks. "He's someone I met in town a few weeks ago and he asked me to be his date tonight. He's really still a stranger, Mairead is just teasing." I glance at my host from under my lashes and she beams at me.

"Tall, dark, and handsome stranger, isn't that how all the best stories start?" Claire says, joining forces with Mairead and earning a laugh from us all.

"There's something there between you two, lass. You won't be able to deny it for long, just you wait and see," Mairead says as she stands to clean the table. "Now you two go on and relax. You have some free time before you need to get ready for tonight."

Claire and I both head up the stairs to our respective rooms, but I stop her before she turns for her end of the hallway. "You really are welcome to come with us tonight. It's not a problem at all."

"Thank you for the offer, but I'm not going to intrude and be the annoying third wheel. Plus, I couldn't live with myself if I let Mairead walk there alone," she answers before she enters her bedroom.

Once in my room, with nothing else to do, I decide to read a book, one of my favorites that I brought from home. Funnily enough, it's about faeries. It's never been a problem for me to read for hours on end, so this should easily pass the time.

Chapter 7

I'm pulled from sleep by tiny hands lifting my hair away from my ears.

"It's time to wake up! You must get ready!"

I open my eyes to see Flynn smiling down at me from the edge of my bed, his pointed ears peeking out from his cap.

I sit up, slowly this time, and give him a sheepish smile. I hadn't even realized I'd fallen asleep, my book still laying open beside me.

"What time is it? How long was I asleep?" I ask, mentally noting how comical it is that just this morning I couldn't believe my eyes at the sight of the creatures. Now, I'm speaking to them like it isn't strange at all.

Another pixie appears from nowhere, this time a female. "It's 5 o'clock! You've been asleep for hours! I'm Bramble by the way," she adds, waving in greeting.

I don't think I will ever fully get used to this.

My eyes grow wide, "Hours? Why didn't anyone wake me?"

Flynn shrugs, "You looked like you were sleeping well, plus, you needed to rest up for all the dancing you'll be doing tonight." He breaks into a silly jig as he says the words.

I give them both a once over. "So do pixies go to the céili? Since you can apparently disappear on command..."

They both nod animatedly. "Yes! We love to watch the festivities and play pranks on the unsuspecting partiers..." Flynn realizes he's told on himself and trails off before he finishes.

I laugh and slide slowly from the bed, trying not to disturb them, and make for the bathroom to start a shower. I close the bathroom door behind me, leaving Flynn and Bramble to themselves. In the middle of washing my hair I start to hear things clattering and moving around. Sticking my head out from behind the curtain, I see the pixies rummaging through my makeup bag. "Just what do you think you're doing? You shouldn't be in here while I'm bathing anyway!" They look up at me in surprise, not understanding the problem. I sigh, giving them a kind look, "Please, I would like some privacy."

They're both gone before I can blink, their tinkling laugher ringing through the room. It's obvious they're mischievous little things.

Before worrying about my makeup, I take the time to carefully style and dry my dark curls so they'll be fresh for tonight. As for the makeup, I've always preferred a natural look, but perhaps tonight a bit more won't hurt.

I hear a small knock on my door and find Claire behind it. "I'm terrible with makeup. I was going to see if you would help me."

Just as I open my mouth to answer, Mairead calls up the stairs, "I will help both of you girls get ready!" In a moment she is up the stairs and ushering us into my room, assessing us both to decide what needs to be done. "I'll begin with Claire since you've already started on your own, dear," Mairead says to me.

I quickly pull my bag out of the bathroom, waving it around excitedly, "I'll work on her makeup while you work your magic on her hair, Mairead." Upon diving into my bag, I notice a few of my items are gone...*pixies*.

As I'm adding the finishing touches of powder, Mairead is putting the last pin into Claire's hair. She's braided the front of her smooth red hair into a pretty headband.

"It looks wonderful," I tell her.

She stands up and moves aside, motioning for me to sit in the chair. "Now it's your turn."

Mairead gets started on my hair now and my stomach has already started doing back flips knowing Maddox will be here soon. I don't even notice my bouncing leg until Claire teases, "Nervous, are we?"

My attention is immediately turned to stilling my leg as I move my eyes to her and grin, "A little, but I really don't know why."

"I do," Mairead laughs, giving Claire a pointed look, "just wait until you see the young man." She pats my shoulder with one hand, "Don't be nervous. You're going to have a grand time with him tonight. Not to mention, he's already besotted with you."

I try to turn and look at Mairead but she stops me, not letting me interrupt her work. "What makes you think that?"

Her answer is assured, "That boy has been closed off since I've known him. He barely acknowledges anyone, let alone strangers, and in just a few weeks you've managed to get him to attend a public dance with you." She leans down next to my ear, "I'll say it again. He's besotted."

I hope she's right. Though I barely know him, there's something about Maddox that draws me in, and I hope it's mutual.

Mairead is finished with my hair now, a half up/half down look fastened with a braid at the back to hold it all together, leaving most of my ringlets down and showcased.

"Thank you Mairead, it's perfect."

She dismisses both Claire and I with a wave of her hands. "Thank me later. You two need to get dressed!"

They both leave the room as I head for the bathroom where my dress has been hanging. Sliding into the blue dress, I'm pleasantly surprised. It fits me like a glove, as if it really was tailor made for me. I admire myself in the mirror for a moment before picking out simple teardrop earrings to accessorize and settling on a pair of black flats for shoes; comfortable enough to dance in, but still dressy enough to not look out of place.

After one last check in the mirror I start for my bedroom door when there's a knock at the front door of the cottage. My heart skips a beat and I'm suddenly acutely aware of just how nervous I am. I press my back against the door, taking in a few calming breaths before building up the nerve to walk down the stairs.

Maddox is just settling himself onto the couch as I start down the stairs. He looks up to see me, his jaw slackening ever so slightly, and is immediately back on his feet to greet me.

I can't help but beam at him as my heart squeezes. He really is devastatingly handsome. The chambray shirt he's wearing, tucked into grey slacks, highlights the blue of his eyes. His unusual necklace sits on the skin left exposed from his unbuttoned collar and the beginnings of a five o'clock shadow perfectly complement the strong planes of his face.

"You look lovely." He brushes a strand of hair off my bare shoulder, the touch leaving my skin tingling in its wake, before leaning down to lightly kiss my cheek. The scent of him makes the fluttering in my stomach start again. He smiles down at me, placing a hand on the small of my back, "Are you ready to go?"

"More than ready."

Mairead hugs the both of us before sending us off, "You two have fun! Claire and I will see you there."

Turning back to wave as we head out the door, I see Claire giving me a thumbs up. The goofy smile plastered on her face, with a pointed look at Maddox's back, forces me to stifle a giggle.

Arriving at the village center, Maddox parks the truck, coming around to help me out. The first streams of music reach my ears as the musicians tune up. "Welcome to the céili, Mhuirnín." Maddox kisses my hand sweetly before tucking it into the crook of his arm.

The town looks magical tonight: fairy lights are strung overhead, streamers and flowers are placed about the area, and dozens of tables are laden with food and beverages. In the center of everything is the dance floor, the musicians warming up just beyond it. The amount of people in attendance is surprising. "I didn't know there were this many people even in this town," I joke with him.

He laughs softly, "No one ever misses the céili. It's one of the only big events we have here."

We walk to a table where his friends are already seated and they greet us cheerfully, apparently getting more comfortable with my presence. Theo, of course, is the first one to delve into conversation. "I heard the other girl is here finally. What's her name? What's she like?"

I laugh outright at his eagerness. "How could you possibly know she's here already? She hasn't even been here more than a few hours."

He shrugs his shoulders, looking quite proud of himself. "I have my ways, and you still didn't answer my questions."

"Alright, alright." Shaking my head, I grin at him, "Her name is Claire, she's from L.A., she has beautiful red hair and is as sweet as can be."

"Is she pretty? Is she here tonight?" he continues with his barrage of questions.

I sigh teasingly at his persistence. "Yes she's pretty and she is on her way here with Mairead now." I give him a stern look before continuing, "but she is very shy, so you need to have some tact about it. Give her time to get settled so you don't scare her off with your flirting." He feigns shock at my accusation. "Don't act like I don't know exactly what you're thinking. You're not as slick as you think you are, Theo." I look knowingly at him as the rest of the guys laugh at our exchange.

It doesn't surprise me to notice the table they've chosen is near the edge of the crowd, as secluded as they could manage here. "So, what's with you guys always looking like the grumpy old men tucked into a corner everywhere you go?" I ask.

Theo nearly chokes on his stout at my question and murmurs something that earns sharp looks from the others, cutting him off before he'd even gotten started.

"No offense," I say, smiling sheepishly at them all. "Just an observation."

To their credit, they all look quite entertained with my question, even if none of them offer an answer.

The band leader stands, grabbing everyone's attention. "The dance floor is now open! We'll start you off with something slower. This is Granuaile's dance." He resumes his place back with the other musicians waiting for people to make their way to the floor.

I know my eyes don't hide the spark of excitement I feel at seeing real Irish dancing, maybe even joining in myself. Apparently Kellan notices, "Don't get ahead of yourself. Maddox doesn't dance."

I turn my attention to smoothing down my skirt, trying to hide my disappointment. When I look up, Maddox is staring at me intently, but my answering smile feels forced and tight. He never breaks eye contact as he stands from his chair, holding his hand out to me. He nods his head toward the dance floor as the first strains of the song start.

My brows raise a fraction, "I thought you didn't dance?"

He throws me a sideways smile, "Tonight, I do."

I allow him to pull me to my feet. I don't fail to notice his friend's surprised reactions on top of Theo's cheer, "Alright, boyo!"

As we step onto the dance floor, someone places a crown of wildflowers on my head. I give Maddox a sidelong look, "I'm warning you, I don't know how to do any of these dances."

He leans in, laughing softly in my ear, "I have no doubt you'll pick it up quickly. Just watch everyone else." He backs away into the line of men as I take my place in line with the ladies, the townsfolk giving sideways glances at Maddox with every move, obviously unaccustomed to him being so near.

We begin a series of slow steps, weaving around each person in the line, stepping forward to meet our partner then stepping back, barely taking our eyes off each other. The lines finally converge and his right hand presses into my left. We slowly circle around each other, his arm finding its way around my waist as he leans in close, "Get ready."

He grins down at me as the music begins to pick up speed, twirling me once and letting go for us to join into a circle, holding hands with the people around us. The circle spins one way and then the other, the ladies joining our left hands in the middle and twirling together as the men clap around us, then duck out of the circle and back into the separate lines. Everyone joins hands with their partners across the way to make an arch for the lead couple to dance through, followed by another, then another, until the entirety of the line has woven their way through.

Maddox grabs me around the waist again and twirls me faster and faster with the music, bright laughter bubbling from my lips. Just as I think I can't stand to spin anymore, the music comes to an abrupt stop and so do we. I stumble slightly from dizziness, but he catches me tightly in his arms as we laugh together, completely breathless. My hands are on his chest, his breath rising and falling as he looks down at me. With one arm still strongly around me, he lifts his other hand to caress my face, his eyes intent. "You're a wildflower, mhuirnín. Never let anyone make you feel like anything less."

My heart squeezes at his words, directly in answer to my confession to him on our first meeting. Looking up at him through my lashes, unable to form the right words to answer him, I blurt out the first thing that comes to mind, "Thank you for dancing with me."

His unique eyes are lit from within and for a moment I think he might kiss me, but in that same moment his eyes are caught by something behind me, the light there snuffed out instantly. He loosens his grip on me and steps toward whatever it is he sees. "Go back to the table." He glances at me from over his shoulder, "Stay with them."

I turn in the direction of his gaze as Claire appears excitedly beside me, "You two looked *amazing* out there!"

I smile at her half-heartedly, still watching to see where Maddox is going. She sees my face and looks around, "Where's Maddox?"

The crowd thins and he comes into view standing with a tall, slender woman, speaking very closely to her, and my heart drops a bit. Claire follows my gaze, frowning in confusion. I shake my head, speaking to no one in particular, "Of course she's gorgeous."

Pale blonde hair falls in soft waves down to her hips. Her features are sharp, giving off an air of cruel beauty. She notices me watching them, makes direct eye contact with me, and smirks, her actions drawing Maddox's attention. He glances over his shoulder at me for a heartbeat before turning sharply back to the young woman, saying something to her. She finally turns, heading away from the crowd as Maddox follows.

Claire lets out a small gasp beside me. "Let's go find Mairead," she puts her arm gently around my shoulder and pulls me along with her.

We don't find Mairead, but we do make our way back to the table where Theo and the others are watching the festivities. Kellan notices that I'm alone and parrots Claire's earlier question, "Where's Maddox?"

I shrug, palms upturned, "I don't know actually. I just watched him walk off with some blonde girl when the dance was over."

The entire group exchange dark looks between themselves, even Theo's normal grinning face has darkened a bit. "Nyx," Fin huffs.

I look between them all, brows raised, "Care to fill me in?"

"Trust me," Theo stands, reassuring me, and I pretend not to notice him moving closer to Claire, "she's no one to him. He's most likely trying to keep you from having to deal with her. Nyx has been a thorn in all our sides for years, especially his."

"You should've seen the way she looked at Carlin though. That's hardly reassuring," Claire pipes up.

Theo smiles broadly at her, "Well, why don't you and I make our way over to the dance floor and see if we can find them out there? To help our friends out, that is."

Claire blushes deeply, looking over to me hesitantly.

A laugh escapes my lips at the amused looks on the faces around the table. I smile encouragingly at her, "He might be goofy, but I think he's harmless. Go on."

She laughs outright at his expression when he hears my words, then puts her hand in his and follows him to dance.

I take Theo's now empty seat, looking around the throngs of people, when Fin catches my eye, "I'll go find him if you'd like."

I nod shyly at him, "Thank you." I look between Thomas and Kellan, both quietly watching the dancers. "I think I'm going to step away for a minute. I need a little break from the crowd." They both raise their glasses of stout to me as I stand to leave.

I walk until I'm a good few yards away from the céili, standing in the night air watching everyone enjoy the party from a distance. In a blink, all the lights throughout the village are snuffed out and the music stops, the murmurs of the crowd the only sound left. But the crowd is stunned to silence when an eerie baying sound rings through the air. I think my heart skips a few beats entirely. There aren't any dangerous animals, especially predators, in Ireland, I'm sure of it. But the sound clearly heralds something fearsome.

"You need to hide. Now!" I nearly jump out of my skin when Flynn appears on my shoulder, vanishing again before I can finish reacting. Someone in the crowd screams, causing a panic, and people scatter. That's when I see them through the thinning crowd: a group of hound-like beasts are facing the villagers, staring them down with large, hideous red eyes and fur so black it swallows up any remaining light around them.

Searching frantically around me, the pub catches my attention only a few feet away. I turn to run just as the hounds are closing in on the gathered villagers, snarling viciously but not attacking, almost as if they're looking for something. I make it through the door of the dark, empty pub, and into the back room quickly, sinking to the floor against the dividing wall, my entire body trembling uncontrollably. With the sounds of the creatures getting unmistakably closer, I struggle to slow my breathing and calm myself, sure that the sound of my pounding heart will give me away.

The door to the pub opens and slow, sauntering footsteps on the hardwood floor send a chill down my spine. The low, guttural sounds of the animals are just outside the pub's threshold. Wishing with everything within me that I could press myself completely into the wall, I quiet my breathing even more, striving to make myself as undetectable as possible.

"Come on out now, little one. I know you're in here." Liam's arrogant voice is unmistakable. I don't even dare to swallow for fear of being found. "I'll call off my pets if you come willingly," he drawls. "No need to be scared, lass. Someone I know is wanting to meet you." The silence that follows is deafening, fixing my attention to the fact that the hounds aren't at the door now. Listening carefully, I hear the sounds of the beasts giving chase to something in the distance.

A loud thud just behind my hiding spot makes me flinch and wrap my arms around myself. Footfalls are heading toward me again and a tall shadow stretches across the threshold of my hiding place. I don't think my body can handle any more terror, but I steel myself for whatever may come next.

"Mhuirnín, it's me."

I choke back a sob, "Maddox?"

He's knelt in front of me now, pulling me to my feet and into his arms for a brief moment before pulling away to examine me, "Are you alright?"

"I think so," I nod, breathless. "Maddox, *what is happening*?"

His eyes are intense as they meet mine, "There's no time to explain, but I'm going to get you out of here while Fin and the others are leading the hounds away." He grabs my hand firmly and pulls me toward the front door, passing Liam's prone body. I wonder only briefly if he's alive or not.

Out in the dark street, the town is eerily still, not a soul to be found. "Where can we go? Back to Mairead's?" I question as he leads me through the cobblestone streets.

"Not yet. That'll probably be the first place they head when they realize the chase they're on is a distraction." As if in direct answer to his statement, the cacophony of the pack can be heard coming back toward the town. Maddox tightens his grip on my hand, letting out a frustrated growl before turning to me.

"Run."

Chapter 8

We run until we come to the edge of the cliffs, the sound of our pursuers closing in behind us. There's nowhere left for us to run. I look over to Maddox, still grasping his hand tightly. "What do we do now?" I breathe out.

"Do you trust me?" His voice is steady and calm, despite the situation. His eyes are locked on mine, waiting for my response. The way he's looking at me suggests that the answer doesn't just apply to our current circumstances.

"Yes." No hesitation, just yes. Despite the fact that he's practically still a stranger, he's gotten me this far without harm.

He takes my face in his hands, making sure that I can see the truth in his eyes, "We're going to be fine, but we have to jump."

A wave of panic crashes over me. *What?*

"Now!" He grabs my hand again, giving me no time to think, and jumps.

We fall and everything around us is moving quickly, my hair and dress flailing wildly through the air, but strangely enough, it also feels as if everything is in slow motion. After what feels like seconds and an eternity all at once, we plunge into the cold ocean, our hands losing their grip on each other. This feeling of weightlessness is so utterly different than the feeling of falling. I panic a little trying to find Maddox, but thankfully the sea is calm tonight and we aren't lost to each other for long.

Finally breaking the surface of the water, we see our pursuers turning to leave. "Come this way," he tells me, swimming towards the thin strip of shore at the base of the cliffs. I follow and soon we come upon a hidden opening in the side of the cliff face. To my surprise, it gradually opens, up and up and up, until it finally opens to the land above. The hole in the cliff is cavernous on the inside with smooth, time-worn stones littering the floor, the sea waves shallowly lapping around them.

Maddox helps me get steadily to my feet and out of the water, finding a large rock for me to sit on. "We'll wait here awhile, just to be sure they're gone." His eyes run over me carefully, assessing, "Are you alright?"

I wrap my arms around myself, looking up at him. "I think so. I'm not hurt, if that's what you're asking, but I'm not so sure that I'm not losing my mind. Actually, I'm pretty sure I am losing my mind."

"You're not going crazy," he answers kindly. "I promise I will explain everything I can when I get you safely back to Mairead's."

I stare off into the space around him, unable to focus. My hands come up to rub my face, worry taking over again as the realization hits me. I turn my wide-eyed gaze back to him, "They were after me." My brows knit together, "Why?"

He kneels to my level, both of us still dripping with sea water. He's looking at me earnestly, but his eyes hold anger, not for me but something else. "Those creatures are hounds of The Wild Hunt, only supposed to hunt one night every hundred years, but this was something different. Someone sent those hounds to take you, but I will never let that happen." He smooths my soaked hair back, soothing my rising fear, and leaves his hand resting on my face. "I promise you are safe with me, Carlin."

I believe him. Everything within me can feel the truth in his words. That almost unnatural steadiness he possesses is unwavering, even now. Looking into his eyes, I can feel my anxious breathing slow, my fear beginning to ebb with the shallow waves around us. I look around the cavern, trying to find anything to take my mind off the night's events. "How did you even know this was here?"

He moves to take a seat across from me. "This is what they call Mermaid's Cove. There's only a handful of people left who even know it's here." He laughs once at my questioning look, "No, mermaids aren't real. At least, not the ones you're thinking of." He looks toward the opening of the cove, "It should be safe to head for the cottage now. Come on."

We make our way slowly up to the ground above where there is nothing to be seen or heard, much to my relief. The only noise is the waves of the sea below and the normal sounds of the night. We start on our trek toward Mairead's, an uncomfortable silence between us for the first time. After a while, I can't stand it anymore. "Where did you go tonight?" I stop walking, the hurt I felt watching him walk away becoming fresh.

He takes a couple of steps before he realizes that I've stopped, then turns to face me. "I'm sorry that I left you. Fin found me and told me you were clearly bothered by what happened." He closes the distance he put between us now. "Who you saw me with, Nyx, she's not what you think. There are things about this world that you don't know, and I was trying to keep you from them. Before they brought themselves to you." He looks pained at the thought.

I rub my forehead, trying to ease my annoyance, "Maddox, I understand that you're trying to protect me from...*whatever* is happening, but I'd rather just know. It's the not knowing and the guessing that makes it a little torturous for me. Please tell me."

He throws his head back to the sky, sighing deeply before meeting my eyes again. "I am a changeling. A human stolen from the mortal world as a child and raised in the Faerie Realm. The others too: Theo, Thomas, Fin, Kellan, even Liam. They're all changelings. We grew up alongside, but never equal to, the Fair Folk."

I can only blink up at him, my mind not producing a coherent thought for a long moment, the still-lingering shock of the night like a heavy fog on my brain. How many more times am I going to be presented with information that hits like a ton of bricks today? I would be inclined to think the entirety of this town had gone mad, but I woke up this morning to pixies in my room. It's not a huge leap to believe what he's telling me now.

"So where does Nyx fit in?" I ask when my mind starts turning again.

He starts walking again and gestures for me to follow, not comfortable with standing out in the open any longer. "Nyx is a type of water nymph, something like a siren, but likes to stay near fresh water. She grew up around us and has always been horrible, only now she's a lackey to one of the rulers of the Otherworld who is even more wicked than Nyx can be." He glances over at me, checking to see how well I'm taking everything in.

"So, Theo was telling the truth when he said you were just trying to keep her away from me?"

"I couldn't let her near you, I didn't know what she might've been there to do. But she was just a distraction. A pawn to get me away so they could come for you."

I'm covered in chills at the thought of being taken by those *things*. I rub my arms, trying but failing to smooth the goosebumps away. Maddox notices my discomfort and takes my hand firmly in his.

"Liam said he could call them off if I went with him. Do you think he sent them?" I ask.

New anger lights his eyes, "No, he doesn't control them. He was there to help take you." His jaw tenses and releases. "He's a pawn too, like Nyx. I don't know what they're up to, but I'm sure it didn't help that I got in the way of whatever it was he was trying to do with you. He's the type that could've been there out of pure spite."

We've just entered the forested part of the road when we hear a low growling sound from between the trees around us. I let out a small gasp, turning to Maddox, fear threatening to freeze me in place. He squeezes my hand to comfort me, speaking in a low quiet voice, "Don't react, just keep walking; they like the chase. When I tell you to go," he continues, "you run to Mairead's as fast as you can and get inside the fence line. It's warded, and they can't come in. Don't look back, don't stop. No matter what happens." He slides his eyes over to me, waiting for confirmation that I'll follow his instructions. I nod, my movements stilted and jerky from fear.

A single black hound stalks slowly from the trees in front of us, blocking our path. Maddox quickly rips the leather string from his neck, uttering a single Irish word, "Fás," sending the sword pendant growing into a life-size broadsword right in front of my eyes. He twirls it in his hand once before settling into a fighting stance, the hound's red eyes drawn immediately to him. In the same breath that the obsidian beast bounds toward him, Maddox growls out the command: "Go! Now!"

I burst into movement as Maddox clashes with the creature. I've only made it a few yards when I disregard everything he told me, looking back to see him land a killing blow just as a second beast is stalking up behind him. I open my mouth to warn him a moment too late. The second hound has already lunged, sinking his teeth into Maddox's shoulder and causing him to drop his sword. It feels like the breath has been forced out of me by a physical blow as the creature knocks him to his back and lunges for his throat. Maddox reacts just in time, grabbing the hound by its open maw, holding its jaws open only inches above his face.

My eyes lock onto the sword lying just behind them. There's no way I can leave him like this. Scrambling back towards them while the horrible thing is preoccupied, I grab the sword shakily. It feels so foreign in my hands, but I raise it anyway, ready to strike however I can. Maddox looks up from the hound, a mix of surprise and fear filling his eyes as he hastily takes in the sword raised in my shaking hands, "Stop, I have to kill it! I have to be the one to kill it!"

The obsidian hound realizes my presence then and turns sharply toward me. I back away slowly, sword warily pointed toward it. Maddox gets to his feet, speaking calmly to me, "Throw me the sword." I hoist the sword toward him, but the sudden movement makes the beast pounce. I fall to the ground, hands up, ready to block a bite that never comes. Instead, the creature falls lifelessly on top of me. Maddox is there in an instant, throwing its ghastly body away and pulling me to my feet. He puts his hand to my cheek, stooping to look me fully in the face. His eyes are searching every inch of me, his chest rising and falling rapidly. "Are you harmed? Did it bite you?"

I shake my head, fighting to keep my breathing normal as the reality of the situation sinks in. "I-I'm fine. But you're not." My eyes fall to the sleeve of his raised hand, soaked in blood. I feel sick not just at the sight of the blood, but at the thought of him being hurt. "We need to get you to a hospital, Maddox."

"We just need to get to Mairead's. She'll have the things we need. Doctors won't know how to fix this," he assures me. Letting go of me, he turns to the limp body of the hound, cutting a tuft of fur from its thick neck and shoving it into his pocket before using the dirt road to wipe his sword clean. He utters another Irish word and the sword shrinks back into a pendant. He shoves it into another pocket and we start again for the cottage.

I heave a sigh of relief as soon as we enter the gate. When we reach the front door, it flies open and Mairead greets me with a tight hug before we can even step a foot over the threshold. "Oh lass, I am so relieved to see ya'. We've been pacing the floors waiting for you two!" She notices the blood on my face and pales. "Are you injured child?" she almost whispers the question.

"No, but he is," I shake my head, turning to Maddox. "He's been bitten."

She ushers us in quickly, "Did you get its hair, lad?" She looks at Maddox, her face serious. He nods, giving her the contents of his pocket as we step over the threshold.

Claire rushes me as soon as we enter, her arms flying around me, "Thank goodness you're okay! Theo got me back here safely before joining the others to distract those...*monsters*." Her gaze turns far off as the last word leaves her mouth.

The sight of Fin, Theo, Thomas and Kellan all sitting around Mairead's home looking rather worried catches me a little off guard.

Mairead pushes Maddox past us, directing him to sit down in one of her dining chairs to examine his wound. "You're going to have to remove your shirt, lad." Using the hand of his unwounded arm to undo his buttons, he slowly slides off his shirt, wincing from the pain. It's immediately obvious that he's been honed for battle, lean but powerful muscles cord his entire body. I only realize I'm staring when he catches my eye, giving me a slow sideways grin. Heat rises in my cheeks as I look away quickly, leaving him laughing softly.

"Carlin, in the kitchen cabinet just above the sink there is a wooden box; I need you to bring that to me, along with a mortar and pestle and some warm water," Mairead instructs me.

I return as quickly as I can with her requested items. Setting them down onto the table within her reach, I steal a glance at Maddox's wound; the holes in his bicep aren't just leaking blood, but a putrid, black substance, and the veins around his wounds are turning black to match. I let out a small breath, having to fight back the nausea creeping in, looking between the two of them with wide eyes, "Why does it look like that?"

Maddox answers, leaving Mairead to empty the contents of the wooden box. "The hounds' bites are laced with venom. It'll kill some-one quickly without the proper antidote."

"What's the antidote?"

Mairead answers this time, "The hair of the hound that bit you, mixed into a balm with a few other healing herbs. But the hair only works if the one who was bitten is the one who slays the creature. Now, I need you to clean his wounds while I mix this." She dips a clean cloth into the bowl of water and hands it to me. I start cleansing away the blood and black poison, trying to be as gentle as I can, but he winces when I touch a particularly painful spot.

"I'm so sorry!" I pull my hands back and start to step away, but he grabs my hand with his uninjured one.

"Look at me. You're doing fine," he reassures me sweetly.

I finish cleaning away as much as I can and Mairead takes my place with the antidote. She covers the wound in the mysterious balm, wrapping it with gauze just as the pixies appear with a clean shirt for him. I'm slightly confused by their appearance, "I take it Claire knows about them now?"

Mairead answers with a humorless laugh, "After tonight, she had no choice but to know about them, as well as other things."

Maddox stands and makes his way to me. "You should rest, you're exhausted." He runs a hand softly over my bare arm.

I shake my head at him, "Not before you explain *everything* to me."

He sighs and rubs a hand over his face, obviously hoping to avoid getting me deeper into whatever any of this is.

I find a spot on the couch and cross my arms, turning my face up to him, "There, I'm resting. Now start talking."

He takes a seat in front of me on the coffee table, forearms resting on his legs. "I don't even know where to start," his hands turn up in a small shrug.

Claire plops down onto the couch beside me. "Uh, how about the fact that you were *all* stolen as children and have been living with faeries for *centuries*?" Our current situation has apparently chased away her bashfulness.

"*Centuries*?" I stare at him, gaping. He doesn't look like he can be more than in his late twenties. "When, exactly, were you taken?" I ask slowly.

He takes in a deep breath before answering, "I was taken as a small child, maybe three years old, sometime during the 1300s."

I can only blink at him again, the only coherent thought I am able to form is, *"How?"*

He answers gently, sensing my rising dismay, "Time passes differently in the Otherworld, and for all who live there."

"They don't call it Tír na nÓg for no reason," Theo says, leaving his quiet twin to elaborate at mine and Claire's questioning looks.

"It means Land of Youth."

Maddox gestures between himself and the rest of the men there. "We all live here now, in the mortal realm, but were granted a form of immortality by the rulers we serve for as long as we serve them."

"So why are you all here, in this particular village, out of all the places in the world?" I ask.

"This village is built very close to one of the gates leading to the Fae Realm, making it a hotbed for fae activity," Kellan explains. "And that particular gate is the closest to the kingdom of the ruler we work for."

"Are you all from the same time?" Claire asks then, eyeing Theo curiously.

Maddox answers her, a little bit of playfulness in his tone, "Theodore and Thomas here are the babies of the group, taken around the late nineteenth century."

Theo gives him a suffering look at the use of his full name as Claire giggles next to me.

"Kellan was stolen around the same time I was," Maddox continues, "and Fin, or rather Fenrir, is the eldest, the son of a Viking berserker. He was the oldest of us all and training to be a berserker himself when he was taken."

That explains the odd accent I picked up from him.

"There are *so* many questions I want to ask," I say, shaking my head incredulously, "but I don't know if my brain can process it all."

Kellan leans himself against the stair rail and raises his eyebrows, "No better time to ask than now."

"Why did they take you? Who are these *rulers* you work for?" My mind is swirling with too many thoughts to voice.

"Faeries steal children for different reasons. Sometimes to keep them as servants, other times to replace a child of their own or because they need someone to do their dirty work in the mortal world." Maddox looks to all his friends behind him, "They were stolen by emissaries from the Seelie Court to be raised as warriors and guards for King Finnbhear and assigned to keep watch over the fae, both Seelie and Unseelie, that cross into this realm. They are required keep them in check if they get too unruly, or draw too much attention when it isn't wanted, and to take them out if they do."

"I was stolen, along with Liam, and raised as a slave to Queen Mab's Unseelie Court, until King Finnbhear saw me holding my own with a group of goblins when I was around ten and brought me back to the Seelie Court to join this lot as a guard." His eyes harden in an effort to hide the sadness there, but I see it. My heart aches for him, to be raised with the wicked creatures from Mairead's story is a horrible existence.

I look to Mairead, reminded of her tale, "How did you know all of this?"

"I was there when it happened, dearie." She smiles wryly at me, moving her hair up to reveal pointed ears that are capped in tufts of grey fur. "I am what they call a Brownie. I've been with these boys since the beginning, helped raise them in Finnbhear's court."

I look to Claire, who is mirroring my astonishment. I didn't think it was possible to be any more shocked by tonight's events.

"So, what exactly *is* a Brownie?" Claire manages to ask through the shock.

Mairead straightens proudly. "Brownies are household helpers. We love to help with everything and anything we can, and don't particularly like being unable to do those things."

All the times she'd denied my help and rejected my refusal of hers suddenly make more sense. "The dress I'm wearing now, did you actually have it just lying around?" I ask, narrowing my eyes.

Her eyes twinkle at her work finally being recognized. "I started making it the moment I laid eyes on ya', dearie."

I open my mouth to thank her, but before I can utter a word she shoots a hand up, "Don't thank me child. Faeries don't like being thanked."

I clamp my mouth shut with an embarrassed grin.

"So wait," Claire asks, looking to Mairead, "you're a part of the Seelie Court then, the good ones?"

She laughs at Claire's wide-eyed look. "Aye, I was, but not anymore. I left and came to this realm when these young men did. I'd raised them nearly their entire lives. I wasn't about to let them go alone." She looks to the group of them, all smiling softly at her, the love they have for each other evident.

"But," she says, holding a finger up, "don't let the names fool you. Seelie, Unseelie...they're arbitrary names made up mostly by humans to help make sense of it all. There are terrible, terrible things from all sides of the realm. And usually, the best of the best or the worst of the worst end up here, and both for different reasons. The human world is a playground for one and a solace for the other."

"And Mairead here is the best of the best of them all," Theo says, putting an arm around her.

Mairead moves from her place at the kitchen table, "Now, it is high time you *all* get some rest after everything you've been through tonight." She gives us all a pointed look. "As for more questions and figuring out why those hounds have shown up, that can wait 'til morning." She looks to the group of warriors, "You're welcome to take turns on the couch, but I think we'd all feel much safer if someone was keeping watch tonight. Not you," she points to Maddox. "I know you're stubborn as a mule, but you've been injured and need the rest more than anyone."

He shoots her an annoyed look but doesn't protest.

I stand to excuse myself to my room and Maddox stands quickly with me, leaving us only a hair's breadth apart. He strokes my cheek sweetly, tilting my head to look him in the eyes; the others in the room quickly finding things to do to give us a few moments alone. He searches my eyes carefully, as if he can read all my thoughts there. "How are you taking this?"

Placing my hand on his chest, I give him a soft smile. "If I didn't have all of you here, seeing and hearing the same things, I would be sure I was losing my mind." I laugh once, more out of uncertainty than humor. "Honestly, I'm terrified. Why would someone send those things after me?" My voice trembles slightly at the thought, panic threatening to grip me tightly again.

He pulls me to his chest, holding me in his strong arms for a long moment, the sound of his heartbeat soothing to me. When he pulls back, he doesn't let me go completely. "We'll figure this out." He cups my face in his hands, "Whatever it takes to keep you safe, I'll do it."

I shake my head at him, my eyes threatening tears, "You could've been *killed* tonight." I look to the floor, guilt hanging over me, "I don't want anyone getting hurt, or worse, because of me."

"Look at me."

I look into his striking eyes and he brushes away the single tear that has started to fall, pressing his lips to mine. A soft, sweet kiss laced with a promise. He pulls away, the kiss over far too quickly, and places his forehead against mine. "Whatever it takes to keep you safe, I'll do it," he says again. "I'm not afraid of a fight, or even death for that matter."

"What? No, Maddox," I cut him off, incredulous. "How can you even say that? I'm practically still a stranger to you."

"I would never sit back and allow even a stranger to be thrust into something like this without fighting," his blue-eyed gaze on me is unwavering. "But you're already more than just some stranger to me; you and I both know that."

Chapter 9

Maddox is dead. The hound's bite landed true and killed him. I'm alone in the woods, the horrible creature stalking me, and I have nowhere to run. The blackness around me swallows everything. All I can see are the hound's red eyes coming closer and closer until they lunge.

"No, please! Maddox!"

"Carlin, wake up," someone shakes me gently. "I'm here, Mhuirnín."

My eyes shoot open. I'm in my room and Maddox is sitting on the edge of my bed, his brow furrowed in concern. Sitting up, I throw my arms around him, breathing a sigh of relief, "I was having a nightmare. That thing had killed you."

He smooths the back of my hair down, soothing me, and speaking into my ear, "I am here and perfectly fine. I came running as soon as I heard you scream."

I pull back and take him in, "I don't think I'll be able to sleep now." Looking to the window I can tell there are still a few hours until sunrise. "Will you stay with me awhile?"

He brushes my cheek with his thumb, a smile pulling at the edge of his lips. "Of course." He moves to lie down on top of the covers next to me, pulling my head to his chest and weaves his arms around me. The scent of him coupled with his steady embrace eases my mind, chasing away the looming terror of the dream. We lie in comfortable silence for long awhile, enjoying the closeness.

"How do you even go outside knowing that something like that might be waiting for you?" I say into the quiet, my mind still spinning with thoughts of the hounds. A chill runs through me at the thought of what else might be out there that I've never known of.

"You can't allow the fear of what might come to hold you hostage. If you allow that to happen, and miss all the good that's out there waiting for you, then they've already won." The soft tones of his voice help to soothe my rising fears.

"I just can't stop thinking about you being raised in that place, with all of those terrible things."

"Don't worry yourself with that. It doesn't bother me much anymore, it's just my life now." His fingers run up and down my arm absently, lost in thought for a moment before speaking again, "At first, as a small child, it was terrifying. But after a while I was almost numb to it. Being there made me stronger. I had to fight if I wanted to survive, and it's served me well working for King Finnbhear all these years."

"Why do you think someone sent those hounds for me?" I ask, all the thoughts and questions from earlier coming back to me.

Maddox lets out a slow breath, "I intend to figure that out. I'm going to have an audience with King Finnbhear tomorrow to make an appeal for his assistance, and for his protection to be granted to you."

I sit up, facing him. "I'm coming with you."

"No." The word is absolute. He props himself up on his uninjured arm. "Mairead was telling the truth earlier. The Seelie Court might be the *better* half of the Fae, but that doesn't mean they're good either. Faeries are different creatures entirely and don't work on the same rules that mortals do. They're all dangerously cunning, especially the rulers, and all too ready to trap a human into a bargain, one that never ends well for that human. Goodness and innocence are a rarity for them. I don't know if they even understand it," he says, thinking out loud. "I don't want to waltz you in there just to become some sort of curious prey."

I tilt my head to the side, "Don't you think it's only fair for me to be there if it's a meeting *about* me?"

He shoots me an exasperated look, my point obviously made.

"I promise to let you do all of the talking and I will stay with you the whole time."

He pulls me back to his chest, huffing a sigh, "Fine, but you have to listen to whatever I tell you. No stubbornness." I nod my head against his chest, and he kisses my hair. "Now get some rest. You'll have another eventful day tomorrow."

I smile in his arms, mixed feelings of excitement and wariness settling over me.

The sound of voices and movement downstairs wake me and I realize I'm alone. I must've been deeply asleep not to notice Maddox getting up. Padding over to the bathroom, I freshen up quickly before making my way downstairs to see the entire group still here, all in various stages of eating breakfast: Kellan and Fin just sitting down to eat, Theo and Thomas in the middle of devouring the food on their plates, and Maddox already done. He sees me and makes his way over to me, planting a light kiss on my brow in greeting.

"Have you been awake long?" I ask.

He shakes his head, "Maybe an hour, not long. You were sleeping too well; I tried my best not to wake you."

"Good morning, everyone!" Claire says as she pads down the stairs behind us, sounding bubbly but still looking exhausted. She comes to stand by me. "Please tell me I'm not the only one who couldn't sleep after last night."

I feel as exhausted as she looks, "You're definitely not alone. I had terrible dreams, but eventually got some peaceful sleep." I share a small smile with Maddox.

Mairead comes through the kitchen door bearing plates of food for me and Claire. "Come now, sit and eat," she bids us over as she sets our breakfast on the table.

"So what's the plan for today? Where do we go from here?" Claire prods, speaking to no one in particular.

Maddox answers as he props himself against the wall closest to me, "Carlin and I are going to the Seelie Court. I've requested an audience with Finnbhear."

Claire shoots me a wide-eyed look at that, her fork full of eggs suspended in midair.

Thomas, ever the silent one, shocks me by speaking up, "You two shouldn't go alone. At least take one of us with you."

Maddox is pensive for a moment before nodding. "You're right. Just in case something goes awry, someone should go with us." He looks to Fin, "I think it should be you. You've been with Finnbhear the longest and he trusts you the most for just that reason." He pushes himself off the wall before he adds, "I have a few more things to take care of before we go." He looks between Fin and I, "We'll leave in an hour. Whatever it is you need to do to get prepared, do it by then." His voice is a little stilted and strained, catching me off guard.

He leaves the cottage without another word and I shoot a glance at Fin, eyebrows raised.

"He's worried about having you there," Fin explains quietly.

"The Fae are always dangerous, no matter what court it is," Kellan adds, nearly parroting Maddox's words from last night.

"I have to say," Claire interjects, "on one hand I'm a little jealous that you're getting to see what the Faerie Realm is like." She shrugs, "But on the other, I'm glad it's not me experiencing something like that."

The reminder of facing something so unknown gives me a sinking feeling in my stomach. "What all do I need to know before I step foot inside that place?" I look between all the changelings.

"Don't eat anything they offer you. Don't drink anything they offer you," Theo says, raising a finger with each rule.

"Why?"

Thomas speaks up again, "Because faerie food and wine will bewitch you. Once they have you enthralled, they can make you do anything they want."

"How did you guys eat and drink then?" Claire asks, every bit as curious as I am.

Theo answers her, "We're in the king's direct service; he granted us immunity. The only one who can enthrall us while we're in his service is Finnbhear himself."

Fin speaks this time, his voice is stern, "Also, don't speak to anyone if you can avoid it. Faeries can't lie but they *can* dance around the truth. They will have you trapped into a devil's bargain before you even realize what's happened."

Mairead, silent this whole time, finally speaks, "I understand she needs to know all of these things, but there is no reason to scare the poor girl." She puts her hands on my shoulders, looking me steadily in the eyes. "They're all correct. The Faerie Realm is dangerous. But as long as you stay with Fin and Maddox, you'll be fine. They're not only skilled fighters, these boys have had ages of experience dealing with the very worst of the Fair Folk and are still alive to tell the tales. You're in good hands." Her tone is, thankfully, reassuring. "Now finish up your breakfast and come to your room. I have something for you," Mairead tells me, picking up the empty dishes from the table.

I can't eat much. My nerves are scrambled but I manage to force down a few bites before making my way to my room where I'm greeted by Mairead, Claire, Flynn and Bramble.

"We're going to help too!" Claire says, gesturing excitedly to the pixies holding up sprigs of baby's breath and grinning widely.

"You'll wear this. It'll help you blend in." Mairead holds up a beautifully embroidered gown like a work of art, helping me slip into it. Ivory embroidered chiffon depicting different flora covers the palest green silk that falls gracefully around my form, the sleeves opening into a trumpet style at my wrists. Claire hands me a pair of intricately decorated slippers made of soft leather and Flynn waves me over to the edge of the bed to sit.

The pixies pull a few curls softly back from my face, securing it all with the sprigs of flowers as Claire applies a touch of makeup.

"You look like a beautiful faerie queen!" Bramble squeals.

I smile at them timidly, not sure if I could ever blend in with the otherworldly creatures. I turn to Mairead, my curiosity peaking, "What does Maddox have to prepare before we go?"

"Himself, lass," she gives a pained smile. "There are no special rituals or rules to get into the Faerie Realm; you just walk right through the gate. He's having to prepare himself for having you so near the very things that have brought him so much scorn and pain all these years."

Her words bring on a sense of guilt. Was I wrong to demand I come along?

"I know what you're thinking," Mairead says, her voice taking on a motherly tone, "but it's a matter that deals *directly* with you. He knows that it's only right for you to be there. Maddox cares a great deal for you and he's worrying over your safety is all."

Her words ease my doubt a little.

"With that being said," Mairead adds, "he only has your best interest at heart, so listen to what he tells you when you're there." She throws me a stern look, knowing I can be obstinate with him sometimes.

I nod my head and grin sheepishly at the old faerie. "Yes, ma'am."

There is a knock at the door and Maddox steps through. "Are you ready?"

The sight of him is a bit of a shock compared to the last time I'd seen him. He has changed completely into light leather armor. The smooth brown material is made into a woven pattern as the sleeves reach his shoulders, his sword no longer around his neck but strapped to his waist. It wouldn't be a surprise if a few other weapons are hidden upon his person.

"As I'll ever be, I think." I let out a deep breath as I stand, trying to ease the nerves creeping back in.

His blue eyes finally take me in completely, his mouth falling open the slightest bit, sending my own into a shy smile as he clears his throat. "We should go. Fin is waiting for us outside."

Mairead and Claire both hug me as Claire whispers conspiratorially, "I'll be waiting for you to get back, and you *have* to tell me all about it."

I follow along silently behind the warrior to meet with Fin.

The Viking is dressed similarly to Maddox, only instead of a sword strapped around his waist, two battle axes are strapped across his back.

"Do all of your weapons change size on command?" I ask.

"They do. It makes them much easier to carry in the mortal world and not be labeled a psychopath," Maddox answers, a slight laugh in his voice. He beckons with a nod of his head. "Let's get going. The sooner we get this started, the sooner it can be over."

We make for the woods just outside of Mairead's fence as a light misty rain begins to fall. We walk along in silence, all seemingly stuck in our own thoughts. A little while later, Maddox stops in front of two oak trees standing only a few feet apart, their branches twined together in an arch overhead.

"Really? This is it?" I look between the two warriors, an eyebrow raised, "Kind of unassuming."

Maddox huffs a laugh at my statement, "That's the point. It'll stay hidden for the most part and catch any *unassuming* humans off guard. They'll step through, making their way to either the Seelie or the Unseelie court, and be lost to the mortal realm until the ruler grants them leave."

I frown at them both, a little disappointed at just how mundane it seems. "That's seriously all we do, just step through?"

Maddox doesn't answer this time, he simply steps through the trees and vanishes. I let out a small gasp, looking behind me to an amused Fin. He nods, signaling for me to follow behind Maddox. I take in a deep breath, steeling myself for what's to come, then step through.

Maddox is waiting for me on the other side and Fin comes through just a moment later. My shoulders fall a bit at what I'm seeing. Everything looks the same, except it isn't raining here. Instead, dappled light ripples through breaks in the green canopy overhead.

"I was expecting something at least a *little* different..." I say to them. They both let out a small laugh at my blatant disappointment.

"Just look closer, Mhuirnín. You'll see," Maddox says into my ear.

So I do just that. Looking slowly around the forest, I become acutely aware of movement stirring in the woods around us as figures, some humanoid, some utterly inhuman, start emerging from the forest. Creatures like women pull away from the bark on the trees to look us over, their skin matching the bark of the trees with hair like vines and branches floating around their heads. Diminutive figures step out from behind rocks and ferns looking just like roots with wide eyes and spindly limbs. Tiny faeries flit through the air like hummingbirds.

I step closer to Maddox, taking his hand, fear and awe battling within me at the sight. He leads me down an open footpath, Fin following just behind. It isn't long before we've reached our destination. We stand before a great yew tree, the size of the trunk big enough to house Mairead's entire cottage. It's joined to a group of other trees through a series of bridges suspended from the massive rooms built into the canopies. The doors in front of us open of their own accord, revealing a foyer leading to stairs built into the trunk of the tree.

We climb multiple flights of stairs, strains of soft enchanting music reaching our ears, before finally emerging into the throne room. The room is spacious but empty of decor, the beautiful architecture leaving no need for any ornament except for the ornate dais housing an imposing throne at the head of it. The branches of the tree twine together into open arches lining the length of the throne room before coming together to create an intricate ceiling.

A few groups of scattered Seelie Court inhabitants watch us closely as we walk toward the throne, but there are no other occupants besides a handful of armored guards and the king.

The seelie king is a formidable figure. A crown of golden leaves sits atop auburn hair falling in thick waves to his shoulders, framing a wise and dignified face. I'm a bit surprised at the age just beginning to show on him.

The faerie king regards us coolly as we reach the foot of his dais. Maddox and Fin bow quickly and efficiently. I follow their lead, executing a quick but graceful curtsy.

"Maddox, Fenrir, it is always a pleasure to see you. Though I gather the circumstances as to why you're here are not as pleasurable," he addresses my companions kindly, his voice a rich baritone. He turns his gaze to me, a small twinkle in his eye, one that doesn't sit well with me. I can't explain it. I know I just met him, but something about him and the way he's looking at me fills me with unease.

"You must be what all of the fuss is about." His amber eyes roam over me, "I don't fail to see why, you're quite the alluring little thing. Wide eyed and demure, just calling for a white knight to rescue her. There aren't many like you left in the mortal realm. Innocence is a rarity these days."

I toss him a pinched smile, unsure if I heard the teasing and suggestion in his tone correctly. Maddox stiffens beside me, apparently not liking the king's tone himself.

"You know, it would be a pity to have you here, as lovely as you look, and not offer you a chance to see more of my home," Finnbhear continues, "Why don't we share a small meal together? Discuss things in a more hospitable environment." The faerie king cocks his head the slightest bit, the look reminding me a little of a cat assessing a mouse it's about to toy with.

"Thank you for the generous offer, sir," Fin speaks this time, "But I think the quicker we can get this matter taken care of and Carlin back to the mortal realm, the better we'll all feel."

I steal a glance at Maddox beside me, his gaze on the king is fiery and it's easily apparent he's biting his tongue. Angering the supernatural ruler, especially one he's indentured to, wouldn't be the smartest idea.

The hardness that has crept into Finnbhear's voice when he speaks this time isn't difficult to miss, "Tell me then, what is it that has brought you here?"

Maddox takes a breath before beginning his explanation, releasing a bit of the tension in his body, "Someone ordered hounds from The Wild Hunt to pursue Carlin and bring her back to them." He glances over to me before continuing, "I was hoping for assistance in finding the one responsible and to ask you to grant her your protection until they are found."

"What do you know at this time?" Finnbhear questions.

"We have reason to believe that a member of the Unseelie Court has orchestrated it. I caught an agent of the court, Liam, trying to coerce her into leaving with him to stop the attack." He pauses to sigh before finishing, "In order to safely remove her from the situation, I used non-lethal force to take him down, in the interest of averting an act of war."

The king turns to me, head tilted in assessment, "Is this true, girl?"

I nod, looking over at Maddox before speaking, "Yes. If it wasn't for Maddox I would've been taken."

The faerie king cocks his head again, this time looking between the two of us. "Even in this short meeting, it is glaringly obvious that you have taken a particular interest in the girl, and she in you." He makes direct, probing eye contact with Maddox, something in his glare that I can't quite place. "And you mean to tell me you haven't the faintest inkling as to who could be behind this, boy?"

What is he hinting at? That Maddox may already know the reason behind the attack? Surely I'm misunderstanding.

Maddox's face slackens for a breath before his jaw clenches, but he says nothing.

Finnbhear stands and smirks. "I thought so." He beckons for Maddox to follow with a lazy hand, "Come, these are matters we must discuss privately."

The changeling warrior nods once to him before turning to me, "Stay with Fin and you'll be fine." And with that he turns, following the faerie king through the doors just behind his throne.

"He shouldn't be long," Fenrir murmurs, gripping my arm softly. "But let's make ourselves scarce." He glances to the gathered courtiers, making me realize more had arrived during our audience, before pulling me over to wait by one of the open arched windows. "The less attention you draw from them the better."

My eyes dart around the room suspiciously before looking back to him. "Do you really think they'd try something with you here? And Maddox?"

"If there is anything we've learned in all our years spent here, it's that you can never let your guard down." His eyes never stop scanning the room, his training as a guard apparent. "They tend to ignore the fact that we were raised among them and know their ways. We know when they're scheming, and they're always itching to test their wiles on humans."

I focus my attention out the window to the mysterious land below, trying, and failing, to ignore the feel of otherworldly eyes on me. For a short while I watch a number of different creatures go about their daily lives below in a bit of a daze, entranced by the madness of it all. I'm startled by the sound of doors being flung open, Maddox stalking out of them.

"Like I said, if you're *truly* worried for her safety," Finnbhear's voice, full of what seems to be teasing, rings from the room behind Maddox, "she is more than welcome to stay here with me. I could guarantee her protection then."

"Let's go home," Maddox says sharply. He won't meet my eyes, but it's impossible to miss the tightness in his own as he stalks for the exit. I shoot a quick glance to Fin, questioning, but he only gestures for me to follow his friend.

I catch up to Maddox, following closely behind as he pushes our way through the gathered crowd of faeries. Suddenly, my wrist is gripped tightly by a creature within the crowd. A bent and withered hag, cloaked in worn grey shrouds of cloth, jeers at me. "I can tell your future."

I blanch, recoiling, but can't pull out of her clawed grasp.

"I see hell there," the hag crows. "You'll soon be gambling with fate!"

Maddox rounds on her, a short sword drawn from somewhere on his person. "Take your hand off of her, crone, or I will cut it off." His voice is sharp and seething.

She loosens her grip at that, and I am able to wrench free, allowing my companions to usher me swiftly to the stairs and down into the foyer below, the crone wailing all the while in the distance.

I'm still trembling when we reach the forest. "What was that?" I ask, my words stilted and breathless from the fear still gripping me. "What could she have seen?"

"She's a banshee," Maddox answers. "They're known to see the future, mostly bad things, but they never tell the entire story." He still hasn't stopped walking, in no mood to dawdle in this place any longer.

"Like we said," Fenrir adds behind me, "faeries can't lie, but they can, and will, evade the truth. Either by omission or wordplay."

Finally, we reach the gate and stepping through this time reveals a much bigger change. Night has settled in the mortal world now. Time truly does pass differently in the Faerie Realm; we couldn't have been there much more than an hour.

"Oh wow," I breath out as hundreds of little blue lights float up from the dark forest floor.

"Sprites," Maddox says, smiling at me, though it doesn't quite reach his eyes. "You'll be able to see any faerie creatures here in the mortal world now, no matter if they're glamoured or not."

I shoot him a questioning look.

"Anyone who has entered the Faerie Realm is granted this *sight*," he explains, glancing toward the glowing sprites. "Go on, they won't harm you."

I step tentatively toward a group of them, hovering just a few steps away. Once I'm close enough I can hear their light, tinkling laughter and whispers. They flit around me, inspecting everything. Weaving around my dress and face before a group of them alight in my curls, emanating their blue glow around my head. A delighted laugh bubbles from my lips at the wonder of it all.

Maddox is staring, awe seeming to slacken his face, but it's Fin who speaks, "They like you."

I smile at the Viking and look back to Maddox whose expression has changed completely. He rubs a hand down his face, almost angrily, before turning away and stalking toward the cottage without another word.

"I don't know what your problem is, but it's not me." I call to his back, drawing myself up indignantly, a little hurt by his sudden attitude.

He stops abruptly and turns back to face me. "What?"

I frown at him from across the clearing, losing a bit of my boldness. "You've been distant all day, but after the audience with Finnbhear, I feel like you're angry with me." I shake my head, "Did I do something wrong?"

Fin quietly disappears into the night, leaving the two of us alone.

Maddox takes a step closer, his shoulders dropping, voice remorseful. "I'm not angry with you. Far from it. It's just, there are things at play here that you don't understand. That's what I'm angry at."

"Then *tell me*, Maddox." I hold my hands out, "Help me understand. It's not just today though," I add. "Since I've met you, one minute I think I know where this is going then the next you take two steps back." I huff out a shaky breath.

He's come closer to me now, just within arm's reach. His eyebrows knit together as he looks at me. "You are in danger, and the closer you get to me the more dangerous it becomes. There are things in my past that are coming back to haunt me, and as much as I've told you, there are still things I can't say. I'm bound to secrecy. And I refuse put you in harm's way. No matter how *alive* you make me feel..." He sighs, looking up into the night air. "It's better for you to walk away now," he says quietly as he turns to leave again.

"But I don't *want* to walk away." My voice comes out barely above a whisper, forcing me to take a deep breath before speaking again. "All my life I've felt a pull toward this place, a yearning. Like there was some piece of me already here, waiting. Almost like a string pulling me here. I could never explain it. But I finally made it here and I've found it, that *thread* tugging on my soul. It was you." I close my eyes against the emotion threatening to overtake me, "Just please don't push me away." I open my eyes and before I realize what's happening, his lips meet mine fervently, his hands twining through my hair, pulling me into him. My initial shock is quelled as the kiss deepens, pushing all the weight of the last few days away, leaving no room for anything but him and I. It's almost crippling, every unsaid word and feeling between the two of us being poured into the kiss. I could melt into him.

We pull away slowly and he rests his forehead against mine, not wanting the connection to end. Our breathing is ragged as we take each other in.

"Promise me, Mo Chuisle," his own voice is thick with emotion when he finally speaks, "whatever may come, you will hold on to me." He pulls back to look at me, running his fingers down my arm until my hand is wrapped in his.

I squeeze his hand, locking onto his striking eyes, unwavering. "I promise."

Chapter 10

When we make it back to the cottage we see Fin waiting patiently, propped up against the gate. He joins us silently, a knowing gleam in his eye, as we walk through the garden and to the front door. We open the door to find the entire group, including the pixies, awaiting our return.

Claire jumps from her seat beside Theo and rushes me, "You're finally back! I need to hear everything!"

Mairead steps up beside the redhead, patting her back gently. "Remember what I told you, lass. It may have been all day for us, but it's only been a short while to them," the brownie laughs. "At least give them time to step inside the door."

Claire blanches slightly but shoots me a grin.

"So, how did it go?" Kellan questions, brows raised.

Maddox, Fin, and I take seats around the dining table while everyone else gathers around to hear the results of the meeting. I've only
just realized myself, after the run-in with that banshee and in the forest
afterward, that I don't know how the audience with the king ended.
But I know it can't be good given Maddox's state when we left the
wooded palace.

Everyone finally stills, awaiting a reply. Maddox takes in a slow
breath before answering, "Finnbhear can't grant her protection."

My heart drops slightly, more for the warrior who has fought so
hard for my safety than disappointment at King Finnbhear's answer.

Kellan straightens from his leaned position against the wall, brows
pinched in confusion. "That's absurd, why?"

"Because she is not a member of his court," Maddox answers tightly,
taking in another breath before continuing, "and neither am I."

Everyone turns sharply to Maddox, shock and confusion warring
on their faces, including me. After a few beats of stunned silence Fenrir
speaks up, his tone cold. "You've been in his service for *centuries*, longer
than anyone here besides me," his head shakes in disbelief. "How, pray
tell, are you not a member of his court?"

Maddox runs a hand over his face, leaning forward to prop his
forearms on the table. "I was taken by the Unseelie Court, raised
there for the first few years of my life and trained as a servant and
emissary to Queen Mab. My service to the Seelie King is, apparently,
only a temporary arrangement until Mab decides otherwise." The
dark-haired warrior's eyes fall, "Technically, I am Mab's liegeman, not
Finnbhear's."

I place my hand on his, trying to offer any comfort I can. The
thought of Maddox being traded like chattel by the very creatures who
raised him makes my heart ache. All of them seem to have come to

terms with being worthless to the fae, but I can't ignore the sadness of it all; the realization of it had to be a horrible feeling.

He looks to me as he continues his explanation, "The way the court rules work in their realm, you can only be granted protection from a ruler if you are a member of their court, or by proxy. Mab would be the only ruler able to do that, and we believe someone from the Unseelie Court is responsible for all of this, so we can't go to her. Finnbhear *graciously* offered to allow you to stay and become a member of his court yourself, just until we get a handle on the threat," he explains to me, "but I don't like the idea at all. He can't be fully trusted either. He's been known to take a keen interest in human women, luring them away out of boredom and curiosity. And, as we all could tell, you seemed to pique his interest."

Fin speaks up again, his expression and voice resolute, "Then we will be her protection." The Viking warrior gestures to the rest of the changelings, who each give their agreements with no hesitation.

"No, I can't ask any of you to do that. I don't want anyone else getting hurt because of me," I object. Guilt hangs heavy on me over this entire situation and being at the center of it all.

Theo, who has been unnaturally quiet this entire time, answers me, "You didn't ask, we offered. So it's settled. No more objections."

I shoot him an exasperated look and notice, much to my amusement, how close he and Claire are sitting.

Maddox looks to each of his friends, "You're all sure?"

Kellan answers, "We've faced countless challenges together over the centuries. We don't intend to stop now."

Maddox nods his head in agreement and looks to me, "We'll also teach you how to fight and defend yourself should the need arise." He shoots a look at the redhead next to Theo, "You too, Claire."

Her head whips to him, wide eyed as she exclaims, "Me?!"

"You've been dragged into this just as much as I have," I answer before Maddox can. "Plus, it will make me feel *infinitely* better to have someone out there looking like a fool with me." I flash her a wide, pleading smile.

"Well, when you put it that way," she gives in begrudgingly. "I guess I'll do it." She holds her hand up, stopping Maddox before he can reply, "But *only* if you guys teach us how to use all those fancy weapons of yours."

The guys all balk at her condition. "I don't know, Claire," Theo says hesitantly.

"There's really no need," Maddox says, trying to let her down gently.

She pouts a little as she looks at the group of them. "Come on. When will we ever get the chance to do something like this again? Please?"

I shrug, glancing at Maddox from under my lashes, "I have to admit, it'd be pretty cool to learn."

They all look to one another and I can see their resolve melting away before they finally agree. "Fine," Maddox answers, a grin pulling at his lips. "We will start first thing in the morning. In the meantime, since I didn't last night, I'll take first watch of the cottage, then Fin after me; everyone else needs to get sleep while they can. We'll change out every couple of hours." He stands, pulling me up to him and enclosing me in his strong arms before pressing his lips to mine. He pulls away and heads out to start his watch, leaving me blushing at the open display of affection, and the rest of our company highly amused.

Claire catches my eye, clapping her hands silently with a big goofy grin spread across her face. "Come to my room immediately!" She hurries towards me, "Now I *really* need to hear everything. Leave no detail out." She puts her arm through mine, almost dragging me up the stairs and into her room.

Claire's room is a mirror of mine, the only difference being the color scheme; cornflower blue as opposed to my blush pink. She flops down hard onto her bed, sprawling backwards, "Start from the beginning: what was it like stepping into the Faerie Realm?"

I walk over to the window seat and make myself comfortable, at least as much as I can with the fine gown still on. "There really isn't too much to tell," I shrug. "The gate to Finnbhear's realm is just between two nondescript trees, joined together by some of their branches. The only difference at first was that it was raining here and dry there, but then the different faerie creatures started showing themselves."

I tell her of all the different creatures, of the amazing palace in the trees and of the faerie king. We spend a long while discussing the events of our respective days. I tell her of the run-in with the banshee, of my argument and subsequent makeup with Maddox, and she gushes over the details of her day spent with Theo. Before I know it, Claire has fallen asleep during our chat and is softly snoring on top of her bedspread.

I step quietly to the door, starting for my room, but I'm nowhere near tired. Changing course, I head down the stairs, creeping past the sleeping guards and through the darkened cottage before slipping out the front door. Maddox sits atop the stone fence looking out toward the road and the moonlit woods beyond. No doubt he noticed my presence as soon as I stepped outside, but he doesn't turn until I am just behind him.

"Come to keep me company, Mo Chuisle?" he smiles over his shoulder.

I return his smile, shrugging. "I'm not the least bit sleepy, so I thought I'd join you."

He stands from his position on the fence and lifts me effortlessly onto the stones before perching himself next to me.

"Anything of interest happening?" I ask.

"Not at all," he shakes his head. "I highly doubt they'll try anything again so soon, but it never hurts to be cautious."

I stare out into the dark woods across the way, the tiny blue lights of sprites catching my attention through the thicket of trees. A small smile tugs at the corners of my lips at their appearance, but my thoughts quickly turn to the darker things of the Otherworld and Maddox's life there. "You know, even though the five of you have lived through such hardship for so long, you all still seem to be happy. I've only scratched the surface of what you've been through, and the fear I feel when I think about it is overwhelming."

His voice takes on a reflective tone as he speaks, "Because we know that, despite the horror we've lived through, despite all the hardships, there must be someone out there who is greater than it all. We've been through countless horrors and dangers throughout our lives. Many could've, *should've*, killed us on numerous occasions. But somehow, we always make it out alive, by the skin of our teeth sometimes, but we've survived. The very fact that we've lived long enough to tell the tale is proof enough for us."

At my questioning gaze, he continues, "I think, somehow, my mother knew what was going to happen in my life. Even in the very few years I had with her, she made sure I knew of one she called The True King. She ingrained it so deeply within me so that I would always hold onto it, and I did. You'll probably know Him by a different name, because He has many. Even the Otherworld has names for Him. All of creation knows Him, even if they choose to ignore or deny it. Some of the fae, like Mairead, even follow Him."

"Do the others feel the same way you do?" I ask, knowing how different their backgrounds are.

"They do," he answers. "Theo and Thomas were raised like I was, but Kellan and Fin were taught by the three of us. We've all seen how real the great evils of the world are. We've lived with them and been cursed by them for centuries, and we've made it through. All of us have felt it, the protection and presence, throughout our lives. It's because of that, that we know there is someone greater than it all. And He must be *for* us."

A true testament of faith, I realize with a small pang of guilt. I thought I had been tried and tested with the things I had been through in my life, feeling triumphant for having made it out the other side with my faith still intact. Now those things just seem like tiny inconveniences, stumbling stones, compared to the horrors these men have gone through.

We sit in comfortable, thoughtful silence for a while after that, mulling over our conversation. His eyes never stop roaming over the quiet landscape, studying the night, his chiseled jaw tensing and releasing. He turns his striking eyes to me again, his brow drawn. "I'm sorry for earlier, in the forest. The last thing I would ever want to do is hurt you." His eyes are earnest as he looks at me, "I'm sorry I made you feel like my anger was directed at you. Between having you so close to those creatures, everything that happened in the meeting, then the incident with the hag...I was stressed more than anything."

"Did something more than what you said happen in that meeting?" I study the elegant planes of his face as he shakes his head, perfectly shadowed by the light of the moon. "Did you really want me to leave?"

"No," he breaths out. "It was the only way to keep you out of harm's way completely. I didn't know what else to do. But I was selfishly praying you'd stay." Our eyes are locked for a silent moment before he turns to dig something out of his pocket. "I had this made for you before we left for the Seelie Court, but I lost my nerve when I saw you in that gown." He runs his eyes along the length of the beautiful dress I'm still wearing. "But after what you said to me in the forest, I think it was meant for me to give it to you now."

His words pique my curiosity, leaving me wondering what it is I said to him that made him think that way. He laughs at my questioning expression, a glimmer in his eye as he presents a dainty golden ring. My heart skitters when I see it.

The entire ring is made up of three golden strands, starting separately at the bottom before finally joining together at the top, fashioned into a Celtic knot. "Threads," I breathe out, an astonished laugh escaping my lips, everything lining up too perfectly for it to be chance. I turn the delicate ring in my hands, taking it in, and notice the inside of the band is engraved with the words *mo chuisle*. My chest tightens with emotion at just how thoughtful it all is. "It's stunning, Maddox." I slide the golden ring onto my finger. "You know, you still haven't told me what *mo chuisle* means," I say, my mouth feeling strange around the foreign word.

He smiles, laughing a little at my pronunciation, "It means my pulse." His words pull me, stunned, from admiring his gift. My eyes lock intently onto his. "I meant it, in the forest, when I said you made me feel alive." The warrior looks away to scan the night, but looks back to me, speaking again before I can form an adequate reply, "For so long I've lived in a haze, numb to the world around me. I built walls and built walls, never letting anyone get close enough to break them down." He huffs a single, humorous laugh, "No one ever cared enough to try, really." His hand sweetly brushes a stray curl from my face, "But then there you were, walking into that room, this bright, *magnificent* little thing, and my defenses were down before you'd even said a word. I could feel my hardened heart begin to beat again. It scared me how much I wanted nothing more than your heart to beat for me like mine was for you in that moment. But you were so naïve and innocent. I was at war with myself every time we were together. How could I drag someone so full of light and goodness into something so dark? But you were dragged in anyway."

His rough, calloused hand comes to rest gently on my cheek before continuing, the look in his eyes as he pours out his heart paired with the enchanting lilt of his voice causes my heart to stir. "Yet, unknowingly, you had staked your place firmly in my heart. And the second I stopped fighting it, the second I let you get close, you were almost taken from me. I can't help but feel responsible for it all." His eyes fall and he starts to take his hand from my face, but I stop him, my hand resting on his.

"You're not to blame for any of this. You've been there to save me every time," I comfort him. Our lips meet ardently. My hands meet the firm muscles of his chest as his find my face, deepening our connection, every pent-up feeling and emotion from the last few days conveyed through the kiss.

We're parted by a single amused cough behind us, belonging to Fin. The Viking's eyes are lit with mirth, causing my cheeks to warm. There is no uncertainty that he saw the whole thing. He suppresses a grin as he speaks, "It's time to swap out. Go get some rest."

I start for the front door before Maddox, embarrassment quickening my movements.

The two changelings speak for a moment before he catches up to me as I enter the cottage. Turning me toward him, he draws me into his arms. "We'll have a full day of training tomorrow, and you'll need all the rest you can get. Sleep well, mo chuisle."

I bounce up on my toes to plant a quick kiss to his mouth before starting up the stairs.

I am awakened by the sounds of the changelings downstairs, already up and preparing for their day of teaching. I drag myself slowly out of bed, still groggy. The time lost in the Faerie Realm sent my internal clock askew. I spent hours lying in bed, wide awake, finally forcing myself to sleep with only a handful of hours until morning.

Padding over the cool wooden floor to the shower, I'm greeted by a group of pixies, Bramble and Flynn among them, digging through my things again. "Getting started early, I see." At the first sound of my voice, they drop everything, startled by my presence. I laugh outright at the guilty looks across their diminutive faces. "Go on, explore all you like. Just don't break anything," I tell them as I start the water. The group giggles and continue delving further into my belongings, paying me no mind at all.

After my shower I feel more awake. Wrapped in a towel, I blow dry my hair, much to the surprise and delight of the pixies. Quickly pulling on a pair of black leggings, a black tee and sneakers, I head downstairs, leaving the pixies to play with my hairdryer. Their sounds of delight and astonishment leave a smile across my face.

When I reach the ground floor, the group of young men have already finished breakfast and are heading for the front door. Maddox walks over to press a quick kiss to my lips and brow before greeting me. "Sleep well, Mhuirnín?"

I shrug, "I guess the few hours I got weren't so bad."

Claire comes bounding down the stairs then, dressed similarly to me. "Good morning, everyone!" she sing-songs.

I tilt my head and frown slightly at her, "Why are you so cheery this morning? Just last night you were groaning about having to do this."

She lifts her head proudly, "I've decided I'm going to enjoy myself. It's an opportunity to learn something I would've never had the chance to learn before. I'll look at it that way." She shrugs and grins at the group of us, her smile lingering on Theo as she brushes her hair behind her ear.

I lean over to her, speaking conspiratorially, "More time with Theo didn't sound so bad either, did it?" Her face immediately reddens but she nods excitedly to me.

Mairead comes through the kitchen door, bearing plates of warm food. "Good morning girls! Come sit, eat, you'll need the energy."

Claire and I obey her motherly order and find our seats at the age-worn table.

Maddox joins his friends waiting at the door, "You two take your time. Come meet us behind the house when you're through." With that, the group of warriors leave to prepare for their day of teaching.

Mairead, Claire, and I enjoy chatting and having breakfast together before we decide to make our way outside. We round the back of the house to find the group of soldiers sparring with swords.

Claire intakes a sharp breath beside me. "Yes! I was hoping to get my hands on a sword today." Her excitement is palpable.

They stop their sparring, laughing a little at her excitement over the weapons. "Not today, I'm afraid," Maddox says, kindly letting her down. "We'll begin with basic self-defense and conditioning, then move on accordingly."

The redhead's face falls slightly as we follow Maddox over to the rest of the group and wait for our first lesson to start.

Maddox pulls me gently out from the group to stand with him, facing the others. "Alright, we'll start with how to escape if someone grabs you from behind." He moves to stand behind me, his arms wrapping gently around my shoulders and neck. "Now, if someone grabs you in a choke hold, this is what you're going to do."

I have to force myself to concentrate on listening to him, and not the thought of how close I'm pressed to his chest, sending the butterflies in my stomach into a tizzy.

The dark-haired warrior continues, "As soon as you feel someone starting to grab you, tuck your chin to protect your airway, grab their arm with both hands and get as wide of a stance as you can."

I mime the movements in time with his instructions.

"Then, you're going to hit their groin, their abdomen, wherever you can reach, as hard as you can with a closed fist. As soon as that's done, bring your elbow straight up and into the attacker's face."

I move through the last steps slowly and Maddox releases me from his hold, stepping around to face me before speaking again. "Okay, now let's try it from the beginning at a normal speed. Move through it as though you're actually in peril." I nod as he moves back behind me. Claire giving a double thumbs up as I catch her eye. Before I know it, his arm is coming around me firmly, just enough to mimic a real-life attacker. I quickly duck my chin and go through the motions with determination. Apparently too much determination. Maddox swiftly loosens his grip on me and braces his hands on his knees, catching his breath after my aim to his groin struck true.

My hands swiftly cover my mouth as I turn to face him, the sound of riotous laughter coming from his friends behind me. "Oh my gosh, I'm so sorry!"

He lifts his head and flashes me a grin, "Don't be. You did exactly what you were supposed to do." He laughs breathlessly at my expression, "Train like you'd fight. Otherwise, the real thing is going to come as a shock." Maddox finally unfurls himself to standing as he motions for Claire to begin her turn.

We spend the better part of the day going through any and every way to get out of possible abductions, stopping to watch the guys spar when we run out of steam and need breaks, until the warriors finally realize that we're worn thin and end our training session. Claire and I slowly make our way back to the house. "I don't know about you, but my muscles already hurt," the redhead groans.

I laugh lazily, too exhausted to put much effort into it. "I'm struggling to move now, it's definitely going to be a challenge tomorrow." We laugh together as we climb the stairs using quite a bit of effort, the two of us heading to our respective rooms with plans to bathe and turn in early for the night.

I decide to fill up the claw foot tub and have a good soak instead of a shower, not wanting to put in the work to stand any longer than I have to. I am greeted by a soft knock just as I am pulling on my soft pajamas. Upon opening, I discover a smiling Mairead, baring a plate of roasted salmon and steamed vegetables. "I thought you girls might like to have dinner in your rooms, where you can be nice and comfy after the day you two have had," she says kindly. I move aside to let her in and she lays the plate down on my bedside table.

"That's very thoughtful of you, Mairead, and I appreciate it," I tell her, taking pains not to just say *thank you*.

She gives me a quick warm hug before heading back toward the door, "I'll leave you be for now, lass. Relax and get some *much-deserved* rest."

I don't realize just how hungry I am until the smell of the food reaches me, my stomach rumbling at the sight of it. I enjoy my dinner in the company of the pixies, answering their many questions about humans and human things, the sounds of the changelings sparring again ringing up through the window from the garden.

Chapter 11

The next few weeks are spent training, day in and day out, with the occasional group outing sprinkled in, a much-needed remedy anytime cabin fever takes hold. Our constant time together allows for a deep bond to form between the seven of us.

Every move they teach us is practiced over and over until muscle memory has kicked in and they start to become second nature. Once we master basic self-defense, we move on to hand-to-hand combat, then finally on to weapons training, much to Claire's delight. We spend time with each of the warriors, learning skills in their area of expertise.

Maddox instructs us with broadswords, Fenrir with battle axes, then onto Kellan with flails, Theo training us in daggers, and finally, the ever-silent Thomas teaches us skills in stealth and archery. In the end, Claire and I are well versed in defending ourselves by any means necessary, and we've each earned our fair share of bumps and bruises to show for it, the group of changelings never going too easy on us and never failing to smugly remind us we'd asked for it.

The days pass by otherwise uneventfully, with no attempt at another attack, leaving everyone on edge with the worry of what might happen next.

"The ball is tomorrow and you all need to be prepared for anything. They've been quiet for weeks, which means they're biding their time, probably saving everything for tomorrow night," I overhear Maddox speaking to his friends after training one day.

"But why there?" I interrupt. The lot of them turn around to glance at me before turning back to Maddox.

He surveys the group before looking back to me, "There are faeries there every year, and along with them comes their trickery." He walks over and hands both Claire and I small pretty daggers, each in a leather sheath. "These are yours. Carry them with you at all times."

I take the knife and store it in my back pocket, my mind catching on something he'd said. "What's with the 'you all need to be prepared'?" I joke, "I guess you're so good you don't have to be prepared, huh?" I elbow him in the side, shamelessly flirting. But the smile he gives is tight, not quite reaching his eyes. Turning to fully look at him, I take in his pinched expression; there's something he's not saying.

He finally meets my eyes, a crestfallen look on his face, "I won't be going to the ball."

My chest tightens. "Why?" I ask, trying and failing to hide the dismay in my voice. I can see the disappointment fill his face, knowing my feelings have been hurt.

"I have to leave tonight to take care of some things on the orders of the Otherworld. It happens every year, same time. I never get to go myself."

I try to control my features, but I know my eyes show every bit of sadness there. "Oh. I know we never talked about it, but I was looking forward to going together. I guess that's what I get for assuming." My voice sounds more cheerful than I feel. "But I understand. Maybe I won't go either," I shrug.

"No," he answers hastily. "Please go, Mhuirnín. I saw the way your face lit up when I told you about it." He puts his hands on my arms, "I know you'll love it, and I don't want to take that away from you. Fin will be glad to accompany you," he says, inclining his head toward the Viking.

The blonde guard steps forward from the others, all pretending not to listen. "Of course. It would be a pleasure."

I smile sweetly at him, nodding, "Thank you, Fin."

He nods once in answer before striding for the cottage, the rest of our friends leaving us alone in the growing darkness of dusk.

Maddox turns to me and draws me into his arms, holding me tightly to his strong chest as I wind my arms around his waist. We stay that way for a long moment, quiet and breathing each other in. The sound of his steady heartbeat has grown to be one of my favorite sounds, always reminding me of his nickname for me and the meaning behind it. He finally pulls back, but only slightly, leaving me to crane my neck to see his handsome face. "I have to go, Mo Chuisle," the sound of the Irish words on his tongue never fails to send my stomach fluttering.

"So soon?" I pout slightly.

"Unfortunately, yes." The handsome warrior plants a light kiss on my brow before starting toward the front of the house. "Go inside and get some rest for tomorrow."

"You know I'm really not looking forward to being there without you," I walk alongside him until we reach the front of the house.

He stops me by the front door and plants an intense kiss on my lips. "I *know* you will love it, and I also know that you will be stunning." His eyes are alight with something I can't quite place as he walks backwards toward the gate. "Who knows? The prince may even steal your heart away."

I laugh, rolling my eyes before looking back at him. "Never."

Maddox laughs as I head through the door, only fully turning to leave once I make it inside.

I am greeted by the smell of a roast dinner, the entire group already sitting down to eat. Mairead gets up when she spots me and scurries off to the kitchen to get my plate. I take the only seat available at the head of the table as Mairead lays my meal out before me. I can only smile at her, still unused to not saying 'thank you' to show my gratitude.

"Claire told me you two were given your own daggers," Mairead says cheerfully as she takes her seat across from me. "You two have really come a long way with your training."

"We've worked hard enough, that's for sure!" I reply with a laugh, Claire nodding animatedly in agreement.

Everyone enjoys the meal and each other's company as I sit quietly observing, not quite up for joining the conversation.

The old faerie notices and speaks kindly to me, "Why don't you go on up to your room, lass? I know you're disappointed and so is that handsome lad. Go get some beauty rest for the masquerade, not that you need it." She winks at me as I stand from my seat.

Bidding everyone goodnight, I head to my room for some much-needed time alone.

The day of the ball passes quickly, dread and excitement warring within me. Dread, because I won't be able to enjoy this with Maddox, and excitement because pretty dresses, castles, and dancing are everything I've always dreamed of.

Claire is beside herself with excitement, she can hardly contain it. We've spent all day distracting ourselves with beauty treatments in my room to pass the time. Mairead bursts through the door, her anticipation also welling over. She clasps her hands together as she speaks, "It's finally time! I can hardly wait for you girls to see your gowns!"

"I can't wait! I know they'll be amazing." I reply.

She ushers each of us to our rooms to begin getting ready, going to assist Claire first, then returning to me. After I finish my makeup, the faerie fashions my hair into a soft, elegant up-do, making sure to leave a few of my signature curls loose around my face. She disappears out of the room, returning a few moments later with my gown in hand, but not before making me close my eyes. She instructs me to keep my eyes closed until she helps me into the dress, wanting me to see it on for the first time. Even with Mairead's help, it's a struggle to slip the garment on blindly. Finally, she fastens it closed and lets me open my eyes in front of the full-length mirror.

Speechless is an understatement. The gown is straight out of a dream. Periwinkle fabric stunningly complements my fair complexion and somehow, without ever trying it on, it fits like a glove. The illusion neckline joins with a sweetheart bodice embroidered to look as if it is made entirely of blue leaves. Turning around to admire the skirt, I'm more stunned than I was before. The A-line skirt is cut and embroidered to resemble individual sparkling faerie wings laying over my waist and legs.

"Do you like it?" my host asks timidly behind me.

I turn to hug her tightly, "Mairead, there aren't adequate words! I couldn't have imagined anything better."

She returns the hug with a delighted laugh before pulling back to gesture toward my shoes and jewelry laid out behind me. "Put the rest of it on and meet me downstairs so I can give you the finishing touch," she says before slipping back out the door.

I slide on my silver heels and a pair of crystal teardrop earrings, making sure Maddox's ring is still on my finger before heading downstairs. Claire comes out of her room just as I start my descent down the stairs and she gasps loudly. "Oh my gosh, you look like a princess!" my friend exclaims as she runs down the hallway.

I am immediately awed by her gown too, its golden color makes her red hair shine. An elegant halter neckline falls into gold and white fabric fashioned to resemble the scales of a fish. Not a fish I realize, but a mermaid, when I see the bottom of her flowing gown embroidered to resemble a mermaid's tail.

We embrace at the top of the stairs, our excitement bubbling over. "You are gorgeous!" I tell her as we start to descend the stairs. The entire group of changelings, minus Maddox, are waiting patiently for us. They all stand when we enter, pleased smiles on their faces at our extravagant states.

They murmur their hellos and compliments as Theo rushes to Claire, his eyes shining with awe. "You look amazing," he says to her shyly.

The redhead looks at him with the same amount of timidness. "You clean up nicely too," she replies as she takes him in.

The four men are dressed in leather armor instead of costumes or suits, and though every piece of their attire is beautifully crafted and intricate, it's not at all what I was expecting. I hold out my hands in question, looking pointedly at them, "You guys look dressed for battle, not a ball."

Kellan shrugs, giving a quick grin, "Fighting leathers are less restrictive, easier to move in if the need arises."

"Plus, they're a whole lot more comfortable than any formal attire," Fin adds. "We'll blend in though, plenty of people will be in costume."

"Boy, you guys really are no-nonsense, aren't you?" Claire says.

They all voice their agreement as Fin admits, "Given the nature of our lives, we prefer to keep it that way wherever possible."

Mairead interrupts us, bearing masks in each of her hands. Claire's is a dark teal green overlaid with a thin layer of shining gold, and directly in the center of the brow is a matching seashell with a single pearl inlaid into the middle. My mask is fashioned to look like dozens of tiny intricate silver leaves laid over one another. "Now go on, don't be late. Thomas and I will see you all there," she gestures to the quiet twin as she leaves to get herself ready.

Fenrir steps forward, giving me his arm. "You look wonderful," he says as he leads me out into the cool night. Much to our surprise, Claire and I are met by a luxury car, big enough to fit us all, awaiting us in the driveway.

"How on earth?" Claire breathes to no one in particular.

Kellan answers from behind us, "We have unlimited resources granted to us by King Finnbhear, monetary resources being one. So, we decided to use some of that to make sure you ladies had a fine ride and not subject you to the old truck."

We laugh, making our gratefulness known as we're ushered into the car.

"Where did Finnbhear get the money anyway?" Claire asks as the car begins to move.

"The Otherworld has fine gems and materials just like in the human world that can be traded for their value," Thomas explains to her. "But the creatures of that realm, the rulers in particular, also have well-off and greedy human contacts that trade their money or finery in exchange for a favor, usually to help them get even farther ahead in life than they already are."

Fin breathes a humorless laugh, "A handful of them are pretty well-known people too, but that's all I have to say about that." His revelation leaves Claire and I begging for their identities, but he remains mum, thoroughly enjoying our guesses for the remainder of the ride to the castle.

We come upon the road leading to the castle quickly, the drive lined with ancient forest on either side. The woods finally open to reveal the massive building, its cylindrical grey towers standing proudly against the darkness of the grounds surrounding it. Many cars are arriving and lining the rounded drive, each dropping off guests at the huge polished wooden doors. Our car is stopped before the doors in no time and we put on our masks, the warriors' being plain brown leather, not ones for flashy displays.

Theo is out of the car first, offering Claire his arm which she gladly takes, Kellan and Fenrir following suit. Fin turns to offer me his hand as I slide, as gracefully as I can manage, out of the car after them. Their chivalry is pleasantly surprising, even if they are visibly uncomfortable with this much pomp. It's not that they have ever been unkind, they're always anything but. It's just that, as warriors, the group of them are typically a little more rough-around-the-edges in their mannerisms.

"You all really know how to be gentlemen when you put your minds to it," I tease. Their answering laughs are lighthearted.

"We were raised in the Faerie Court. We know the ins and outs of courtly life better than most," Kellan answers with a smile as we pass through the great wooden doors, stepping into a spacious foyer.

The inside of the castle isn't at all what I had expected. Instead of cold stone walls, it's obviously been updated from its original medieval state to a more warm, palatial interior. Across the room is an imperial staircase leading to the doors of the ballroom. Some guests choose to enter through doors just underneath the stairs, while others climb the staircase to enter from the second floor.

Claire drags Theo up the tall staircase, saying something about a grand entrance. The sight of the two enjoying the night together causes my chest to tighten.

"He would be here with you if he could, you know," Fin offers kindly, noticing my slight change in demeanor as we trail along behind them.

My mouth tightens into some semblance of a smile, but the pang in my chest deepens.

We enter the mezzanine over the grand ballroom, Kellan just behind us, and start toward the staircase, twin to the one in the foyer. The cavernous room is filled with guests, many of them human, but scattered throughout the groups of mortals are throngs of Faeries, a mixture of Seelie and Unseelie, glamoured to look like humans. I'm not sure whether it's a gift or not to see them through the magic, with the sight now gifted to me from visiting their otherworldly realm. Worry quickens my heart when I see my companions exchange quick but concerned looks.

"Are there normally that many faeries here?"

"No," Kellan says, all traces of lightheartedness gone. "We need to be on our guard."

Claire looks around, confused, before her eyes settle on me. "What are you talking about? I don't see anything."

"Anyone who enters the Otherworld and returns can see them," I explain to her.

Fenrir looks to each of us, "Do you both have your weapons?"

Claire pats her skirt over the spot where Mairead has sewn in a hidden pouch to store her dagger, while my mind goes directly to the weapon in its sheath strapped to my leg, the individual panels of my skirt making it easy to get to the weapon if needed. We each nod to the Viking.

"Good. Claire, you stay with Theo at all times. Carlin, stick with me or Kellan. Don't go anywhere alone tonight," he tells us, command and concern lacing his words.

With that, we start our descent down the grand staircase and I'm finally able to take in more of the room. The white plaster paneled walls are mostly bare, only broken up by an entire wall of French doors and windows along the right side of the room which causes my eye to drift toward the many chandeliers hanging over the polished wooden floors. Further up, an opulent ceiling is made up of painted panels depicting the story of the stolen prince. The entire space, except for the head of the room, is encircled by the mezzanine overlooking the dance floor. At the head of the room sits a single carved wooden throne unoccupied atop a dais, doors flanking either side of it.

As we step onto the ballroom floor, a herald announces the arrival of the prince. Immediately, the room goes silent except for a few quiet murmurs in the crowd. The sea of people part to make way for the prince to move through, pushing me and my companions a few rows back. The entire room feels electrified with the building anticipation of seeing the so-called cursed prince.

One of the doors behind the dais opens and the mysterious royal steps into the room. I can only catch glimpses of him through the crowd. Dark hair, a navy-blue ceremonial uniform, and a dark mask are all I see as he moves through, greeting individuals in the crowd.

"Do you want me to get you closer?" Fin asks, a strange twinkle in his eye.

I shake my head dismissively, not too worried about whether or not I see the supposed prince. "Thank you but no, it's not that big of a deal."

My companion nods his head once as he scans the crowd, but I catch a small twitch from his lips as he fights back a grin. Before I have much time to think on his odd behavior, the herald speaks again. "The prince will now choose his partner for the opening dance!"

The women in the crowd begin murmuring excitedly now, all hoping to be the one chosen. Their anticipation and eagerness bring on a smile as I look on, curious to see who the mysterious man chooses. On my tiptoes, I see the prince beginning his stroll past the rows of guests in front of us when he turns his head our way. The room seems to draw a collective breath as they part for him, waiting to see who the lucky one is. As I watch him make his way through the onlookers I step back, giving him room to get by, only to realize he's stopping in front of me.

His tall form bows gracefully before he offers me a hand, "I would be honored if you would allow me the pleasure of the first dance." His eyes lock on mine as he straightens, awaiting my reply. But I'm frozen, a hazy sense of familiarity dancing on the edges of my mind. I fight to find it, but it is just out of reach. He smiles at me, and I realize I've waited a beat too long to reply, leaving him hanging. He's lowered his hands behind his back, fidgeting his fingers idly.

Ignoring the small tug in the back of my mind, I quickly lower into a graceful curtsy. "Of course."

The first strains of a waltz begin from somewhere on the mezzanine and the throngs of guests clear the floor as he takes me into his arms, spinning me into the dance. The moment his hands are on me, the unnatural haze clears from my mind with that familiar touch, like magic dancing across my skin. The little things that make him who he is are no longer hidden: the little bit of brown just in the corner of his eye, or the elegant planes of his face that I'd memorized over these weeks together. How had I not figured it out before? I had still believed it was some made up tale, despite all of the impossible things I'd seen since I'd been here.

My breathing hitches, mouth falling open in shock as I try to form a coherent thought, but before I can gather myself to speak, he interrupts me in a low voice. "Not now, Mo Chuisle." Maddox smiles down at me, my heart swelling at the sight of that devastating smile. "There will be time for that later, and you must be ready." I nod up at him, still struggling to find words as he twirls me around the opulent ballroom, my gown swaying beautifully with the movements of the dance. We spin by our friends as guests begin to join the waltz.

"Do they know?" I ask, still breathless, shifting my eyes to where they stand watching. Claire, ever the supportive friend, sends a big cheesy grin my way as Theo ushers her to the floor.

"Claire doesn't," he huffs a laugh at the sight of her, "but the rest do, Mairead included. They were bound to secrecy, just as I was," he explains.

It all feels like I'm dreaming, like I can't quite gather my thoughts to process any of it, not quite sure it's real. My wide-eyed gaze keeps searching him over, making sure he truly is there. He is the stolen prince, Maddox, the man I have completely and utterly fallen for. My head is spinning with thoughts of our entire lives and how it all played out, everything leading up to this moment.

The last notes of the waltz start to fade and Maddox's eyes take me in again. "Have I told you that you're magnificent?"

I beam up at him, my eyes answering the warmth in his own.

The music stops, but before he steps away he warns me quickly, "Go back to Fin, I have to keep up the charade until the time comes. Be ready for anything, Mhuirnín; and trust me." I curtsy, my eyes still on him through my lowered lashes, silently conveying my understanding. He bows deeply and then we part. I head for the Viking warrior just across the room as Maddox starts mingling with other guests.

"Enjoy your dance?" Fin looks at me out of the corner of his eye, the look there entirely pleased. He knows I've figured it out.

I shoot him a small smile and a look that tells him everything he needs to know. "Thoroughly." I lean closer to him, speaking as quietly as I can, "What happens now?"

The blonde guard never takes his eyes off the crowd, always scanning for potential threats, something I've noticed they all do. "At some point," he begins, "the herald, who's a lackey for Queen Mab, will announce that it's time to try your hand at naming the prince. Women will start shouting out random names, never truly understanding how it all works. Of course, it's only expected since they don't know anything about the Otherworld or just how *real* the curse is; it's just a game to them. And The Unseelie Queen enjoys the spectacle." The blonde changeling stops scanning the crowd and looks me in the eyes then. "At least, that's what normally happens. But this year I expect there to be more of a challenge."

At my questioning look he continues, "Judging by the attack at the céilí, Mab knew you would be the one to break the curse. No doubt she'll try her best to keep you from doing it, hence all the faeries here.

We need to be ready for anything." A shudder runs through me at the thought of what unknown things could await me later. Fin notices and reassures me, "We are ready for whatever they throw at us. We will keep you safe; your training will keep you safe. The only thing you should worry about is getting to him." I nod, swallowing down the rising fear threatening to take hold, readying myself for whatever may come.

Chapter 12

Claire and I spend the evening dancing with our friends, each surprising us by asking us to dance, not wanting to let us miss out on experiencing the ball. The changelings take the opportunity to fill Claire in on what might happen tonight, as much as they can without breaking their bond of silence. As grateful as I am for the distraction of dancing and enjoying the evening, I can't shake the looming sense of dread hanging over me. I feel on edge, my stomach heavy with that dread and anxiety anytime my mind drifts to the moment I'll have to break the curse. The unknown of it all leaves all manner of things swirling in my imagination.

Then I hear it.

THUD. THUD. THUD.

My heart skips a beat with each sound of the herald's gilded staff as he waits for the room to go utterly silent.

"It is time to break the curse!" he gestures theatrically at the prince, at Maddox, standing stiffly just in front of the dais. "Any lady who believes she truly knows the prince and can sever the bonds of the curse, come forth to try your hand." He takes a quick step backward, moving away from the surging crowd.

I look to my group of friends, eyes wide, my heart thundering in my chest. Kellan nods to me, silently urging me on. I look to the massive crowd, surging ever closer to Maddox, all manner of names being shouted over the din. Not one of them knows the darkness behind it all, only believing it's a game for their shallow entertainment.

Then, across the room, I see movement. Nyx, stepping away from a dark, foreboding figure who can only be the Unseelie Queen, is striding closer to Maddox.

Fin follows my gaze. I know he sees them, but I give him no chance to react as I begin pushing my way through the crowd.

She's going to name him, on the orders of Mab.

She's going to name him before I can.

I don't know what happens if one of them breaks the curse, but I won't stand by and watch it happen. He could be bound to her, or the wicked queen, forever if she gets there first.

Now I know why so many of the Unseelie faeries are here. They're here to make sure I never make it to him. As soon as I begin my approach, they shed their glamours, sending the humans in attendance into a panic. The ballroom breaks into complete chaos. Behind me, I hear the weapons of the changeling guards being commanded to grow. I spare a glance over my shoulder to see the group of them pushing back the undulant crowd of humans and faeries alike. Turning back to the front of the room, I push through the bodies around me until I spot an opening. Sprinting for the gap in the throng of guests, I make it only a few steps before someone grabs me.

"Oh no you don't," Liam's seedy voice breaths into my ear as he tries to haul me backward. Luckily, my training kicked in the moment I felt his hands on me, my dagger unsheathed without him even realizing. Stomping down hard on his foot with my heel, he curls over in pain, and I take that chance to sink my dagger anywhere it will land. I feel the blade plunge into his skin and he lets go of me entirely, his hands flying to his stomach. I have to force down the horror of what I've just done. I couldn't let him take me, and Nyx is inching ever closer to my prince, my Maddox.

I have to get to him. There are only a few more feet between us as I begin to run again, his hopeful eyes on me the entire time. I crash into him with enough force to knock him back a step, pulling back to look into his beautiful face as I say loudly, "Maddox! Maddox O'Connall!"

The lights are snuffed out as soon as the words leave my mouth. The glass windows and doors lining the ballroom shatter, a furious wind howling through them. Queen Mab stalks toward the dais, her black hair never moving an inch in the unnatural wind. Her black eyes are seething, furious at the turn of events. She could be beautiful, but the wickedness underneath isn't something easily hidden.

Maddox grabs me tightly. "Hold onto me, Carlin! You must hold on to me!" he screams through the howling gale. Immediately I do as he says, my arms winding tightly around him as I rest my head against his chest. His strong arms wrap around me firmly, like a shield covering my petite frame. His mouth is at my ear as he speaks, voice low and serious, "No matter what may come, hold on to me." The same words he spoke in the woods after the meeting with Finnbhear. He was trying to prepare me even then.

"Let's see just how much you love him, girl!" Mab yells over the cacophony of beasts starting to converge around us. I only let my eyes drift up long enough to see the other warriors fighting them back with

force, even Claire holding her own next to Theo. But I force my eyes
closed as a few terrible creatures slip through, placing their faces inches
from mine, teeth gnashing and claws grabbing at us.

The wind howls even stronger, threatening to pull us apart and we
tighten our hold on one another as an unnatural rain begins pelting
into us. Suddenly, I feel Maddox begin to shift, his movements strange.
Pulling my head back to look at him, never letting go of his body,
my heart stops altogether. What I see before me is not Maddox, not
wholly. His form is beginning to blur and stretch, changing rapidly
into all manner of nightmarish and inhuman things. My eyes are wild
as I look at him, tears starting to form.

"Maddox?" I can barely choke out the word around my terror.

"Whatever you're seeing, Mo Chuisle, it isn't real!" he yells over the
deafening noise around us, his form still horrific. "It's me, Carlin. It's
me." He pulls my head back to his chest, "I would never hurt you. Just
close your eyes and don't let go."

I let out a sob and shut my eyes tightly against the nightmare happening around me, trying my best to calm myself. Maddox places a
comforting hand on my head, covering my ear from the noise surrounding us, and I hear my favorite sound, his heartbeat, strong and
steady. It's a sound I've grown to love so much, and it soothes me, if
only for a moment. In a breath, his heartbeat is drowned out by the
increasing havoc around us.

The cold rain pelting our bodies turns to searing heat, like acid
falling onto our skin. Letting out a cry of pain, I dig my nails into
Maddox's jacket, refusing to let him go. I hold onto him through all
the increasingly terrifying forms he takes, feeling his body shift and
change within my arms. I don't dare look up again, afraid of what I
might see.

But in a moment, the feel of his body is no longer there, only emptiness, forcing my eyes to flash open as a red-hot coal is forming in my grasp. The immediate, searing pain causes my fingers to loosen, but a voice behind me makes my hold tighten again, the burn pulling a strangled cry from my lips.

"Don't let go, don't let go!" Fin yells behind me. "You must extinguish it!"

My mind racing, I force myself to stand, turning for the closest body of water I can think of: the lake beside the castle. I can only pray I get there through the onslaught of Unseelie creatures bent on stopping me.

As if reading my mind, Fin answers, "We'll hold them. *Just go!*"

I sprint for the now shattered glass doors to the gardens, the burn of the coal almost too much to bear, but I don't dare let go. Tears of pain and fear stream down my cheeks as I push my body faster through the moonlit night. The lake is just a few feet away now, but I can hear something or someone closing in behind me, though I'm not brave enough to turn back and see. Tamping down my rising fears I push myself even harder, building my momentum, and jump for the depths of the lake, the burning coal tucked tightly against my chest.

The relief of the cool water is immediate, and the once red-hot coal is now black as night. But there's no time to relish in the relief before I'm swiftly yanked downward by something taking strong hold of my ankle, the coal knocked from my hands. Forcing down the cry threatening to peal from my lips, I reach for the coal now floating away as I'm pulled down farther and farther into the dark water. Making every effort to hold onto the breath left in my lungs, I turn in the water to face whatever it is that still has its grasp on me.

There's no holding in the scream this time as I take in the sight of the creature dragging me away. Some twisted blend of horse, human, and sea monster stares back at me. Huge white eyes set deep into a long, ghastly face flash as it looks over its shoulder at me. One of its long muscled arms is stretched out behind, holding me in place with a clawed, webbed hand. It's eel-like tail cuts swiftly through the water, dragging me deeper and deeper. I kick and fight against its clawed grasp with everything in me, but it refuses to loosen its hold.

My lungs are burning now. If I don't get free soon, I'll be lost to these depths forever. I kick again, but my strength is already waning as blackness is creeping into the edges of my vision. I am nearly out of breath when I feel something wrap firmly around my waist, a flash of light cutting through my line of sight. My head swivels to the source of the movement, my eyes wild as they land on Maddox, sword in hand, severing the creature's hold on me.

He swims quickly for the surface, keeping me held tightly against his skin. We break the surface of the water and the first intake of breath is just as painful as the burning I felt in my lungs down below. Maddox pulls me to the shore, both of us panting wildly as Fin and the others rush to haul us fully out of the water. But Maddox waves them off, "You take care of her. I'll be back."

"Wait!" My voice is hoarse as I try, but fail, to stop him from disappearing back under the surface of the lake. Claire pulls me to my feet, still panting and coughing as Fin wraps his jacket around me. The dissonance of sounds from the chaos in the ballroom has stopped, leaving the night eerily still and quiet as we wait for Maddox to return. It feels like the whole world is holding its breath.

Mab's cruel voice breaks the silence, sending the changelings snapping back into defense mode. The faerie queen is vibrating with rage, fury written all over her features as she aims a finger at me. "You might've succeeded this time, you little chit," she spits, her voice barely controlled with the anger, "but this is *far* from over."

Just as the words leave her mouth, a splash sounds from behind us. The head of the monster from the lake lands with a sickly thud just in front of Mab's feet.

"It's over." Maddox's command sounds from the shore as he comes to a stop just in front of the Unseelie Queen. She stares at him for a silent moment, her jaw setting indignantly before she vanishes into the night.

Maddox turns to face me then, his eyes searching me over fervently. "Are you hurt?"

I shake my head slowly at him, mind still reeling from the events of the night. His hand on my arm snaps me out of my daze and I realize with a start that I'm not hurt at all. "Wait," I turn my hands and arms over, confusion twisting my features, "I'm not burnt. How am I not burnt?"

"You broke the curse, Mhuirnín," Maddox explains. "Everything connected to it was reversed the second it was broken."

My eyes begin to search him over only just realizing, with no small amount of embarrassment, that he's nude; his clothes apparently not surviving the brunt of the curse. Mairead, as if in answer, appears bearing blankets for the both of us.

"Are you alright? That *thing* didn't hurt you, did it?" I ask him, barely able to speak from the effort of holding back a flood of tears. The adrenaline is wearing off me now, releasing all of the panic and fear it had staved off.

His blue eyes go soft as his hand brushes over my disheveled hair, as if he's trying to lend me some of his calm. "I'm completely fine and so are you. It's done, and we made it." He leans in to rest his forehead against mine, his voice laced with emotion, "You did it, Carlin. You broke the curse." His lips meeting my forehead sweetly is enough to send my emotions over the edge and I let out a strange mix of a laugh and a sob.

"Then why does it feel like it's not really over?" My thoughts are unable to completely turn from Mab's threat.

Maddox shakes his head, his voice assured, "There's nothing more she can do. She has no hold over me now." His eyes are steady, but the elation there is impossible to miss. "You've been through more in the last hour than anyone could ever dream of. It will take a while not to feel on edge, but I promise you are safe." No longer able to hold back, our lips meet, the world around us melting away.

A cough from Kellan pulls us from the moment as our friends look on, amused. We step away from each other, but Maddox doesn't fully let me go, keeping his arm firmly around my waist. Our friends are just as disarranged as the two of us. Claire's arms are wrapped tightly around herself, seemingly trying to hold herself together. The redhead's eyes are tired as she meets mine. I step away from Maddox to wrap her in a comforting hug.

"I saw you holding your own out there. Thank you, thank you for everything," I say to her as tears start streaming down both of our faces, relief and happiness washing over us.

She laughs through the tears as she hugs me back, "I am so happy for you. A prince! Who would've thought?"

Mairead's arms come crashing tightly around the both of us, Flynn and Bramble on her shoulders, smiling broadly as she joins our hug, "I am so *proud* of you lasses!" She pulls back to look at me, a familiar twinkle in her eye. "I knew you would be the one to do it." Mairead makes her way to Maddox then, glowing with pride as she throws her arms around him tightly before stepping back and assessing him. "Now, I know you're my king now, so forgive me for speaking out of turn, but you should find some clothes, lad."

"Unless you fancy going for another skinny dip. The lake should be safe now." Theo's wisecrack breaks through the seriousness of the night, sending the group of us into a peal of laughter.

Maddox shakes his head at his friend's antics before addressing Mairead again, "Please don't treat me any differently. I'm no different now than I was yesterday," his discomfort with being called *king* apparent.

Mairead assesses him seriously, "You are the direct descendant of the very king who ruled this place all those centuries ago. The curse is broken, *you* are the one who rules over all the fair folk here. Take your rightful place as king."

He smiles wryly down at her as we all walk for the castle, "Technically, I am no king yet. We haven't had an official coronation."

Mairead scoffs at his refusal, hitting him playfully on the arm, "Alright then, I will see to it that you have a grand coronation," the old faerie adds with a look of pure love in her eyes. "You deserve it, lad."

The warrior stops to hug her again before we step through one of the shattered doors and into the ballroom. Claire's quiet gasp and the sound of shattered glass under our feet is the only noise from our group as we take in the state of the room in such sharp contrast to what it was just a few hours earlier. The once grand ballroom is now only a shell of its former self. Darkness hangs where there was once beautiful golden light, and an eerie stillness has settled over the place, the others in attendance either fleeing or hiding the moment they got the chance.

"Right," Theo looks around, disrupting the silence, "tell us where to find a broom in this place and we'll have everything back to normal in no time."

"Don't you dare even think of cleaning this up. Just leave it to me," Mairead protests.

Theo gives her a disapproving look, "We're not about to ask you to clean all of this up on your own, Mairead."

The elderly brownie places her hands on her hips, "You're not asking, I'm offering. So it's settled."

I can't hide my smirk as I observe his disgruntled face at his own words being used against him. Mairead calls the pixies back to her, who have taken the liberty to explore, and asks them for help with the cleaning.

"How are you going to let them help you, but not us?" Theo asks, feigning offense.

She gives him a pointed look, "Because they can help in ways that you can't, it'll make this much quicker."

More than just Flynn and Bramble appear, and the gathering of faeries begin sweeping their hands in an upward motion, from the floor to the broken windows, all concentrating intensely on their task. The shards of debris slowly lift from the ballroom floor, making their ascent toward the wall of windows, and nestle neatly back into place as if someone rewound the world. The ballroom is once again pristine, as if nothing had ever gone wrong.

Claire and I gape at Mairead as she smiles wryly at us, dusting her hands. "I always have a few tricks up my sleeve," she says proudly.

"Is that how you keep on top of literally everything at the cottage? The cleaning, the cooking, the *dresses*..." I say to her, astonished.

Claire laughs, shaking her head, "You know, I don't feel nearly as bad as I did for not insisting on helping you more."

The jovial faerie chuckles in return, "I only use magic to clean when it's a big job. I prefer the old-fashioned way." She gives us a sly wink.

"Your help, with everything, will always be appreciated, Mairead," Maddox says to the brownie before speaking to the whole of our group. "You're all welcome to stay here. For the night, or as long as you'd like. I had rooms prepared while some of the Unseelie servants were still keeping up the castle. Just in case." He looks to me, eyes aglow, "Now, if you'll all excuse me," he looks down pointedly at himself, still wrapped in the blanket, "I'm gonna go get dressed."

Claire squeals, practically bursting with excitement at getting to see more of the castle and pulls Theo along behind her to explore. The rest of our gathered group says their goodnights before heading to find their respective rooms, leaving me alone in the quiet ballroom.

My thoughts are interrupted by Maddox's voice from behind me a few minutes later. "Walk with me?" I turn to find him approaching me, a single dark eyebrow raised in question. Somehow, even with this silly expression, he still manages to be unfairly handsome.

I nod silently at him, a wide grin creeping across my face. Placing a gentle hand on the small of my back, he leads me to a pair of the French doors lining the wall and out into a beautifully manicured garden. We walk among the pristinely shaped hedges and flowers in comfortable silence for a moment, enjoying each other's company and the calm night surrounding us.

Lights come to life in the hedges as we pass, but only upon further inspection do I notice that they aren't lights at all. "Sprites," I breathe with a wonder-filled laugh as a few of them flit gracefully around us.

Maddox grins down at me, "Fin was right, they like you."

"Have you lived here all this time?" I ask, gesturing to the castle behind us.

Maddox shakes his head, "No. I've had access to it, but it was too painful. I live in the old boathouse, just there on the other side of the lake." He points across the sparkling lake to a tiny, aged cottage I hadn't had time to notice earlier, and gives me a sidelong glance. "I'll take you there sometime soon."

"Why did Mab allow you to be traded to Finnbhear?" I ask, voicing my musings as I stare out at the night. "Especially if there was a chance you could be sent here, giving you a greater chance at having the curse broken?"

"Fairies are bound by their word. That's why they're so careful with how they speak, talking in circles to make sure they aren't caught with the short end of the stick," he explains. "And to every curse, there must be a counter-curse, so to speak; that's the way their magic works. They're not powerful enough to have that final say. So, when she cast the spell, there had to be a way to break it, hence the ball. But that doesn't mean she believed it would ever happen. I was hidden away in the Otherworld for years and years, even with Finnbhear, until they got lax. By that time, even *I* didn't think it would ever be broken. And as far as being traded, it's all a game to them and we were just their pawns to move about and use and spend as they wish."

We fall back into silence for a while as we walk until we both try to speak simultaneously. The dark-haired prince bids me to speak first as we come up the center of the garden to a stone fountain bubbling there.

"What happens now?" I ask him, curious about where we go from here. I remember the rest of Mairead's tale about what could happen next, but I don't dare voice her words for fear of sounding like I'm expecting anything from him.

He stops walking to look me in the eye, taking one of my hands in his, "What happens next is we figure this out together." He takes in a breath before speaking again, "I have thought about this since the meeting with Finnbhear, and I know Mairead has been talking, so you probably know this is coming..." He fumbles through his words, nerves making him uncharacteristically flustered.

I fight to control my own nerves, my beating heart, as I anticipate what is coming next.

"I know this is a big undertaking, so please don't feel obligated to answer now. Think on it, if you have to," he tries again.

A delighted laugh bubbles from my lips at his bumbling on. "Are you ever going to get around to the question or not?" I tease.

He laughs with me, a lightness within him that wasn't there before, the sound of it like wonderful music to my ears.

"For centuries, I prayed for you," the nerves are gone as he begins speaking this time, back to his normal, steadfast demeanor. "For so long I almost lost hope. But the moment I had almost given up completely, there you were, after all that time, waltzing into my life like a beacon in the darkness. One look at you and everything fell into place. From that first moment, I think I knew you would be the one to save me. Those beautiful, bright eyes seemed to see right through me. Because of you, there was a hope that hadn't been there before."

"None of this," he gestures to the castle around us: the manicured ground, the fields and forest beyond, before taking my hands in his, "none of it would be worth a thing without you. It would be a great honor, Mo Chuisle, if you would share this life with me and stand beside me as my wife and queen." His eyes are questioning as he waits for my reply.

We've only known each other a short while, but I've never felt more like myself than when I'm with him; not that I needed him to complete me, no. But it's like he amplified what was already there, bringing out the best version of me, like we could take on the world as long as we were together.

A whirlwind of nerves and happiness overtakes me as I answer him, my voice breathless, "Without a doubt, yes." Before the words are completely out of my mouth, he scoops me into his arms, twirling me around. His lips meet mine as he sets me gently back on my feet, only pulling away to take out a simple golden ring, a small emerald cabochon set into the top.

"It was my mother's," he says, the love in his voice apparent, but laced with pain. "Of course, you'll get your own, but I wanted you to have something that's special to me," he adds quickly, clearly worried I won't like the ancient jewelry.

I hold out my hand for him to slide it on, "I don't need anything else at all, this is perfect."

Relief is written on his face at my acceptance of the beautiful ring. "As much as I would love to spend all night out here with you, we both need rest. We will have new things to deal with in the morning." He takes me by the hand and pulls me back into the ballroom, smiling over his shoulder, "I'll show you to your room. I had it prepared especially for you."

He leads me across the ballroom, through one of the doors flanking the dais, and into the hallway beyond. The medieval wooden floors continue throughout the castle and vaulted beams line the ceiling, showing the antiquity of the expansive building. At the end of the hallway, we climb a large stairwell that opens onto the second floor, passing by a handful of doors until we come to the end of the hall.

Before us are two beautifully crafted wooden doors. Maddox opens one and ushers me into the room beyond. A gasp escapes my lips at the sight of the room, lovely and expansive; the entirety of Mairead's cottage could probably fit into it. The ancient wooden floor continues throughout the space, but is covered with a massive Victorian rug. Powder blue and cream seem to be the theme of the decor, from the elaborate rug to the damask walls. The intricately carved head and foot boards framing the bed are gilded on the edges with a gorgeous crowning canopy overhanging the head of it.

I immediately make my way to the window seat, partially hidden behind elegantly draped curtains. "I love this," I breathe out as I lower onto the pillow-lined cushion. It's a pleasant surprise to see that along with the original medieval windows, the ancient stone walls were left exposed in the little alcove.

Maddox huffs a deep, velvety laugh behind me. "You seemed to enjoy the window seat at Mairead's," a grin pulls at my lips at the memory of him poking fun at my disheveled hair that morning, "so I made sure you would have one here."

I cross the room and throw my arms around him, standing on the tips of my toes to reach all the way around his neck. "It's wonderful," I whisper to him, "all of it."

He pries me away, just enough to look at my face, "You haven't even seen the entirety of it." he laughs again.

"I don't need to, just the fact that you thought of me is enough," I answer.

His eyes are lit from within as he smiles sweetly down at me, "I have thought of you every second since the moment I first saw you."

I bounce up on my toes again to meet his lips. His returning kiss is a little more restrained, apparently conscious of our location and taking great care to remain chaste and gentlemanly.

"I hate to kick you out," I say sheepishly as we pull apart, his thumb brushing my cheek sweetly, "but I can barely hold my eyes open." I look up at him from under my lashes, his hand still on my face as he leans in to plant a light kiss to my brow.

"Goodnight, Mo Chuisle," he says softly as he heads for the doors. He turns as he opens one, "My rooms are just at the other end of the hallway if you need me."

I turn around in place, slowly taking in the bedroom more closely as the door clicks shut. Remembering that I have no other clothes here, and being still in my damp gown, I head for a door to the right of the window seat thinking I might find a closet. Instead, I'm surprised to find a sizeable bathroom built into one of the rounded towers of the castle. Underneath the windows encircling the tower, a huge bathtub is built right along the most curved part of the wall, giving another view of the lovely gardens below.

Finding all the toiletries and supplies I could possibly need in a small linen closet, I make quick work of washing my face and brushing my teeth, unwilling to delay sleep any longer than I have to. But I still have no idea what I'm going to wear to sleep as I walk back into the bedroom.

As if on cue, Flynn and Bramble appear bearing my old, comfy pajamas. "Maddox had us go back to Mairead's to get you these. He thought you might need them," Bramble grins, giggling at the warrior's sweetness.

I smile down at the little creatures, grateful for my comfortable clothes. "I couldn't have slept well without them." They giggle again, crooning a goodnight as they vanish.

To my frustration, getting out of my gown without help is more difficult than I expected. I finally manage slip out of it and into my well-worn cotton shorts and tee, feeling wholly out of place in the grand room now. Too tired to dwell on it, I climb into the silky powder blue sheets, exhaustion quickly pulling me into a deep sleep.

Chapter 13

The warm sun coming through the ancient windows wakes me gently. It takes a moment to realize where I am, the stupor of sleep still hanging over me like a fog. My mind begins to clear, bringing on a pleasant smile with the memories of last night: the lovely moments after the curse was broken, after the terror of it all. It almost feels like it happened in another lifetime in this soft morning light, like a nightmare chased away by the light of dawn.

Vases full of beautiful white anemones, my favorite flowers, have been placed onto both bedside tables, and I remember it was something I had told Maddox in passing during our weeks together. My small grin grows into a bright smile as my chest swells at the thought of him remembering such a tiny detail. But the rumbling of my stomach pulls me from admiring the lovely flowers, reminding me that I haven't eaten since before the ball. Dragging myself out of the luxurious bed, I pad quietly into the hallway.

Just as I pull my door shut, another door opens from somewhere behind me. Claire emerges, stretching her arms in the air and yawning as she steps into the hall.

"You're up early," I say, startling her.

"I couldn't force myself to sleep any longer. I am *starving.*" She groans as I meet up with her, beginning our search for the kitchen.

As we descend the grand stairway, I laugh and gesture to our surroundings, "I feel like I should be dressed better. I stick out like a sore thumb among all of this."

She waves her hands to her fuzzy pajama set, depicting her favorite childhood cartoon, "Tell me about it. I felt like I was somewhere I shouldn't be in my room last night."

We turn down a hallway, searching for anywhere we might get sustenance, when we hear the voices of our friends through an open door. Claire and I step tentatively into an impressive dining room.

At the back of the space, Gothic arched windows reach from the floor to a gorgeous vaulted ceiling, letting in the bright morning sunlight and leaving no need for the iron chandeliers suspended there. Intricate tapestries hang along the light stone walls, their colors beautifully complimenting the large royal blue rug running the length of the twelve-person table.

At the head of the table sits Maddox, the rest of the warriors taking their seats around him. Surprisingly, they don't notice our presence until we reach the table, too deep in their conversation.

I take the empty seat adjacent to Maddox, Claire claiming her spot beside Theo as she proclaims, "Why on earth are you guys already awake and dressed?"

Theo laughs at her, sweetly running his hand along the back of her hair, "Training, love."

She pouts slightly. "You trained without us? You could've woken us up."

"We thought we would let the both of you rest," Maddox explains. "Last night was something neither of you could've imagined. You deserved to sleep in."

Mairead comes through a door behind us then, bearing plates of breakfast and humming all the way. "Good morning, dears!"

I whip my head around to survey the men, "You couldn't have made your own breakfast and let *her* rest also? Or at least offer to help?" They all hold their hands up, proclaiming their innocence.

"You know how she is. We asked, but she insisted. Wouldn't even let us near the kitchens," Kellan assures me.

"I know, but it still feels wrong not to help her," I say, still unused to letting someone wait on me hand and foot.

She sets our plates in front of us before taking a seat herself, looking to me conspiratorially, "That's a beautiful new ring you've got there, lass."

My hand flies to the golden ring still on my finger, I couldn't imagine taking it off last night and had forgotten I still had it on this morning, already accustomed to the feel of it on my hand. It would be futile to fight the bright smile that blooms across my face at her knowing comment.

Claire crooks her head to see for herself with a questioning look, mirroring that of the changelings.

Their combined reactions cause Maddox to laugh, that wonderful rich sound, and share a secret smile with me before addressing them, "I was waiting to have everyone together before sharing the news and discussing plans for my court. *Our* court actually," he corrects himself, taking my hand across the table.

"Are you..." Claire leaves the question hanging in the air, her anticipation palpable.

I nod at her, beaming again, holding out my hand across the table for her to see fully.

"I can't *believe* I didn't notice first thing this morning! I must've been exhausted to miss that," she exclaims as the changelings congratulate their friend.

The rest of breakfast is pleasant, happiness hanging in the air around us. Mairead makes quick work of clearing the table when everyone is finished, but Maddox stops her before she can disappear into the kitchens to clean. "Mairead, please come sit. You are just as important in this discussion as the rest of us."

She smiles at him, pride lighting her face as she takes her seat again.

"Obviously, we must discuss plans for a coronation," Maddox continues, his eyes bright, "and a wedding. But before we get into that, I want to ask you all to be a part of my official court." He looks around the table, meeting everyone's eyes questioningly.

The gratitude on their faces is clear. "Of course we will," Fin answers for the group, "but how is that going to work out with Finnbhear?"

"I met with him last night. He will honor my rule over the otherworldly inhabitants of this realm, you all included. He releases you four: Fin, Theo, Thomas and Kellan, from your sworn service," Maddox answers. It seems he was already hard at work while the rest of us were sleeping. "All he asks is that you uphold your duties in keeping the citizens of the Faerie Realm in line, should they become a problem here," he adds, looking between the group of them.

Kellan laughs, a trace of bitterness there. "So, exactly the same. Only without being bound to act on his every whim."

"No," Maddox stops him, "it will be your choice. You are free to do as you wish, but I will need help asserting my rule over the faerie creatures here, especially the few who will try to slip through and cause havoc. Finnbhear is allowing us to keep our spelled weapons, but we lose all other gifts from him. No more pay, and no more eternal youth. We will begin to age naturally again from this day on."

The changelings, Maddox included, look as if they are warring with the emotions they feel at that statement. Shock, awe, and relief would seem to be a few. Fenrir, the longest serving guard in Finnbhear's service, looks up with wide eyes. "It's really over? We're done?"

The ever-silent Theo speaks, apprehension clear in his quiet, steady voice, "There's no catch?"

"No conditions, no catch, no bargains," Maddox answers. "We're free."

Something about it feels almost too easy. It's strange that the faerie king would so willingly relinquish some of his best warriors. But I don't dare voice my concerns for fear of ruining their relief and happiness. They all seem lighter, as if the burden of their bonded service was a physical weight upon their shoulders for all those centuries.

"Now, onto the matters of the court," Maddox continues again, looking to the jolly brownie. "Mairead, I want to ask you to be the steward of this castle. You would be in your element here, making things run smoothly anywhere that help may be needed."

Mairead clasps her hands together, "Of course I will, lad! I am honored and delighted that you want to keep me around." She gasps excitedly before speaking again, "Does this mean I will be in charge of planning the coronations? The wedding?"

Maddox and I both laugh at that. "Mairead, you would be a part of that no matter what," I assure her.

She smiles proudly at me before standing from the table, "If I may be excused, I would like to start planning a special celebration for you two. A celebration for the curse being broken and of your engagement."

"You don't have to ask permission to leave the table, Mairead. I am the same Maddox that I have always been. Nothing has changed," the blue-eyed warrior insists.

Her look to him is one of pure love. "No, but you are to be a king. A good and just one, I believe, and I owe you my respect," she answers before she turns to leave the room.

"A faerie planning your parties...are you sure you shouldn't have just made her Master of Revels?" Theo jokes as soon as the brownie walks out of earshot, an eyebrow raised to Maddox.

I shoot him a teasing look, "Careful, or you'll be Court Jester." At that, the entire table bursts into laughter.

The rest of the morning is spent bestowing various positions to the group. Claire is given the option to become my lady-in-waiting once Maddox and I are married. She leaves the decision until later, wanting to think over everything the commitment would entail. Leaving her home and her family is, understandably, a huge part of her hesitation.

Thomas, with his gift of stealth, knowledge in poisons, and covert attacks, is named Spy Master. Fenrir is given the position of Commander of the Guard and is also tasked with finding more men to join the castle guard, which all of the changelings will be a part of. Kellan is chosen as Fin's second-in-command, and Theo is named emissary to Maddox as king. The whole of our group will be recognized as the king's Private Council.

After our breakfast meeting, Claire and I decide to take the car, still here from the night before, back to the cottage to collect our things and bring them back to the castle. "I know we could've walked, seeing as we only have two suitcases between us," I say to Claire as she gets into the driver's seat, "but I really didn't feel like dragging them all the way here."

Claire shakes her head in agreement before starting up the car. "Not gonna lie, I'm a little nervous about driving on this side of the car," she says, grinning toward me. "So be glad that this is only a one lane road!" We both laugh as she pulls onto the main road, steering us for Mairead's cottage.

We arrive at the country house with only a few snags in the drive over. "Was it just me, or were there more cars in town *and* on the road than usual?" I say to Claire, my thoughts drifting to the handful of panics the redhead had at having to pass cars on the usually empty one-lane road.

She shoots me a suffering look, "Don't even remind me. That was *torture* on my nerves."

I laugh, shaking my head at her dramatic reaction to the short trip as we step inside the cottage, both heading to our respective rooms to pack our things. I'm barely able to get more than a handful of things folded and packed before Claire bursts into my room. Her eyes are wary, voice climbing in pitch as she speaks, "When was the last time you checked your phone?" She shifts her eyes to something on her own screen, then back to me.

I stop what I'm doing and grab for my phone, discarded on the bedside table. "I haven't touched it much at all since I got here," I answer, picking my phone up, "only to let my family know I made it safely and to check in occasionally."

Shock and confusion run through my mind at the number of notifications I see. Calls, texts, emails, some from family and friends, others from people I haven't spoken to in years. The majority of them are from my mother and Natalie. Most of the messages are loaded with questions about news articles, videos or screen shots attached, all about the scene that played out at the ball last night. Of course, someone in attendance recorded their experience of the madness on their cell phone, sharing it for the entire world to see.

I meet Claire's wide-eyed stare, my own matching hers. "I don't know how I feel about this," Claire says, "and I'm not even in the forefront of it all. I can only imagine how you feel."

I move my eyes back to my phone, studying the pictures of Maddox and I huddled together in the midst of the chaos. "How much do you want to bet the extra cars around here are a result of this?" I say, moving my eyes to her as I gesture to the phone.

"Do you really think the news would be here that quickly?"

I nod, "They'll be racing to be the first to get an exclusive story or an interview with Maddox."

"And you," she adds.

A sigh escapes my lips at that. I haven't quite wrapped my head around being a key component in all of this.

We make quick work of packing our things then, no longer worried about placing them neatly into the suitcases. "We should get back to the castle as soon as possible. We need to warn the others. But first, I should call my family." I close my bag, pulling out my phone again as Claire says something about doing the same.

My mom answers on the first ring, bombarding me with a million questions I can hardly get a word in edgewise. After finally calming her down, I make sure she knows that I'm okay before trying to explain everything as quickly and as well as I can. She finally relents, stopping her barrage of questions and allowing me to hang up and get back to the castle.

I walk down the stairs to find Claire waiting at the front door. She grins at me as I take the last step down, "A lot of explaining to do?"

I give an exasperated laugh and nod in answer as we leave the cottage.

"Looks like we're a little late." I say as we come up to the front of the castle. News vans and rented cars filled with reporters and paparazzi are lining the round drive. Our car is instantly swarmed once we park, leaving us no room to even open the doors. A few seconds later, the crowd is parted and pushed back by the changelings. Theo and Maddox come to our rescue, opening our doors, putting their arms around us and ushering Claire and I through the onslaught of questions from the crowd.

"Should we all be worried about those creatures?"

"What's your connection to them?"

"Can we get the whole story from any of you?"

"Why have we never heard of you before, Maddox?"

"Is that an engagement ring on your hand?"

"Was this all a publicity stunt?"

Finally, we make it through the front doors, shutting out the noise on the other side. I give Maddox an exasperated look before glancing to the entire group. "We came to give you a heads up about all of that," I gesture to the door and the crowd beyond, "but it appears we were too slow."

Maddox laughs at my annoyed face, "You two weren't far behind them actually, they've only just gotten here."

"How did they even know?" Kellan asks, arms crossed in irritation.

Claire and I simultaneously pull our phones from our pockets, opening the video taken last night and display it for them to see. Claire looks between them, "Do you guys not have cell phones?" They all either shake their head or shrug.

"Never really needed them," Kellan answers.

"All these years and no one figured out anything about the Other world...until now?" Theo says, incredulous.

"The faeries never showed themselves in force before," I say to them. "There was no reason for them to. No one had ever even come close to breaking the spell. Of course, in this day and age, something like what happened here isn't going to stay secret for long."

Fin indicates the reporters outside with a nod of his head, "So what are we going to do about them?"

Everyone looks to Maddox, who in turn runs a hand down his face. "As much as I hate it," he sighs, "we're going to have to talk to them; give them something."

I loose a breath, nodding. "I agree. They'll never go away if they think there's a secret they can sniff out."

Before we can decide anything further, Mairead comes through one of the doors behind us leading deeper into the castle. "There is a group of townsfolk outside, along with Lord Mayor Murphy, asking for an audience with you," she says to Maddox. "I just got back from a trip to town and came in through the back. I had to sneak around to avoid being seen by that lot out there," she clarifies at our confused looks.

I glance at Maddox, raising an eyebrow, "Two birds with one stone?"

"We might as well," he smiles, shrugging before addressing the brownie. "Mairead, if you will, please tell our guests to allow us half an hour to prepare, then we will grant them all an audience."

I take in my own worn jeans and casual top before speaking, "We should probably change into something a little more presentable."

"All of our clothes are still in the car," Claire answers, no shortage of exasperation in her voice.

Maddox smiles between us, "I'm sure you'll both find something satisfactory in Carlin's closet upstairs."

"My closet?"

He huffs a laugh at my confusion, "You were apparently too exhausted to notice last night, but there is a door just beside your bed. It leads to a dressing room I had prepared for you. Claire, I'm sure she won't mind sharing until we get your own closet equipped."

The redhead and I share a cheesy grin before her look changes. "There's no way we're the same size though," she says. She's right. Although we have a similar build, she stands quite a few inches taller than me.

Mairead puts her arms around both of us, "Leave that to me," she says with a wink. "Just let me take care of the crowd outside and I'll meet you there."

Claire and I are giddy with excitement when we set our eyes on the walk-in closet. It's nearly the size of my bedroom and filled with an array of items from dresses to shoes to accessories; anything we could need. My eyes are immediately drawn to the display of jewelry on the far wall where there is a note from Maddox atop a small pillow stating that a crown is being commissioned for me at this very moment. Claire comes over from inspecting the shoes and reads the note over my shoulder.

"Oh my gosh, how romantic!" she gushes over the sweet gesture.

I can't contain my giggle as my excitement matches hers. "Okay, we have to get ready. We've wasted valuable time gawking."

We begin searching through the clothes as Mairead walks through the door. "I hope you love it, lass. I've been helping him put these rooms together for weeks."

I give her a sidelong look, questioning, "Even though you didn't know if I would break the curse or not?"

"I had all the faith in the world," she says as she squeezes my arm.

Claire makes a triumphant noise behind me and I turn to see her pulling a pair of tailored trousers from their hanger, holding them up to herself to see if they will fit her taller frame.

Mairead stops her before she hangs the pants back up, "Put them on, dearie. I can fix them." She then flicks her wrist as Claire pulls the pants on. They fit as if they were tailored just for her. The redhead puts on a lightweight sweater and classic black flats before finishing her look off with pearl earrings.

As she's finishing up, an emerald green wrap dress catches my eye and I quickly pull it on. I complete my look by sliding on some nude heels and accessorize with delicate golden earrings to match the rings gifted to me by Maddox.

Before we know it, it's time to let the assorted crowd in. Mairead rushes down the staircase before us to gather the guests into the ballroom as we meet up with the changelings in the council room just behind the dais.

Maddox kisses my lips swiftly as I come to stand beside him, "You look wonderful, though, you always do. Even with bedhead." He smiles teasingly at me as I take in his form in a well-tailored suit.

Before I can complement him, Mairead comes through the door to the dais, "They're all waiting for you."

My heart feels like it's in my throat at her words and I force myself to take a calming breath. Maddox, sensing my nerves, pulls me to him and plants a sweet kiss on my forehead. "You will be fine, Mo Chuisle." He gives me his arm as Mairead opens the door for us to step out.

Clicks of the cameras are all I can hear in the otherwise silent room as our friends take their places flanking the bottom of the dais. I try to pull away to join them, only to have Maddox stop me with a soft hand on my arm.

"They're here to see you, not me. I'm not anything special," I whisper to him.

With that, he breaks his stare over the room, turning to look me in the eye. "You are everything." His eyes gleam as he grips my arm gently, running his thumb soothingly over it, "And, you are to be my queen. They're here to see you too."

His words hit me like a ton of bricks. Just yesterday I was an unknown girl from an unknown town, and now I'm being thrust into the spotlight, set to take on a huge political role.

"I don't know anything about being a queen, Maddox," I whisper, shaking my head. I'd agreed so quickly to his proposal. Of course I want to marry him, there was no question about that, but I hadn't given much thought to what agreeing to that actually meant; the reality of it all is daunting.

"We will all help you," he says, glancing pointedly at our friends. "And I will be right here by your side. We will face this together."

My heart thunders at the look in his eye and I resolve to stay there beside him.

Maddox addresses the group of locals first. "Lord Mayor," he nods to the older man at the head of the townsfolk, "what can we do for you all?"

The man bows, "Please, call me Paul." He continues speaking, gesturing to the people behind him, "We were all witness to what took place here last night. After learning of your true heritage and being informed of what you have done for our people here," the man glances to Mairead, who smiles proudly, "we have unanimously decided to allow for you to claim your birthright and make you our leader. To become a crowned republic of sorts, under your protection."

Maddox stiffens beside me and I know his mind is running through all of the years he was treated as a pariah, respected now only *after* they've seen the things he and the other changelings have protected them from for so long.

The steady warrior takes a breath before answering, chasing away his annoyance, "Though I'm grateful for the recognition, I am not sure how that could work with the modern government."

"If I may interrupt," a middle-aged woman shyly steps out from behind the mayor, clearing her throat nervously. "I found a loophole in some of our old government documents, one that, seemingly, wasn't there before, presumably hidden from us just as you were. In the event of a royal descendant returning," she eyes him pointedly, "and the members of our village agreeing unanimously, the government will have to legally recognize our request. It would just be for our county for now. But, judging by the whispers we've heard from the wider, larger government, some of whom were here last night, it could spread to other regions of the country." The woman curtsies quickly as she retreats into the crowd.

"I will think on your proposal and give you an answer within a week, after the party Mairead has planned for the village," Maddox says to the crowd.

Before his words have completely filled the room, reporters are hurling questions at us. We answer them as quickly and efficiently as possible, avoiding reciting the entire tale starting centuries ago. It would only cause them to overstay their welcome, wanting more and more of their questions answered. But it seems what little we do answer appeases them enough to leave, rushing to be the first to put out the story, much to our relief.

Chapter 14

The subsequent week is full of deliberations pertaining to the town's request, along with decision making regarding the final preparations for the party Mairead is planning. It's to be another céili, to make up for the disaster of the last one, only this time it will be during the day to soothe the fears of the townsfolk.

"I'm still not sure," Maddox says as we sit at the table in the council room, his warring thoughts plainly written across the elegant planes of his face. We're alone now, after another long discussion with our friends. It was the last meeting before the céili, filled with debate after debate over the people's request. Maddox is the only one that is still undecided.

I look to him, a comforting smile on my lips before I speak. "The townspeople want your protection, and after what they've seen," I give a small shrug. "I can't blame them."

He rubs his hands over his face, trying and failing to chase away his mounting anxiety. "I know, Mo Chuisle," he smiles softly at me, letting me know it's not me that he's frustrated with. "I agree with everyone on that. I'm confident I can give them safety. It's just the prospect of being their leader; It's daunting. Just a few weeks ago I was an outcast. Everyone I passed glanced at me sideways, preparing to bound away if I so much as moved wrong." His blue eyes are puzzled underneath his knitted brow as he admits his fears to me. "And now, just like that, they want me to lead them? Who's to say they won't turn on me just as quickly again? I'm not even sure I would make a good ruler; I can't even make a final decision on this."

Rising from my chair, I make my way to stand in front of him, placing my hand in his. "I think that's a good sign." I huff a laugh at his confused look, "You're not taking this lightly, you are weighing out every possible aspect. That shows me how much care you will give to all matters as a leader." He strokes his thumb across my knuckles absently as I continue, "I know it's daunting to you, but think of all the innocent people who could've been saved from those creatures if only they would've had someone to stand in their way and show them the darkness hidden behind the beautiful surface. Even now there are people who would never stand a chance, being stolen, or tricked, and walking into a situation unaware of the trap that lies in wait for them, like it has been for thousands of years. But we could change it. *We* could give them a fighting chance, pulling back the curtain so they at least *know* what they're getting into if they make that choice. Everything could stay just as it is, or *we* could change it."

Maddox takes me in silently; I can practically see his thoughts swirling in his eyes like a tumultuous sea.

"It's getting late and we have a big day tomorrow, but I want you to know that whatever decision you make, I trust that it will be the right one," I assure him.

He pulls my hand to his lips and lays a gentle kiss there, "Go to bed, Mhuirnín. I will be here a while longer."

I bid him goodnight with a soft kiss of my own before leaving him to his thoughts.

"Wake up!" Claire bounds into the room enthusiastically, "It's time to get ready!"

I feel my hair being tugged on lightly before I can even sit up, giggles abounding; apparently the pixies are with her. I groan as I sit up on the edge of the bed, "Someone's excited..."

She flops down at the foot of the mattress, "I barely got to experience the last céili before those awful things showed up. I'll actually get to enjoy this one!" She smiles to herself, no doubt thinking of Theo. "Do you think he'll dance with me? Like Maddox did with you? I just keep picturing it and how romantic it was," she sighs.

"Of course he will!" I assure her. "I don't even know why you had to question that, he's completely enamored with you. Besides, didn't he dance with you at the ball?"

"He did, but you and I both know he hates it."

"Yes, but he *loves* you," I assure her.

Her cheeks redden at that before she pops up and heads for the hallway, "Let's go have breakfast with the guys and then we'll have some girl time for primping!"

I trail her through the hallways and into the dining room where all but one of the guys are sitting around the table. "Where's Maddox?" I ask as I take my seat.

Kellan shrugs, "He wasn't at training this morning, maybe he's sleeping in."

I nod, "He was up late last night, even after I finally went to bed. There was a lot on his mind. I'll go check on him if he's not down after breakfast."

"Has he made a decision yet?" Thomas prods gently.

I shake my head, "I don't know. He was still going back and forth with it when I left him in the council room. He has a lot of worries and doubts playing tug of war in his head. I figured leaving him to sort through them alone, without any outside voices, would be better for him." The room nods in agreement and we eat in silence for a while, lost in our own thoughts.

"We'll be going straight to the village after breakfast," Fin speaks up. "As much as she hates to accept it, Mairead is going to need help with finishing everything this morning."

"Is she there already?" Claire asks, slightly stunned. "The sun hasn't been up for long."

"She never sleeps. Literally," Theo answers her. "Plus, she's in her element with things like this; she was probably chomping at the bit waiting for an appropriate time to get out there."

We all share a laugh at Mairead's enthusiasm as the changelings finish up their food and make their way out to help her. Claire and I finish up shortly after them and head back up the stairs, but we go our separate ways at the landing. Leaving her to start getting ready for the céili, I go to check in on Maddox.

I knock, but the room is silent beyond the doors as if he's still sleeping. I slip in quietly, not wanting to wake him. He must be exhausted if he's sleeping this late; it isn't like him at all. The room, a masculine mirror of my own, is dark as I step over the threshold. Walking to the window, I open the curtains to let in the morning sun. His bed is empty but tousled, so I know he's been here. Biting back the tiny bit of wariness creeping over me, I search his adjoining rooms to no avail. He is nowhere to be found. I survey the room again, nothing seems out of place and the castle is spacious, he could be anywhere, but something just feels...off.

Leaving the room, I shake off the looming unease; maybe he just needed more time to think. Claire is inside my room, talking with Flynn and Bramble when I enter.

"How's Maddox?" she asks, looking up from her pile of skincare products.

I shrug, "I didn't find him." I look to the pixies, "Have either of you seen him this morning?"

"We haven't seen him since- " Bramble is cut off by a sharp look from Flynn before she continues sheepishly, "since he went to bed last night."

That was strange.

Sensing my worry, Claire reassures me, "I'm sure he's still thinking things over, he probably just needed some space." She ushers me into the massive closet and starts picking things out to try on. A handful of hours later, we're dressed and ready for our day in the village. Thanks to Mairead working her magic, the beautiful blue dress I wore to the first céili is in wearable, almost pristine condition, even after an involuntary swim in the ocean. A small thrill runs through me at the thought of dancing with Maddox again.

Claire decides on a pretty yellow dress, perfect for twirling through the reels.

We rush through the halls, heading for the front doors and our awaiting car. "Hurry, we're going to be late!" the redhead says over her shoulder.

I decidedly ignore the fact that it was her who spent way too much time trying to get loose waves to set in her pin-straight hair.

"It certainly looks as if everyone has gotten over the incident from last time," I say as we arrive. The town square is full of villagers all looking cheerful and light. Mairead outdid herself on this one.

Delicate Irish lace ribbons lining the town blow in the breeze, floral arrangements hang from the top of a massive tent set up for shade and dining. The village's business owners are manning carts with their wares, ready to serve the community, and lively music is already being played, with the first dancers taking their places.

The cheerful faerie meets us as we step out of the car, hands on her hips. "You girls had all day to get ready and still manage to be late," she chides playfully.

"That's just what happens when you're not around to help, Mairead," I grin down at her.

She leans in conspiratorially, "It's a good thing to be fashionably late sometimes." She winks at us and we laugh, letting her lead us through the crowd.

"Is Maddox already here by chance?" I ask as she shows us to a table reserved just for us.

Mairead shakes her head gently at me, "No lass, the boys told me he hasn't been around this morning, but don't worry. He will be here." She pats me on the back, "I have no doubt about it. If there is anything I have learned about him over the years, it is that he does as he promises."

I return her smile, the truth in her words reassuring me. He's always been there, never giving me cause to worry.

Instead of taking a seat at the table, I decide to mingle and enjoy the villager's carts. After a while of strolling through the square, I meet up with Fin as he is leaving the pub. He joins me and we walk back toward the tent together when I notice Maddox skirting the crowd, trying to remain unnoticed, and heading for us.

The smile that pulled at my lips at the sight of him fades as he draws closer and doesn't return it. Out of the corner of my eye I can see Fin look between us, just as taken aback as I am. Something is off with Maddox. He seems withdrawn, distant.

A sense of dread begins building in my chest, but despite it, I return the smile to my face as I speak to him. "It's nice of you to finally show up to enjoy the céili with me," I tease. "I've been looking for you all day, where have you been?" I try to take his arm in my hand, but he is completely rigid. Stopping short, I tilt my head to meet his haunted eyes, a question in my own.

"I'm not staying," he says, his words short and clipped.

The tightness in my chest grows. Something is wrong, there's no doubt. Fin has tensed behind me, sensing the same. My eyebrows draw together in confusion, "What?"

"I'm not staying. I'm leaving."

"Why? Maddox, what's wrong?" I question, anxiety causing the pitch in my voice to rise.

"I can't stay here anymore. I have to go away." The cold way he is speaking to me and the look in his eyes is so foreign, devoid of all emotion as he starts to step away from me.

I know something must be exceptionally wrong for him to be so out of character. Trying and utterly failing to fight past the lump in my throat, my voice breaks when I speak again, barely a whisper, "I'll go with you."

He meets my eyes again, just before he turns and disappears into the crowd completely, "I don't want you to come with me."

Chapter 15

I take a step after him, but Fin's strong hand around my arm stops me. Wide-eyed and speechless I turn to him, a million thoughts and questions swirling through my head. "What just happened?" I blink up at him, fighting back a flow of tears.

"I don't know and that's why I can't let you follow him." His voice is calm and steady, the direct opposite of my own, but I can see the worry behind his eyes though he reins it in well.

He opens his mouth to speak again but I cut him off, "Please don't ask me if I'm okay." I swallow down the rising lump in my throat. "If you do, I'll lose it, and I prefer not to in front of all these people."

His eyes are full of sympathy as he nods at me. "Let's go find the others." Putting his hand on my back, he starts leading me gently through the crowd of people. Fin signals to Thomas and Theo through the crowd as we converge at our table. The rest of our group quickly notices and follows suit.

"Where's Maddox?" Claire asks, looking around. "I thought I saw him talking to you guys just a minute ago."

I take a steadying breath before I try to answer, but Fin beats me to it, explaining to them what had just happened, thankfully saving me from having to try to speak through the emotions washing over me.

"Are you sure it was really Maddox?" Claire prods gently.

"It was him...but not. He was so different; it was eerie," I explain to them all.

The boys look between each other, a silent conversation seeming to pass between the four of them.

Mairead puts a comforting arm around me, "It must be something to do with the Otherworld. There's no doubt."

"It has to be. The only question is *what*?" I say to her. I shake my head, thinking out loud, "I *knew* it was too easy for you all to be released, I could feel it. From what I've gathered, faeries are selfish, greedy creatures and the group of you were some of their greatest possessions."

"You're right," Kellan says. "We should've known it wouldn't come without some sort of catch. With all of us free and Maddox ruling here, it would be easy to undermine their schemes. We know their games, their tricks, and with us in their way we could easily cut off their access to innocent people. They're not gonna give that up willingly. We may all have a target on our heads."

"That's it. I'm going to the Otherworld," Fin says. He looks between the other warriors there. eyes fierce, "Kellan, you come with me. Theo and Thomas stay with the girls. We can't leave them alone not knowing what's going on."

Mairead puts a comforting hand on my back as a stray tear escapes down my cheek, my worry and fear finally spilling over. "Come on, lass," Mairead beckons to Claire, "let's all go back to the castle."

I stop her ushering me and gesture toward the crowd still enjoying the céili, as if everything hadn't just been turned upside-down. "What about them? Someone is going to have to tell them something, they were expecting Maddox."

"Leave that to me," Fin says, nodding once at me before Mairead begins pushing me back toward the castle.

"Shouldn't you be sleeping?" Thomas' quiet voice from behind me in the kitchen causes me to nearly jump out of my skin. I'd snuck down here in the middle of the night to get something to drink and pass the time, not expecting anyone.

"Geez, Thomas. I know you're the stealthy one and all, but you really have to stop doing that to me."

He laughs once, a small grin pulling at his lips, no doubt thinking of the many times he'd startled Claire and me, "Sorry, I don't mean to."

"But to answer your question, I can't sleep."

He watches me silently, propped on the counter beside me now, waiting for more of an explanation.

"It's been nearly a week, why haven't we heard anything from them yet? I've not been able to sleep for worrying about Maddox, and now I'm beginning to worry about Fin and Kellan too. I know time passes differently in the Otherworld, but shouldn't we have at least heard something? Or seen them by now?"

Thomas doesn't reply, only shifts his eyes away from where I'm standing, his head turning slightly.

"Thomas, I know you're not one for much talking, but it would make me feel at least a little better if you'd say someth-" His hand comes up quickly, a single finger raised to his mouth, silently bidding me to be quiet. Pushing off the counter he was leaning on, he rises to his full height.

"Someone's here," he says almost silently.

My head whips around, looking for any sign of a break in.

"Not here. Outside. Stay behind me." He steps past me and toward the kitchen door leading to the castle grounds. I peer over his shoulder as he opens the door, revealing a man standing at the threshold. No, not a man I realize, but a faerie, human-like if it wasn't for his pointed ears. He's wearing Finnbhear's crest on his tunic.

"King Finnbhear would like an audience with her," the faerie says, glancing past Thomas' shoulder to me."

"Now?" I ask

"Yes, miss. He's waiting to be allowed in."

I look to Thomas, questioning.

"You can't allow him past the wards. If you do, he'll be able to come and go as he pleases."

"Then we'll meet with him outside." I quietly plead with an apprehensive Thomas, "He might know something."

Thomas nods once, keeping himself just in front of me as we follow the faerie to his awaiting king.

"Not very hospitable, making me meet you outside in the dead of night," Finnbhear drawls.

Thomas doesn't miss a beat, "Very rude to call for a visit in the dead of night, don't you think?"

Finnbhear laughs once, his eyes gleaming in the moonlight as they shift to me, once again reminding me of a cat assessing a mouse it's toying with. "Now, now. I've only come to see how our little queen is faring."

"What do you know?" I ask. "Do you know where he is?"

He holds a hand up, in surrender or command I'm not sure. "Your bodyguards have already interrogated me, and I can tell you no more than I told them. I cannot say where your Maddox is."

"Can't or won't?" Knowing how faeries dance around the truth with carefully chosen words, I can't help but feel that's what is happening here.

"I have no more knowledge of his whereabouts right now than all of you."

Thomas speaks again beside me, "But do you know what happened?"

Finnbhear laughs again, a deep velvety sound, "What makes you all think something happened? What if he just...left? The tasks ahead may have been too much for the boy and he got cold feet. Marriage, ruling a kingdom, no matter how small, it's a daunting prospect if you're not up for the challenge."

It would be impossible to miss the insult and teasing in his words, but I tamp down the annoyance, unwilling to satisfy him with a reaction. "He may have been in your service for centuries, but if you think that Maddox is one to run away from anything, you truly don't know him at all."

The faerie king steps toward me, but Thomas plants himself between us, making Finnbhear's eyes flash again, this time with annoyance. "Forgive me, Carlin. I didn't mean to upset you. I truly only wanted to make sure you were alright," he says, looking down at me over Thomas' shoulder. "For what it's worth, I think he's made a grave mistake. You would make quite the beguiling little queen."

I know he's supposed to be the more benevolent of the Otherworldly rulers, but tonight's interaction has me questioning whether he deserves even that title. There's no way he's here out of the goodness of his own heart.

"I don't care anything about being a queen." I wrap my arms around myself, fighting off the mounting discomfort at our meeting and hoping to hold my broken heart together. "I only care about finding Maddox."

Finnbhear takes me in for a moment too long, causing unease to wash over me. "All little girls grow up wishing for something like this to happen to them. You can't tell me some part of you isn't disappointed; not getting a crown, a prince. Everything that was *just* within your grasp."

"I only ever saw him for who he was, not what he could give me. None of that matters if Maddox isn't here," I snap, this time not bothering to hide my anger.

"I think this meeting is over," Thomas says, surprising me by just how forceful his usually quiet tone is.

"Very well." Finnbhear steps backwards, still looking at me with those cat-like eyes, "If you ever find yourself in need of *anything*, my doors are always open."

Thomas bids me to go inside while he waits for the two faeries to disappear entirely. Once we're both inside, we wake the others to tell them about our encounter.

Theo speaks after being informed of how strange the entire visit was, "Honestly, I think it's time for you to go home."

My head whips to him in disbelief, "What?"

"I think you're in danger here. Nothing about Finnbhear coming to you was normal. You're like a sitting duck so close to the gate."

Before I'm able to protest, Fin's voice at the entrance of the room startles us all, "He's right."

I look to both Fin and Kellan expectantly as they come fully into the room, but they both shake their heads.

"We found nothing. No leads, no traces of him anywhere," Kellan says gently.

I hold my hands up in question, "How does someone just vanish like that?"

"Mab definitely knows something, but there's no use in trying to get her to divulge anything." Fin fills us in on their efforts, "I think Finnbhear does too, but Maddox's absence plays into his hand. Which is why his appearance here is not surprising, but questionable, to say the least."

"What do you mean?" Claire questions, "From the outside looking in, he seemed so benevolent, so amenable. I mean, he did let you guys go. Are you sure he could be involved?"

Fin shakes his head, "It was all a guise, him letting us go, acting like he's bowing out gracefully. We should've known something was up. We should've *seen* it. We've witnessed his bait-and-switch before, but I think we were all too willing to grasp our new-found freedom and didn't want to question it." The Viking sets his eyes on me seriously, "But I think he may have his eyes set on you."

"What?" I say, shaking my head in confusion. "Why?"

"Who knows?" Kellan shrugs. "Fae are fickle creatures with little to no impulse control. Which is exactly what makes them so dangerous."

Fin meets my eyes again, adding to Kellan's statement, "And why I think it's the best choice for you to go back home. They're like vultures circling, waiting for their chance."

Claire is the one who protests this time. "But you guys are here! You can protect her. I'm sure she wants to help find Maddox."

I stop her with a hand on her arm, offering a comforting smile. "I think they're right, Claire. Besides, I think our best chance at making any progress will be if all the guys are searching. They can't keep leaving someone behind to babysit me."

As much as it pains me to admit it, I know I should go. I'm only a liability right now. If there is any hope in finding Maddox, it'll be due to the warriors and their knowledge of the Otherworld. And I can't stay cooped up behind the castle walls, hiding behind my bodyguards until they find him. So, home it is.

The next day Fin drives me to the airport after an emotional morning. Long tearful goodbyes were shared between Mairead, Claire, and I, the warriors even offering up their own gentle goodbyes. It breaks my heart in two to think I'm headed farther away from where Maddox could be and away from a place that feels more like home than anywhere else ever has.

"We'll find him, you know. I promise," Fin tells me, watching me wipe away silent tears that are still spilling over.

I can only nod silently at him for fear of sobbing. He offers me a tight hug and watches me board my flight home.

My eyes drift to the window as the plane takes to the skies, searching the emerald landscape as if I could somehow see all the way to where Maddox is."

"Where are you?"

Chapter 16

"Please go out with us tonight. It's been almost a year; shouldn't you be better by now?"

I'm pulled from my daze by my friend's pleas. After Maddox left, Fin shouldered the load and made the announcement to the awaiting crowd that he had gone. He spun some tale to them about Maddox needing more time to think through the major responsibility of ruling a people and, thankfully, convinced the press that what happened at the ball was just a publicity stunt for the unknown prince after all. His tale gave me the freedom of coming home without reporters following my every move, prodding for more of an explanation of the things that happened that night and after.

I've been home in my small Southern town, trying to go on with my life as normally as possible. The time has been torturous in a town where everyone thinks they're entitled to knowledge of your personal life, and with this being the biggest thing that's happened in years, it isn't dying down.

Sometimes I can't decide if the worst part is well-meaning people asking questions and giving their unwanted opinions, or supermarket shrinks whispering their thoughts just loud enough for me to hear: what they think I did wrong and how they think I've gone crazy because they catch me staring into space sometimes. It's a fight everyday not to just scream, *can we all just act like nothing ever happened*?

What they don't know is, ever since leaving the Otherworld, I can see little creatures everywhere now. At home, in the stores, in class; they're everywhere. Staring into space and ignoring them seems to keep their attention from being drawn to me. The last thing I need is for someone to see me interacting with invisible creatures and perpetuating the rumors.

"Does it ever really get better, or do you just get used to it?" I ask my friend, tucking away the chain I've been toying with around my neck when she moves her attention to it. The rings hanging there thud lightly against my skin. She knows the whole story and the weight I carry with those tiny trinkets, "And, I don't know, Nat. You know going out like that has never really been my thing."

"Just face it, you got swept up in a whirlwind romance that was bound to end badly. Nobody blames you; it could've happened to anyone. You can't keep pining over it."

"You don't understand," I bite back the annoyance in my tone as I answer her, "He called me *his pulse* like it was my name. I know he loved me. Something had to be terribly wrong. He literally disappeared! No one has heard from or seen him in a year. It's like he never existed at all."

Nat is a little scornful this time, apparently tired of me bringing it up, "You know he's probably in *fairyland,* after running off with that siren thing..." She waves her hand dismissively at the last few words, bringing her voice down to avoid drawing attention. The brunette meets my eyes, less callous this time after seeing the hurt there, "You *still* haven't heard from him?"

I shake my head, not wanting to start this conversation again.

"Not even that Fin guy?" she prods. "No more letters?"

I can't stop the frustrated sigh that escapes at that, "Please don't bring that up again. Something still doesn't sit right with me about it."

My friend barks a laugh, causing other people in the cafe to turn and look, "Of course not! Your ex-fiancé's closest friend sent a letter trying to swoop in and take you for himself. Why would it sit well with you?"

The image of the short note is still clear in my mind, the scrawled out handwriting on the crumpled piece of parchment etched into my brain:

I know you're still hurting, and I am sorry for the pain he caused you, but you could still be a queen. You and I could rule together. All you need to do is choose me. Think on it,

Fin

Just the memory of the note fills me with unease again. "But the thing is, I *know* Fin, and he never struck me as anything but loyal. I can't understand why he would do something like that."

"You *thought* you knew him. Jealousy brings out a lot of unseen things in people," she says matter of factly.

I shoot her a flat look. Understandably so, she doesn't quite grasp the fact that they've been loyal friends for centuries.

She takes one last sip of her coffee, then is back to her initial appeal, "Just come with us tonight. I know it's not your thing, but it's just karaoke night. You don't even have to talk to anyone, just make fun of their singing."

"Fine..." I sigh, standing from my chair to leave. "But only because I know you won't stop until I go. I guess I'll see you in a few hours."

"Yay!" She claps excitedly, "I'll let everyone know you're coming."

Later in the evening, while finishing the last touches of my makeup, I'm interrupted by a knock on the door. Opening it, I am met by a sing-song chorus of, "Hey!" Apparently Natalie decided to invite her entire new friend group along to pick me up.

I step back to allow them entry as Natalie greets me sheepishly, "I just thought we could all meet and leave from here. Are you ready to go?"

Trying to hide my annoyance at the intrusion, I plaster on a tight smile. I've never been one to have a large group of friends, only a handful of close ones. I gesture to my body, "Just let me change clothes really quick and we can go."

Telling the group to make themselves at home, I head to find something to wear to combat the looming Autumn chill. I decide on a drapey blouse tucked into dark skinny jeans, throwing on some ankle boots and gold earrings, and quickly fluff up my curls as I leave my room.

"Woah, look at you! You'll catch some eyes for sure," Nat exclaims as I emerge into the living room.

I purse my lips at her, "You know that's not what I'm going for, so don't you dare try and set me up with anyone. I only agreed to go out to appease you."

She laughs off my mood, threading her arm through mine and leading me out my front door. It only takes a few minutes to walk to the local bar, the unfortunate source of our entertainment for tonight. Bad, drunken singing can be heard before we even reach the door and I'm already annoyed. Being much more of a homebody, packed crowds, especially inebriated ones, are a far cry from my version of fun.

Natalie's friends burst through the doors, obviously not holding the same sentiments. Nat drags me through after them and I immediately regret my decision to come with them tonight. In a town as sleepy as ours, karaoke night is what everyone in the entirety of the town, besides me, looks forward to.

The space is packed wall to wall, forcing us to shoulder our way through to find a clear table. We all take seats around one of the last open tables, a girl in the group shouting over the music, "I'm going to get a tab started, what does everybody want?"

"Just water for me," I answer after the others rattle off their random drink orders. This turns their attention directly to me, obviously confused by my drink of choice. But instead of anyone commenting on it, I'm caught off guard by the question coming from another girl in the group.

"You know, I've just been dying to ask. What was it like being with a prince? What was he like?"

I shoot Natalie a look, her brown eyes just as irritated as mine as she turns on the group of girls, "Didn't I tell every single one of you before we even left my house *NOT* to bring that up?"

Her friends get up, murmuring something about going to mingle and dance, obviously disappointed about not getting any gossip, and Natalie's statement makes me wonder what kind of conversations they were having while I wasn't there.

Natalie looks at me pleadingly, "I'm sorry! I swear I warned them all not to talk about any of that."

"It's fine, I believe you. It's not that big of a deal," I say, smiling gently to soothe her worry, but the pang in my heart is hard to ignore.

I slide from my chair, telling Nat I need the restroom, and leave her there sitting alone. The bathroom is empty and thankfully muffles some of the obnoxious noise from the bar outside. I had to step away, I could feel my annoyance rising and needed a minute to decompress. Leaning my hands on one of the sinks, I fight to keep my thoughts from trailing to Maddox and anything to do with the Otherworld. But when I look to my reflection in the mirror, I'm no longer alone.

My heart leaps to my throat at the sight of the crone just behind me, realizing with no small amount of fear that it's the banshee from the Seelie Court. I turn, trying to slip past her without incident, but of course she's not going to let that happen.

"Do you remember me?" she jeers.

Determined not to let my fear get the best of me, I swallow it, looking down my nose at her. "I'm not afraid of you." I say, though my pounding heart would suggest otherwise.

She cackles out right at me, sending a chill through my spine, "No need to be afraid of me, girl. I'm only a messenger."

"I don't believe you." My heart in my throat causes my voice to come out barely above a whisper, my brave facade slipping as I look at her. Her grey robes float of their own accord, on some phantom wind, and her words from a year ago echo in my mind.

She raises her eyebrows almost in challenge, "I can't lie."

"No, but you can twist and toy with words until they're bent enough to only masquerade as truth."

She smiles at me, her jagged teeth causing panic to rise in my belly, "You'll see soon enough. Probably sooner than you thin-"

"That's enough!" I cut her off, my fear coming out as anger just as Natalie opens the door beside us.

"Are you alright? I could've sworn I just heard you talking to someone." She looks around the bathroom, concern limning her features. "You look like you've just seen a ghost."

If only you knew.

I shake my head as my eyes drift around the now empty room, the hag nowhere to be seen. "It's nothing. I'm fine," I say as I squeeze past her back into the bar, not sure if I'm trying to convince her or myself.

On our way back to the table, Natalie glances over to where her friends have started getting flirty with a table of guys, her look of longing impossible to miss.

"Go. You know I don't mind being on my own. I'll be just fine right here," I assure her as I return to my seat.

With my dismissal she bounds over to join in their fun, leaving me to people watch from my chair in the far corner of the bar. Turning my head from a particularly terrible karaoke singer, the sight of a familiar blonde head coming through the crowd catches my attention, two more familiar forms just behind. I stand from my chair so fast I almost knock it over in the process. Quickly moving through the crowd, I meet the three of them halfway, "What in the world are you doing here?"

"We could say the same to you," Theo teases in answer, his eyes taking in the packed bar.

At my still shocked expression, Kellan adds jokingly, "We figured you'd be happier to see us than that."

"Of course I'm happy!" I shake off my bewilderment, hugging them all, "I just didn't expect to ever see any of you here." Leading them through the space to our still empty table, I notice Fin still hasn't said much beyond greetings, a tight look on his face.

I force the memory of the letter to the back of my mind, not wanting to bring it up at all, "So, why *are* you guys here?"

"We found Maddox," Fin finally says.

My hand instinctively reaches for the delicate necklace around my neck, grasping the rings hanging there. "You've still been looking for him?"

"Absolutely. We've known him for ages, literally, and nothing about him that day was normal," Theo says.

I look between them all, waiting for more information, "And?"

Fin's expression darkens even more before he speaks, "He's in the Underworld."

Chapter 17

It's like all the noise around me has stopped at the words from Fin's mouth.

I look to him, blinking slowly. "He's dead?" the words come out weak and whispered around the knot forming in my throat.

"No," Fin is quick to reassure me. "No, he's very much alive."

I let out the breath I didn't even realize I was holding, looking around the table at all of the men. "But, you said he's in the Under-world. What does that mean?"

Before they have a chance to answer my question, Natalie and her posse cut through the din around us, making themselves known. "Well, hello!" one of their group drawls to all three of the warriors sitting around me, obviously pleased with their appearance. "Who are your friends, Carlin?" she says to me without taking her eyes off them.

The other girls are just as flirtatious and giddy at the male presence here. It only takes Natalie a moment to recognize them, cutting her eyes to me in question at their presence here. I try to convey to her the importance of our interrupted conversion with only a look; thankfully we've been friends long enough that she reads my plea easily. "Hey, why don't we go get our new friends some drinks? I'm sure they'd appreciate that," She suggests to the group.

They all giggle and enthusiastically agree, quickly heading for the bar. I shoot Natalie a silent 'thank you' as the changelings and I slip out from the table and exit the bar altogether. It would've been too hard to speak privately there anyway. Despite the crowd and loud music, just their presence alone draws attention; they can't help it. It seems to follow them wherever they go, like people can tell the changelings aren't quite their own kind. But I suppose they aren't, never really of this world or the other.

The sidewalk is filled with too many people passing in and out of the building for us to speak freely, so we head back down the street toward my house.

Not wanting to let the heavy silence keep hanging between us, I look to Theo, "Where's Claire? I'm surprised she isn't with you."

"She's still at home. She missed her family and wanted to spend more time with them. But she plans on coming back to Ireland soon, on a more permanent basis." A pleased smile spreads across his face at that.

I mirror his smile, happy for the two of them, but surprised that Claire didn't tell me that she was going back during one of our many phone conversations.

Theo glances down at me, apparently reading my thoughts. Speaking gently he says, "She didn't want to bring anything up that might cause you pain."

I nod, smiling at him again. She knows the memories of my time there are still a tender spot for me. She's spent all this time carefully skirting around any mention of it.

We reach my home and I usher them inside. Closing my front door, I give them just enough time to sit before I round on the three of them, "Tell me everything."

"Well, we all knew something wasn't right when Maddox left," Fin says gently, stopping for a moment to read my emotions before continuing. "We've been chasing down any lead possible as to where he was or what happened. A few weeks ago, Thomas had a run-in with a púca trying to lure some locals through the gate. In exchange for being let go, he told Thomas of something he had overheard while skulking around the Unseelie Court." Fin looks me over carefully, silently weighing whether I'm ready for his next bit of information.

"Just tell me. It's not going to hurt me more than I already have been," I assure him.

Fin releases a breath before speaking again, "Mab pays a tithe to Áed, King of the Underworld, every seven years to avoid having to marry him; mostly in the form of discarded lovers."

Kellan swiftly interrupts at my shocked look. "Maddox would never," he assures me. "Mab would've liked that, given half a chance. But this time, her pick for the tithe was purely out of spite."

Fin leans forward, a grave look on his face as he tells me bluntly, "She came to the castle that night to take *you*."

I can physically feel the color drain from my face as I look at them, wide-eyed. "He went in my stead." My voice is a breathless whisper as I plant myself in the chair closest to me.

The warriors watch me closely, taking in my reaction.

"You're sure?" I urge them after a silent moment.

Kellan speaks gently, "Some of the pixies witnessed it all that night, but were too afraid of Mab to say anything until pressed."

"She somehow found her way around the wards, slipping into the castle while we were all sleeping. Except Maddox," Fin explains the pixies' story.

I knew he wouldn't sleep well that night with so much weighing on him, and now knowing what Mab had planned, part of me is thankful for that.

Fin interrupts my thoughts, "He caught her on the landing before she could get near you and offered himself in your place as long as you would be spared."

I am speechless for a long moment, my mind far off as I process this new information. Looking to each of them for a moment, I direct my question to no one in particular, "What do we do now?"

Theo moves to place a comforting hand on my shoulder, making me look him in the eye. Instead of his normal jovial mood, his voice is staid and earnest. "We're going to get him back. That's why we're here."

I blink up at him, slowly realizing what he meant. "You mean the Underworld is *here*?" I ask, pointing my finger to indicate my hometown, brows raised in bewilderment.

"Not *here* in your town, but in America," Theo clarifies. "California to be exact."

I can't help the laugh that escapes me at that. "The Underworld is in California. Why am I not surprised?"

Theo's jolly mood returns at that, sharing in the humor for a moment before Fin interrupts to reveal their plans. "We're leaving first thing in the morning, and we have an extra plane ticket if you would like to join us."

"Of course I'm coming! Maddox has always been there to save me. It's time I returned the favor."

We're interrupted by knocking at the door and I'm nearly bowled over by Natalie pushing her way through before the door is entirely open. "You disappear without a word after the friends of your *magical* ex show up out of nowhere and expect me *not* to panic?" she rants, plopping herself onto the couch between Kellan and Fin. "I need an explanation!" she says, throwing her hands up in exasperation.

I look between the changelings in the room before settling my eyes back onto my friend, "We're going to California."

Chapter 18

"Excuse me?" Nat blinks at me.

I fill her in on what the changelings have just told me, also clarifying to them that she knows everything about Maddox, the Faerie Courts, and changelings.

"So you're just gonna fly across the country with the guy who tried to swoop in and take you for himself when Maddox *left* you?" she exclaims, much to my chagrin.

The three warriors look between each other, shock and confusion written on all their faces.

I close my eyes, pinching the bridge of my nose against my rising annoyance. I wasn't planning on bringing the letter up, especially not in front of Theo and Kellan. Letting embarrassment get the better of me, I excuse myself to my room for a moment.

I've only just sat on my bed when there is a soft knock on the door, Fin cracking it just enough to peek through, "What was that about?"

I wave him into the room silently. He comes in just enough to shut the door behind him, but no more, waiting on an explanation for Natalie's outburst.

I let out a steadying breath, not entirely ready for a conversation I never thought I'd have to have. "She knows about the letter you sent me."

I scan his face for recollection, but all that's there is utter confusion. His brows knit together tightly. "I didn't send you a letter."

Stretching to the side of my bed, I pull open a drawer in my nightstand, fishing out the crumpled parchment I had shoved in there after its arrival, not wanting to see it any longer. Without a word, I present the note to him, crossing my arms and waiting while he surveys the paper.

Fin's frown deepens as his eyes move over the few lines of script. Unease settles in my stomach as I watch his face.

His arm goes slack leaving the paper hanging loosely by his side. "I didn't write this." He shakes his head disbelieving, "Do you really think I would do something like this?" He holds up the letter and stares at me in disbelief, a flash of hurt crossing his features at the accusation.

I rub my fingers across my brow, trying to chase away my mounting frustration with Natalie for opening her mouth. "No, I don't," I say, finally meeting his eyes. "And I've told Natalie as much. I made it clear to her that I knew something wasn't right, but she tends to have a flair for drama, and where there isn't any, she'll create it. I've pleaded with her repeatedly not to talk about it, but..." I trail off, throwing him a humorless grin. "Do you have any idea who could've sent it? And why they would pretend to be you?"

He shakes his blonde head, propping himself up on the door frame, strong arms crossed in thought. We sit in silence for a moment before he holds the small piece of paper up again, "Can I keep this? I'll see what I can find out after we get Maddox."

I nod to him, not caring to hold onto it any longer. Standing from the bed, I take a deep, cleansing breath. "We should get back in there," I nod towards the living room pointedly. "They're all going to want an explanation after that."

The blond warrior steps to the side, opening the door and ushering me through. We interrupt a quiet debate between the rest of the company. No doubt about the two of us, given the immediate silence when we step into the room.

Nat turns her eyes, full of question, to me. I give her an exasperated look. "He didn't write it, like I've tried to tell you for *months*."

My friend crosses her arms and sits back into her chair. "I don't buy it. I mean, how do you know for sure?"

My anger rises at her, sharp and hot, so set on creating a problem where there isn't one. Before things escalate further, Fenrir steps forward and picks up a pen from my coffee table, copying the words of the note onto the empty space around it. Holding the parchment up to Natalie, he calmly says, "See for yourself."

She gingerly takes the letter from his hand, her eyes darting between the original handwriting and Fin's. Not one to ever admit her mistakes, she hands the paper back to him without another word.

We quickly catch Kellan and Theo up to speed before moving on to the more important matters at hand.

"So where exactly in California are we going?" I ask the group as I take a seat.

"Los Angeles," Fin answers. "There's a nightclub there, conspicuously named The Underworld, that King Áed uses to disguise the entrance to his realm."

My eyes roll involuntarily, "You mean to tell me it's actually called *The Underworld* and people still go?"

Kellan laughs, somewhat humorlessly, "The majority of people aren't going to have any idea that it's more than just a club until it's too late, and a lot of humans are completely oblivious to what's really going on around them. Even if it is, quite literally, right in front of them."

The room goes thoughtfully silent for a moment at that.

"We'll discuss it more when we get there tomorrow," Fin says, breaking through the quiet. "One more thing before we all get some sleep," he continues, his eyes stopping to rest on me seriously, "Have you kept your training up?"

Panicking slightly, I think of the handful of times I tried to practice what they had taught me after I got home, only to drop it shortly after. I'd felt so silly for trying to keep it up when I was sure I'd never need it again. For a second it crosses my mind to lie to them, they spent a lot of time and effort teaching me when they didn't have to, but I settle on telling them the truth. I almost can't stand the look of sympathy written all over their faces at my explanation.

"Do you think you remember enough to hold your own if you have to?" Theo questions tentatively.

Searching my mind for a moment, I quickly go through everything Claire and I were taught all those months ago. "I think so. I'm pretty sure if we find ourselves in certain danger, it'll all come back to me," I joke with them.

"The most important question here isn't whether or not you'll remember the training," Fin says, eyeing me seriously. "It's if you still have the strength and stamina to carry it out?"

"I mean, I'm far from a couch potato. I do exercise daily," I shrug. "Whether or not that's enough to get me through if the need arises...I guess we'll just have to see."

Natalie, who has been uncharacteristically quiet, stands and stretches before talking through a yawn, "Well, it seems you four have quite an adventure ahead of you tomorrow. I'll just be here...stuck in this backwoods town, not getting to see L.A..." she trails off, really putting on a pitiful act.

"Nat, it's too dangerous. You know nothing of the creatures we're up against and it would be an extra burden on us trying to look after you. Besides, it's not like we're going for a vacation." My voice is kind as I try to soften the blow of leaving her out. "I promise I'll keep you updated as much as I can," I say, giving her a quick hug before she heads out the front door. I turn back to the guys, "Alright, who's sleeping where? I only have two bedrooms, so two of you are going to have to share, or someone is stuck on the floor."

It's impossible to hide my mirth at the sight of the hardened warriors playing rock, paper, scissors to decide who goes where. Kellan wins the spare bedroom, Fin the couch, and Theo the floor. Theo, ever the good sport, shrugs it off. "Eh, I've had worse."

After digging out spare blankets and pillows for the three of them, I make my way to my own bed. Unsurprisingly, sleep doesn't come easy. My mind is plagued with thoughts of Maddox, what could be happening to him and how we're going to pull off getting him back, leaving my stomach full of knots and my body unable to relax. Eventually though, the pull of exhaustion takes over, the rings around my neck clutched tightly in my hand.

I pry my eyes open, still heavy from deep sleep, at the sound of a knock on my bedroom door. The morning came all too quickly.

"Carlin, it's time to pack up and leave." Theo sticks his head into the room.

I nod, dragging myself out of bed, not quite awake enough for speech. He laughs at my drowsiness and disappears back into the hallway. After rubbing the sleep from my eyes, I pull a large duffel bag from my closet, filling it quickly with things I might need. Uncertain of what we'll be needing, especially for the nightclub, I pack a few changes of clothes.

Rummaging around my top drawer, I find the dagger gifted to me by Maddox. Unsheathing it, I look it over, running my finger over the cool metal of the blade and down to the gilded hilt. I haven't looked at it since the day I convinced myself I'd never need it again, shoving it angrily into the back of the drawer, not quite ready to get rid of it completely.

Another soft knock sounds at my door and Fin enters, "You ready?"

I nod, but a frown creases my brow when a thought hits me, "How are we going to get stuff like this on the plane?" I hold my hand up, indicating the dagger there.

He gives a small shake of his head. "We can't," he shrugs. "If we were still liege-men to Finnbhear, we could spell it into a pendant; but since we lost that privilege when we were freed, we can't." He holds up the leather string from around his neck, showing his crossed axes hanging there. "We'll have these though, if we need them. They were imbued with fae magic upon forging, no magic needed on our part to use them."

I cross my arms over my chest, "What about me? I told Natalie she couldn't go because it would be too much of a disadvantage to watch after her with no way to defend herself. I'm not about to be a liability myself. You three can't afford to be worried about me if something happens."

A crooked grin spreads across his face at my assertion, "Oh, we're going to get you a weapon." He crosses his arms over his chest, mirroring my stance and grins down at me, "But we are always going to watch after you."

My chin lifts in defiance, "I am not incapable."

The Viking holds his hands up, calmly curbing my temper. "The five of us have always watched out for each other, almost our entire lives," he says referring to his friends. "You are now a part of that. Claire too. Does that mean we think you two are incapable? Of course not. We think you're too important *not* to protect you if needed."

"I'm sorry." I give him a small satisfied smile, feeling a little guilty for my assumption. "I think I'm letting my nerves get the better of me."

"I know," he says kindly, understanding written all over his face.

Kellan pops his head around the door then, "Ready you two? The car is here."

Nodding to him, Fin and I follow, gathering up my things.

We arrive at LAX all too quickly for my taste, dread warring with anticipation inside of me and making the four-hour flight miserable. To my surprise, the warriors have everything lined up for us already;

an SUV is waiting to take us to our next destination when we step outside.

Kellan loads the bags as the rest of us climb in, Fin in the driver's seat. Looking around the fine interior, my curiosity is peaked. "I thought Finnbhear cut off your assets when he released you. How did you guys manage all of this?" I ask, thinking of the plane tickets to get from Ireland to America, then to California, and now the luxury car.

Kellan laughs as he climbs into the passenger seat, grinning back at me. "You don't think we spent all those centuries squandering our money away, do you?"

I huff a laugh at that as we leave the airport behind. "Where are we headed now?" I ask, watching the city pass us by.

Theo grins beside me, "Claire's apartment."

I whip my head around to him, "Does she know about this?"

He shakes his head as he explains, "No, but that's the most inconspicuous place to go right now."

Kellan answers my look of confusion, "With King Áed being here, he will have thralls or even members of his court anywhere and everywhere. A hotel could be infiltrated with them, and we wouldn't have the element of surprise on our side."

"What's a thrall?" I ask. "Like a changeling?"

"The Underworld doesn't have changelings." Fin meets my eyes in the rear-view mirror for a moment, "Thralls are humans who have come into The Underworld, willingly or otherwise, and have been placed under a kind of spell, almost trance-like in nature. Áed controls their every move and thought. They only see, hear, or do what he wants them to. He can spin elaborate illusions, making them believe they're somewhere completely different, all while trapped in his service. He himself is an illusion, appearing like a young, handsome man, but he's ancient; even more so than the other fae rulers. Sometimes I wonder if he's something else entirely."

"Who would go willingly into something like that?" my voice is bleak with somberness, the question rhetorical. Thankfully, they ignore the fact that the very person we're going to save went willingly.

Theo answers my question anyway. "Some go because they think Áed can give them whatever they desire. They're empty and grasping for *anything* to fill them up, and think that's the only way. And for a while, he does give them their desires. He draws them in with it, but it always ends in a nightmare. He's cruel and cunning, as are most faeries," he adds. "But King Áed is worse than them all. He enjoys their torment and despair, thrives off it, and that's how it always ends for them."

My throat is tight with dread as I listen to his words. This is who we might have to face to get to Maddox? A chill runs down my spine at the thought of what Maddox has been facing this entire time.

The car ride is silent after that, everyone's thoughts likely drifting the same way. We arrive shortly in front of Claire's brick apartment building, Theo leading the way to a door on the bottom floor and knocking as we all wait on the sidewalk behind him.

A bleary-eyed Claire opens the door a few minutes later, making me realize it's still early morning here. But it only takes her a moment to recognize the dark-haired man standing at her door. "THEO?!" she squeals, all drowsiness gone as she flings her door open and wraps her arms around him. "What are you doing here?" she asks as she pulls away, only then noticing the rest of our group behind him. She rushes to me, "What are *you* doing here?" she exclaims again as she hugs me.

I hug her back tightly, realizing how much I've missed my friend. "Can we come in? We'll explain everything," I say to her.

She notices the seriousness in my eyes and immediately ushers us inside. We spend the next hour explaining our sudden appearance to the redhead, her frequent interjections lengthening the conversation.

"So what's the plan?" she says as we finally catch her up to speed.

Theo and Kellan look to Fin, waiting for him to answer. He stands from his propped position against the kitchen bar behind us, walking to the middle of her small living room. "The nightclub is underground, housed in the center of subterranean tunnels that the city has long abandoned. As I was told, inside that club is the door to the actual Underworld, which is housed even deeper below the club." He moves his eyes to me, "That's where Maddox will be. I don't know what the layout is like, but we'll split up and find it. Carlin and I will go to Maddox. Theo, Kellan, and Claire, you'll be there to watch our backs as we get him out. We're going in pretty much blindly, so we'll all need to keep on our guard and blend in."

"How do we blend in?" Claire questions.

"King Áed has made the dress code black, so we'll need to have all black on to even make it past the entrance."

Everyone nods quietly, minds obviously not on clothing.

"Have you guys had breakfast? I'm starving," Claire asks, getting up from her couch and walking into her kitchen. Come to think of it, none of us have eaten since yesterday; food wasn't exactly in the forefront of our minds this morning.

The guys quickly make it known how hungry they are, so I join my friend in her kitchen to help prepare some food. Taking my place next to her, I begin cracking eggs into a bowl.

She shifts her attention from the bacon she's placing in a pan and over to me, speaking quietly, "How are you doing?"

The concern in her voice immediately has tears threatening to leave my eyes. I've always hated that about myself; I can mostly hold it together until someone shows concern, then it's like they've cracked open a dam of emotion.

I shrug, not meeting her eyes as I blink away the tears "I'm not sure actually." I feel her gaze on me as I whisk the eggs, keeping my face down. "I was so hurt by Maddox leaving, and convinced myself I'd never see him again. But even now that I know where he is and what really happened...it still hurts." I shrug again, fighting off the growing knot in my throat before I look at her, "I think I just haven't really had time to wrap my head around it all."

She reaches over and squeezes my hand once, her eyes full of understanding, before she turns and starts to cook the food we've prepared. Thankfully, not pushing any further.

Chapter 19

"How about this?" Claire's arm shoots out from around her closet door, holding a black mini dress on a hanger.

Surveying the very short and very tight little number, I scrunch my nose and shake my head, even though she can't see as she digs even more clothing out. "I don't think that's a great idea, Claire. It's not very practical if we have to run or fight."

Her red head finally pokes out from around the door, mouth set in a pout as she looks at the dress, "I guess you're right." Her shoulders slump ever so slightly, "It's just so cute and I've never had a chance to wear it." Disappointment written all over her, she places the dress back where it came from.

We've spent the last hour getting ourselves ready for the night. The sun is just beginning to set, and Claire has been searching for the perfect outfit for a good part of that hour.

"Have you thought about what you'll wear?" She pokes her head back around to look at me.

I huff a laugh, "I brought a few things to pick from, but I'm not too concerned about clothes right now."

My friend comes around the closet door, sitting on the edge of her bed beside me. "I know you're worried about tonight, but we will cross that bridge when we get there. This," she says, gesturing to the clothes, "is what's pressing for now." She pops up off the bed to dive back into her closet.

I sigh at her persistence; I really don't care about my clothes at the moment, but the time to leave for the nightclub is looming ever closer. Pushing myself off the bed, I make my way to her spare room to rummage through the clothes I hastily packed. My hands meet a bundle of cool, smooth fabric in the bottom of the bag. Pulling it out, I take in the sleek, black, faux leather leggings. They're not typically my style, I'd only gotten them at the behest of Natalie, forcing me to try something other than my usual, softer style, but they'll have to do. Pants are obviously preferable in this situation. The rest of my outfit comes together quickly with a billowy black camisole tucked into the pants and black leather boots finish it off.

Claire walks into the room as I finish zipping the shoes up around my calf. "Oooh, look at you!" she says as she wiggles her eyebrows.

I give her a pinched expression, "This is so far out of my comfort zone, it's not even funny." I'd only been brave enough to wear the pants around my house until now, feeling utterly silly in them. But what I'm wearing isn't the most important thing to me at the moment, the task in front of us is, and I am ready to get it over with.

"I'm serious," she assures me, "you look amazing."

Giving her a smirk, I gesture to her attire, "I see you went with the mini dress anyway."

She looks down at her outfit before shrugging back up at me. "Eh, I couldn't pass up the opportunity," she grins cheekily at me, "and if I flash someone while fighting for our lives, I think that'll be the least of my worries."

We both let out a peal of laughter at that, heading for the living room where the guys are waiting for us. I have to hold back more laughter as we step into view, particularly at Theo gaping silently at Claire. I slide past him, mirth painting my features, "You trying to catch flies in that mouth?" I poke at him.

His mouth clamps shut as Kellan and Fin look on with amusement.

"Come on," I look between the two of them, nodding my head towards the front door, "let's give them a minute."

We load up into the dark SUV, joined by Claire and Theo a few moments later, then head off to face The Underworld.

It's not long before we pull up across the street from an abandoned hotel building in the middle of downtown Los Angeles. The blonde brick building still stands tall, but the years of neglect are evident in all its features.

Climbing out of the car to stand beside Fin on the sidewalk, I survey the dingy building. "Are you sure you know where we're going?"

He doesn't take his eyes off the hotel. "There are multiple entrances all over the city, but this is the shortest tunnel to the center."

Claire interrupts as she gets out of the back door, adjusting her dress, "The entrances are open to just anyone?"

"No, they're guarded either by thralls or faeries under Áed's rule," Fin tells her.

She looks between the three warriors as Theo and Kellan join us on the sidewalk, confusion on her face, "Won't they recognize you three?"

"Not on this side of the pond. The Otherworld is just as big as the human one," Theo says as he subconsciously wraps an arm around Claire's waist, sending an ache through my chest.

Fenrir then turns to all of us, but looks pointedly to Claire and me. "Don't eat or drink anything. It'll subdue your senses until you become enthralled and at the mercy of Áed."

He gestures between himself, Theo, and Kellan, "Stay close to us and let us do most of the talking when possible. The Underworld will be full of faeries and humans alike."

I rub a hand up my arm as Claire and I nod, trying to soothe away the fear rising within me. It makes me think back to the day Maddox took me with him into King Finnbhear's court. I thought I was afraid then, but it doesn't compare to this. From what I know of the two, King Áed is much more dangerous.

Fin's eyes are on me now, his question apparent in them. I take a steadying breath, "I'm ready. Let's go."

He leads the way across the street and the rest of us follow. The warriors form a sort of wall around us: Fin leading, Claire and I just behind him, and Theo and Kellan at our backs as we make our way down a flight of stairs just beside the abandoned building.

A man steps out from a door on the landing at the bottom. No, not a man at all, I notice after blinking a few times, but a glamoured faerie. Trying hard to keep my features neutral, I force myself not to react as I see the nightmarish creature beneath. Dark, spindly limbs block our way as the faerie steps out of the shadows in front of Fin, every bit as tall as the Viking. Large pupilless yellow eyes survey our entire group, completely unblinking.

"What are you here for?" The voice of the creature is a horrible, croaking whisper, and his bat-like ears twitch as he waits for an answer.

I halfway wonder what Claire sees and hears, since she can only see the glamour.

"We're just looking for a good time," Fin says, sounding every bit the oblivious tourist. "We were told this was the hottest club in town."

The creature doesn't answer for a moment, only stares, swishing his long black tail behind him.

Fin turns and ushers us to turn with him, silently urging us to follow his lead. "I guess we're at the wrong place, girls. Come on, we'll try somewhere else."

We give whiny sighs of disappointment, playing along with the ruse. Theo places his arm around Claire, and I feel Fin's hand on the small of my back as they make to usher us back up the stairs, but before we can make it any further, the dark faerie calls after us.

"Wait! You're right, it's here." He opens the door behind him, the sneer evident in his harsh voice as a jagged smile spreads across his face. "Enjoy The Underworld."

We step through the doorway into the gloomy, dirty tunnel beyond.

"Well that wasn't creepy at all," Claire whispers as we traipse through the damp ruins of old train tracks.

A humorless laugh escapes my lips, "You didn't even see what it actually looked like." A chill inches up my spine at its depthless eyes. "What even was that?" I ask the warriors.

"A púca," Theo answers. "Foul creature."

I whip my head around to him, thinking of the faerie Thomas got our information out of. "*That* was the thing trying to lure villagers into the Faerie Realm? I don't see something like that being successful."

"They wouldn't look like that; they can change their appearance at will. Púcas can look like anything a person desires. There are far worse things in the Otherworld than that though," Kellan says as he helps me over a piece of fallen debris.

"And you guys actually survived growing up around those things?" Claire looks at the three of them, incredulous.

Fin, the longest serving in the Faerie Courts, gives a single, humorless laugh. "We had no choice."

The contempt in his voice brings me a pang of sadness for the group of men; being raised by the very things that ripped them from everything they knew as children, and having to fight those same creatures tooth and nail just to survive.

It isn't long before the faint thump of music lets us know we're getting close. With every few feet closer, the thrums get louder and louder until we reach a set of massive metal doors that have been fitted into the old tunnel.

Two more faeries, horribly bent and twisted, step into our path from their position against the wall, but only to pull the heavy metal doors open. The music beyond holds the beat for a moment, like the room is holding its breath with us as we step across the threshold, the singer's voice the only sound before the music swells to life again. If the music was loud before, it was nothing compared to the volume beyond those metal doors; It's almost mind numbing.

The doors lead us onto a mezzanine attached to stairs leading down into the main part of the club. The shock running through our entire group is palpable as we get our first full view of what we're up against. We all stand there in silence, surveying the cavernous room.

Flashing lights coupled with the electronic music make it hard to concentrate on anything. It's obvious no one was prepared for the sheer size of this place, let alone the number of humans and faeries alike packed into the space below. There must be literally thousands.

Claire's voice is barely audible beside me as she yells over the noise, "How can this even be possible? The tunnels aren't that big."

"I think we entered the Otherworld when we stepped through those doors," I answer her. "Can you see anything other than humans here?" I turn to watch her face. If she sees them, we're definitely in the Faerie Realm.

Her eyes cautiously scan the room, growing wide as she notices the faeries littered throughout the room, horror and wonder warring on her features.

"Remember what I told you," Fin says. "Don't eat or drink anything, and stay close."

Our companions' eyes never stop scanning the room as they lead us down into the fray. My anxiety skyrockets as we reach the lower level, thrust into the mass of writhing bodies. On impulse, I grab for the back of Fin's shirt, afraid of getting lost in the crowd.

He doesn't turn, only reaches back, wrapping a strong hand around mine, making sure he has a firm hold on me and not the other way round. My grasp could easily be broken if someone wanted to separate us, but with his strong grip on me, parting us would be a much more difficult task.

I look back to see Theo shouldering himself and Claire through the masses in the opposite direction and Kellan breaking off to push his way up the middle of the room, everyone's eyes scanning for the entrance to the place where Maddox should be.

When I turn around, I'm accosted by a club-goer, his hands grabbing at my body, trying to pull me into him. Before he has a chance to grasp onto more than just my clothes, Fin rounds on him. The Viking's free hand is around the young man's neck before he has a chance to realize what's happening. *"Back off."* Those two growled words are all it takes. The random man disappears quickly into the crowd as soon as my blonde companion loosens his hold. Without another word, Fin pulls me to his side, placing a protective arm around my waist before continuing along our intended path.

It's worrying how easily we come upon the door described to Thomas. I tell Fenrir as much, but there's no doubt he already knows. He slides his grey eyes over to me, silently acknowledging my worries before opening the unlocked door and ushering me through quickly.

He stops at the top of a landing of stone stairs before turning to me, sliding a dagger from his boot and holding it out to me. "Take this and stay on your guard," he says in a low voice.

I take the knife, noticing it's one of Theo's, shaking off my nerves as I prepare my body to strike if needed. Cold, sinewy fingers of fear snake their way up my spine when we reach the bottom of the dark stairwell.

The music from above is somehow muted, allowing for sounds of torment to flood my ears. Moans of pain and cries for help drift through the dark stone passage, along with echoes of skin being ravaged by the cracking of a whip. I fight back the bile rising in my throat at the fear of what we might see as we come to an opening in the path lit only by torches.

I don't even have to round the corner to know he's here.

Chapter 20

"A cailín álainn," his deep, lamenting voice reverberates through my entire body, causing my heart to pang with every note of the Irish song, "a dtug mé grá duit, Ó bí ar láimh liom, mo mhíle stór..."

I am glued to my spot, recognizing the song as he sings.

Oh beautiful girl to whom I gave my love, give me your hand my dearest one, tell me you're my bright love and there will be happiness upon me instead of sorrow...

He had sweetly whispered the English words into my ear one night as a musician sang in the pub. For a moment, the memory floods my mind before I'm pulled from my thoughts by a soft touch on my back. Fenrir has moved to my side, his eyes scanning me closely.

Realizing tears have started to spill, I fumble to wipe them away before taking a quiet step around the corner.

The sight of him sitting, chained against the cold stone wall, makes my heart feel as if it will crumble. I can only see the side of him, but it's enough. Enough to see new scars marring his shirtless form, weariness practically radiating off him as he props his arms on his knees, head hanging low. He's filthy, covered in grime, and clothed only in brown leather pants that look to be quite a few inches too short. The cell he's housed in is one of many in a long curved hallway, the sounds of other prisoners suffering is a constant resonance in the background.

Realizing I've been standing there dumbfounded for too long, I make to take a step toward Maddox, but am suddenly jerked back into the hall we've just emerged from.

Quicker than I can react, I'm shoved against the dark stone wall, a warm hand covering my mouth to keep me from making a sound. Fenrir shakes his head silently, staring at me intensely. He flicks his eyes back in the direction of the cells in answer to my questioning gaze.

Just a moment later the sound of multiple sets of feet come into earshot, then the sound of keys jingling. "It's showtime for you, *boyo,*" a harsh voice grunts as we hear the clanking of chains being loosed.

Shadows pass by the archway where we're hiding and Fin chances a look around the wall, his eyes troubled as he tries to piece together the situation. Without a sound, he hurriedly pulls me back to the staircase we had just descended.

"What's happening?" I whisper to him as loud as I dare.

He glances quickly over his shoulder at me, never stopping his ascent, "I don't know, but we need to find the others."

Almost as soon as we slip back into the massive room, we're met by a frantic Kellan. "There's something you two need to see." Without another word, he starts shoving through the thick of the crowd, leading us toward the front of the room where Theo and Claire are already waiting.

My thoughts go completely blank at the sight of Kellan's distress. The edge of the dance floor surrounds a huge pit, reminding me of a gladiator's arena. People and faeries alike are gathered around, shouting and jeering at the participants battling on the dirt floor. Maddox is in the center, fiercely facing down opponent after opponent.

With a shock, I realize the fighters aren't all faerie creatures, some are human. The skilled warrior strikes them down nonetheless.

"He's killing humans too," I whisper into the din, a knot in my throat.

It's a shock when Fin answers behind me, apparently realizing the cause of my horror. "It's a cruel thing, but it's life or death. He has no choice."

Maddox is the last one standing, left exhausted and panting in the middle of the stadium. The delighted screams of the crowd at his victory are deafening as he's led back into an archway across the arena.

My eyes follow his form until he disappears into the shadows beyond. My gaze drifts slowly up the wall above the doorway, finding a platform sitting just above it that I hadn't noticed before. My body freezes to the spot as my eyes climb higher, scanning over a black throne, and then meeting a pair of icy blue eyes staring right back into my own.

"It would seem we have a queen in our midst." The room goes silent at the first sound of the smooth voice, a slow amused smile spreading across the face belonging to those eyes. "Well, almost."

I feel the warriors stiffen just behind me, Claire letting out a shocked gasp at the insult.

The crowd follows his gaze, turning their attention to me.

"I've been waiting for you."

The male faerie doesn't look to be more than in his late twenties, but Fin was right, there's something ancient and dark there looking back at me, barely concealed behind the beautiful guise; something that has my most basic instincts on high alert, making the hair on my neck prickle.

Pale, perfect skin, long black hair, and thick lashes accompany those cold blue eyes. He's handsome and serene, but the darkness behind it isn't easily hidden, and his words give me pause. He knew we were coming.

I give him no answer, no reaction to his taunt except to raise my chin in defiance, leveling my eyes to him. I refuse to show my fear, despite how tightly it's gripping me.

My boldness seems to entertain him, his sneer spreading into an outright smile displaying blindingly white teeth. "Let's see how brave you are without your bodyguards beside you."

Before I know what's happening, with a wave of his hand I'm standing in the middle of the fighting pit, alone. There is a commotion behind me but I only dare take my eyes off the wicked king for a moment. The others are fighting to get to the very edge of the pit, only to be held back by a multitude of people; thralls, I realize. I meet Fin's furious eyes for a breath, shaking my head once before turning back to face King Áed as my companion's protests go silent.

Holding my hands out I shrug, my voice thankfully sounding more confident than I feel, "Here I am."

The dark king leans his head on his hand, eyes flat as if he's bored of me already. "You've come to take your true love back, hmm? I'm sorry my little show threw a wrench in those plans." He pouts at me, voice full of condescension, "I do enjoy my entertainment, as you can see." He flicks his eyes around the entirety of the room.

I take a steadying breath, straightening my shoulders before confronting him. "Maddox was wrongfully given over to you, he wasn't Mab's to trade anymore."

"As far as I'm aware, he came willingly. And..." Áed leans forward in his chair, pouting at me again, "he was always Mab's to give, even while in his mother's womb."

My careful mask of composure slips entirely then, and the wicked faerie delights in it, laughing outright.

"You don't know the whole story, do you? I suppose not," he answers his own question, shrugging indifferently. "Neither did the poor boy until a short time ago. Very well, I'll tell you too. I love a good story," he says haughtily before I even have the chance to say a word. Áed leans lazily back into his black throne, "I'm sure you all know the story of the poor little prince, stolen from his loving mother and father by the *evil* Unseelie Queen." He flicks his eyes over to my companions and then back to me. "Well, that isn't *quite* the truth. You see, as much as he *hated* the faerie kind, your prince's very own father was seduced by Mab. And, as is known, Mab came for him to be given as a tithe to me."

My chest feels heavy at his last words. I already know where this is going, and my heart is crumbling all over again.

"The king, being just a tad selfish, offered up his unborn son in exchange for escaping the fate meant for himself," Áed waves a hand in dismissal. "So you see, he was always going to end up here."

Swallowing past the tightness in my throat and hoping my voice sounds bolder than I feel, I ask, "How do I get him back?"

The dark king throws his head back in laughter. "My, you're a brave one. I wouldn't normally do this, but your bravado entertains me," he says, raising a long slender finger. "I'll give you one chance. If you can convince your love to go with you, he's free." He waves a slender hand and the doors beneath his platform start to open.

My eyes are mere slits as I survey Áed's face, knowing there must be a catch, but I can't refuse the offer. I have to try everything I can to get him back.

"That is, if you can get to him."

I take a step toward the open doors but am stopped short by three figures stepping from the darkness beyond. At first, as they step out of the shadows, I think they'll surely be faeries, horrid creatures of Áed's court, or fighters from his twisted games. But as the first one starts to rush me, with hatred and wrath filling his eyes, it only takes a breath to realize they're not fighters or monsters at all, only human thralls, slaves to the King of the Underworld's dark whims.

I stumble back, the sudden attack shocking me, making me lose my footing. He's on me in a moment, but I quickly land a kick between his legs, sending him rolling off of me, giving me a split second to get back on my feet.

Behind me, I hear Fin roaring to the dark king, "Bring me down! I'll do it, I'll fight!"

Áed only smiles at the Viking's clear distress, wagging his finger, "No, no. It must be the girl. She bargained; she has to be the one to set him free."

In the few breaths it takes for the thrall to regain his footing, I make the decision to avoid hurting them as much as I can; they're victims, their minds toyed with by Áed. They're not coming after me, but whatever it is the evil king has put into their heads.

As the man closes in on me again, using all the strength I can muster, I hit him with the handle of my dagger, knocking him unconscious. Before I even have enough time to breathe a sigh of relief at sparing the thrall, I hear Áed chide behind me, "You're not taking the easy way out of this, girl. For every one you leave alive, I'll send out two more. This is your only warning."

I feel like a physical blow has hit me at the realization of what he's wanting me to do. He wants me to kill them. But I can't. They're people, innocent people, they don't deserve this.

In the middle of my spiraling thoughts, I'm close-lined by the man I had just knocked unconscious, the breath knocked from my lungs as I land hard on my back. He's on me again and now he's even more crazed than before. The dagger I had apparently dropped on my way down is now clutched in his hands and coming for my throat. Grabbing what I can of the hilt, I push back with every bit of strength I have, managing to keep the point of the blade just a couple of inches above my skin.

Panic sets in, causing my breathing to hitch and tears to spring to my eyes. I can't do this. I can't take an innocent life like this. Surrender is on my tongue, making its way to my lips as I hear Fin's voice just above me over the pit. "Look at me, Carlin. Look at me."

I only dare take my eyes off my opponent for a split second, but it's enough to see the warrior's intensity as his eyes bore into mine, his voice as calm as it can be over the nearly deafening crowd. "You have no choice. They are enthralled to do his will, whatever that may be, and his will right now is to kill you. It's either you or them. This is no reflection on you or who you are. It's a reflection on who he is and his evil. He's given you no other choice and you *need to fight*."

I'm trembling with a mixture of fear, anger, and adrenaline as I take in what Fin has just said to me. He's right, I have to fight for my life. The only other way out of this is death, and I refuse to allow the wicked king to take my life. My newfound resolve takes over, pushing my strength beyond its limits just enough to turn the blade toward my opponent. Closing my eyes, I sink the blade into his skin. As much as I know I had to do it, it doesn't make it any easier.

The fight against my last two opponents, another young man and a young woman, is over quickly, their crazed state making them sloppy.

But the memory of their faces will live with me forever. I don't know what's worse, the silence in my head or the roar of the crowd around me, hungry for more.

The doors underneath Áed's throne open again and I turn warily, expecting another fighter, but it's Maddox who steps through this time. I hesitate a moment before moving to stand before him, his handsome face emotionless. "Maddox," I say softly, "let's go home." My hand twitches to move toward him.

I barely have time to react when he moves, his sword slicing the air between us, and the silent crowd erupts anew, delighting in more violence, Áed's laughter resonating above it all. Thankfully, my muscle memory kicks in and I manage to dodge his next few swings as I shift into defense mode. He trained me; I know how he fights. But I've barely been able to get the better of him on my best days. I've never faced him like this, already weak and weary while he's just getting started. My only hope is to move fast and avoid him swiftly if I'm going to last any length of time against his centuries of skill.

I duck another blow before facing him again. "What are you *DO-ING*?"

His beautiful eyes are wild now as he continues his attack, growling out at me, "*You're not real.*"

Panic tightens its grip on me as I realize what's happening. He's been thralled, only knowing what the wicked king is allowing him to see. I'll have to keep up my defense as long as it takes to break through this enchantment, and pray neither one of us is hurt in the process.

"It's me! I'm real and I'm here to take you home," I tell him, my voice urgent, breathless. The months I wasted without training are already causing me to slow.

"You're. Not. *REAL*," he says through gritted teeth with each of his strikes toward me, his movements frenzied.

By no small miracle, I manage to knock his sword from his hand. My thoughts are just as frantic as his attacks as I search my mind for anything, any memory, to pull him from the spell.

"Remember the cliffs, Maddox...and running from the rain...dancing with me! The first time you kissed me with the glowing sprites all around-" Try as I might, I can't stop my voice from breaking completely as I list off all my most precious memories with him, hoping in vain that something would reach through the fog in his mind and snap him out of the thrall.

He comes for me empty handed, swinging with fists now. Áed's cruel laughter still rings over the cacophony of the crowd. "This isn't some old curse, silly girl. This isn't something that can be broken with *true love's kiss*," he croons, his honeyed voice laced with venom.

Tears flow freely from my eyes now, the emotional and physical struggle taking its toll.

"He did resist me for a while, actually," Áed says matter-of-factly. "Droning on and on about some *great king* something or other, blah blah...but he broke eventually."

My angry gaze is immediately drawn to the wicked faerie.

His answering scoff fuels my anger even more, "Don't tell me you believe in that ridiculous story too?"

I pay for the moment of distraction when I'm suddenly disarmed. Maddox stalks around me, waiting for another opening to attack. The scrambling in my mind stops as I suddenly realize what will likely wake him, one thing I know he would never do willfully.

The warrior moves toward me, blue eyes predatory as he closes the gap between us and I stand there, completely unmoving, every muscle in my body tensing as I ready for what's about to happen.

His free hand grabs my arm tightly, holding me in place, and I lock my eyes on his. My breath hitches, feeling a horrible, searing pain in my abdomen as the dagger blade pierces my stomach. My hand instinctively flies up to grip his arm against the pain. The wildness in his eyes vanishes almost instantly as the first inch of the blade slides into my skin, replaced by sheer panic as he looks to the knife in his hand, removing it quickly.

His brows knit together tightly over his horror-filled eyes as he meets my own pain-stricken ones. "Carlin?"

Chapter 21

He throws the blade away from him before his hand flies back to my stomach, holding steady pressure against the dark spot slowly blooming on my shirt.

My own eyes have drifted down to survey the wound, blinking rapidly at the blood starting to drip over Maddox's hand. I raise my wide-eyed stare to him, his own beautiful eyes clear now, not a trace of the haze of his thrall. They rapidly survey my face before turning hard as he rounds on the cackling form of King Áed,

"YOU," Maddox snarls at the evil faerie, his hand itching to leave my abdomen and head for the king. I've never seen him so enraged.

Áed stops his laughter, holding his hands up in mock defense, "Don't look at me. boy. You're the one who did it." I vaguely register his cold eyes sliding to meet mine, everything feeling far away. "I didn't think you had it in you. But, as promised, you're all free to go." He lazily waves a slender hand and instantly we're next to our awaiting friends.

Fin rushes to my side, trying to examine my wound, but Maddox scoops me up into his arms, noticing me swaying on my feet. "She'll be fine. The wound isn't that deep, but I think she's in shock." I can feel the steady timbre of his voice through his chest as I rest my head there. "We just need to worry about getting her out of here. *Now*." He starts forcing his way through the leering crowd as Áed's poison-filled voice rings through the room.

"Just don't forget, *girl*, you took something from me."

His words settle over me like a dark cloud. It takes all of my strength to lift my eyes and look to Maddox, trying to convey my dread. He doesn't acknowledge the faerie's words, but his jaw is set and the storm brewing in his eyes at the wicked king's threat is enough to make even the most hardened of warriors crumble beneath it.

We make it back to the street above in what seems like minutes, Maddox surveying me carefully every few seconds, his eyes locking mine in place, drawing me out of the daze I keep falling into.

"You're alright, Mhuirnín. We'll patch you up soon," his voice is reassuring and gentle as he places me onto the cool seat of the SUV, climbing in beside me as his hand comes up to place pressure on my stomach again.

Fin drives like a madman towards Claire's apartment, the rest of our group silent with worry. We reach the front of Claire's home and I protest weakly as Maddox goes to lift me into his arms again. Having regained a bit of my alertness, I try to wave him off gently, "I think I'm okay. I can walk."

"No, Carlin," he objects. "You're hurt. No stubbornness, I'm carrying you." Maddox scoops me into his arms before I can reply, carrying me up the sidewalk and through the front door before settling me gently onto the couch.

Claire rushes through her living room and heads straight for her kitchen, coming back quickly with a first aid box in hand. "This should have everything you need, I paid extra for a stitch kit." She hands the box over to Maddox, stepping back out of the way, and rubs her arms to comfort herself.

"I'm alright, Claire," I try and reassure my friend. "I think the worst of it is over; the bleeding has pretty much stopped."

Maddox kneels beside me, starting to cut my shirt away from the wound, but Fin steps forward, putting a hand on his friend's shoulder. "I can patch her up, you should go get cleaned up and changed." After taking in the sight of himself, bare torso covered in grime from the dungeon and hands now stained with my blood, Maddox concedes with no small amount of reluctance.

Claire steps forward, quietly showing him to the bathroom as Fin kneels down next to the couch and gently peels back the portions of my shirt Maddox had started to cut. He looks over his shoulder for a moment to Kellan, "I need you to mix warm water with some salt. I need to flush the wound before closing it up."

Kellan makes quick work of his task, only taking a minute before returning with the solution.

Fenrir opens the syringe from the first aid kit and fills it with the liquid before turning to me, placing a gentle hand on my arm, "This is going to hurt, but it has to be done."

Nodding, I watch him move the syringe into place, steeling myself for the coming pain. I grit my teeth against the saltwater burning through the open wound and have to stifle a whimper. As quickly as he started, it's done and he's digging through the medical supplies, ready to move on.

Sometime during the procedure Maddox had crept silently back into the room, now standing, arms crossed, against the archway leading to the hall. He's dressed now, in jeans and a plain black shirt, the filth from the Underworld washed away, but his thousand-yard stare and guilt ladened posture suggest the stains left by that horrid place are far from gone.

I'm brought back to the moment when Fin turns away from the medical kit and back to me, surgical needle and sutures ready in his hand. With another quick warning, he pierces my skin with the needle. It's impossible to stifle the cry of pain this time. I don't know what's worse, the sharp sting of the needle or the tooth-grinding discomfort of the thread being pulled through my flesh. The horrid sensations are nearly overwhelming. Out of habit my eyes dart straight to Maddox, searching for any form of comfort, but his eyes are so full of shame I can't bear it and I force my eyes to close against the wave of nausea crashing over me. I only open them when I feel Fin placing a bandage onto the area, noticing Maddox has left the room again.

Claire steps forward, helping me sit up against the pain, then gently pulls me to standing. "Come on, you should change and get some rest," she says softly, leading me towards her spare bedroom. My protests die on my lips as I realize just how exhausted I actually am, and surely Maddox is too. I want to talk to him, but our reunion will have to wait.

After a night of fitful sleep, the morning comes all too soon, bringing with it soreness and extreme fatigue. Noticing sounds of movement in the living room, I drag myself out of bed, stifling a groan at the pain in my stomach, and head for the source of the noise. Kellan is returning from outside, picking up the other's bags before heading back out to the car.

"We're leaving already?" I question to anyone who will answer.

Theo passes by me, carrying Claire's suitcase, his usually light mood gone flat, "Thomas just phoned. We're needed back home immediately."

Before I'm even able to get the question out of my mouth, I'm startled by the sound of Maddox's voice just behind me. "Multiple people from the village have started to go missing."

I turn to face him, my heart sputtering at the thought in my mind, "Does it have anything to do with Áed?"

He shakes his head, rubbing the back of his neck, "We don't know, that's why we need to get back."

I wrestle against the rising guilt of possibly being the cause of this new attack, Áed's threat echoing in the back of my mind.

The dark-haired warrior gently wraps his hand around the back of my arm, "Carlin, we should talk."

I can't help the stiffness that creeps into my muscles at his touch, so familiar, but at the same time foreign after so long apart. My desire to see him and speak to him is suddenly overshadowed by awkwardness and anxiety. "We will," I answer, my voice sounding more cheerful than I feel. "But I should get my bag and get ready to go. We don't need to waste any more time." His hand falls from my arm as I skirt around him and back to Claire's spare room.

I spend the next twelve hours on the flight fretting about the looming conversation. As bad as I feel about the missing townsfolk, I'm grateful for the delay. I've spent the last year longing for Maddox, thinking that if I just had him back I would automatically feel better, but I don't. My heart still lays in pieces.

We've barely made it up the long driveway when Mairead's small form scrambles out of the front doors toward our car. She gives Claire and I only enough time to slide out of our seats before she crashes into us with a hug, "Oh, how I've missed you lasses!"

My happiness at seeing the kindly faerie again chases away my lingering sadness for the moment. She wastes no time in ushering us through the front door, leaving the changelings to unload our bags. "Come on girls, I have food waiting on ya'. You all must be famished after such a trip."

Claire and I exchange gleeful glances at one another, both of us having missed Mairead and her cooking greatly. We allow her to push us to the dining room and into our chairs, an Irish roast dinner spread before us. The warriors aren't far behind, coming through the doors just as the brownie has fixed our plates. Thomas has joined them now, taking his seat before beginning to fill us in on the disappearances of the villagers.

"The first, a young man, went missing almost as soon as you three left for America," he glances between Theo, Kellan, and Fin. "I didn't think too much of it until the next day, someone else went missing, and as of now, two more."

"It's obviously something to do with the faeries, but have they ever been that bold before?" Claire interjects.

The changelings all shake their heads, Maddox answering, "Not in all our years with them. One or two abductions every year or so, but all from different places."

"Do you think Finnbhear knows?" I ask.

The warrior's stunning eyes settle on me, sending mine darting back to my plate. "Perhaps, but before we know for sure who's behind this, I don't want to bring him into it. Did anyone else know about your trip?" Maddox asks, turning his attention to Fin, Kellan, and Theo.

"No, just the few of us around this table," Kellan answers.

"Is it possible that someone in the Otherworld knew something about it?" I ask, my mind brought back to my most recent run-in with the banshee and Áed's words.

"It's always a possibility," Theo says. "Why?"

"Áed made it obvious that he knew we were coming and... I had another run-in with the banshee from the Seelie Court," I explain, "just minutes before you three walked into the bar."

Fin shoots me a concerned look, "Why didn't you tell us?"

"With the shock of seeing all of you there, and then the news you brought," I glance quickly to Maddox watching me steadily, "I just forgot. But she was insistent on reiterating her words to me from before. Do you think someone from one of the Faerie Courts knew and sent her? And that the disappearances are tied to that somehow?"

The table goes thoughtfully silent for a while before Mairead interrupts, her gentle but irritated voice resonating through the room, "Enough of this troubling news. Why don't you all go take some downtime before starting into the next problem? You've barely brought yourselves out of the last one!"

Our entire group is noticeably grateful for the excuse of a short reprieve before diving into the looming situation. Everyone excuses themselves from the room, heading their separate ways as the old faerie begins to clear the table.

I start for the door, but am stopped short by a name called out behind me, "Mo Chuisle." Hearing him say that name again makes my heart jump into my throat. I turn slowly to face him, swallowing past the sudden dryness in my mouth.

His eyes are weary as he takes me in, his voice soft, "Please talk to me."

"What do you want me to say?" I breath out, walking to the arched windows, watching the dusk falling over the grounds. My heartbeat speeds up to the point where I'm sure he can hear it when he comes to stand just behind me, his hand coming to rest on the small of my back.

"You've avoided me since we left Claire's house, not even looking at me for more than a moment. We have to talk at some point. Just look at me. Say *anything*," his voice is pleading, begging me to speak. So I tell him, everything flooding out unfettered: about how it hurt me to see him walk away, the way it felt wondering what could've happened to cause him to do it. The ache it caused to know that, even after we'd promised to face the world together, he'd walked into literal hell alone, leaving me to think he'd abandoned me. The words just spill out and I can't stop them, the hole he'd left within me as he walked away still holding me captive.

He takes a seat in a chair by the window, calmly sitting there taking blow after blow of my angry words, though I know each one strikes true. The understanding written all over his face breaks me even more.

"I would have fought for you," I berate him, gesturing down to the still fresh wound in my side. "I *did* fight for you." I finally break eye contact with him, looking out the window for a moment to steel myself back into a sense of calm. "I loved you so deeply, so quickly," my words are barely above a whisper. "When you walked away without any explanation, you shattered a piece of me."

He finally looks away from me, his face turning to the ground, body crumpled. "You don't think I know that?" His voice is ripe with guilt.

"I'm still trying to pick up the pieces, Maddox." My voice finally breaks a little around his name.

He stands, striding to place himself just in front of me. His beautiful eyes are intense as he locks them onto mine, searching as if he can see the shattered pieces there. "Then let me mend it."

I close my eyes against the tears threatening to flow. "I understand why you did it," I whisper, "and I will *forever* be grateful that you saved me from that fate. But I just need some time, Maddox."

He reaches up, wiping the single tear that has escaped down my cheek. "I'll wait." His voice is soothing as he assures me, "I'll wait until the sun fades away into nothing, if that's what it takes."

I leave him standing alone at the window, walking into the hallway and softly shutting the door behind me. The sight of Mairead standing just outside the door makes me pause, my face heating with the knowledge that she's probably just heard our entire exchange.

She stops me as I try to walk past her, looking me firmly in the eye. "You know there aren't many men who would sit there and take that like he did after what he's been through; sitting there and letting you tear him into pieces too." Her words add even more weight to the crippling guilt I feel after the way I just unloaded on him. He'd gone to hell and back for me, and I thanked him by tearing into him, my hurt and sadness coming out in the form of anger instead.

Ashamed, I can't meet her eyes until she places a gentle hand on my face, "I'm not reprimanding you, lass." My tears finally spill over at the kindness in her voice. "I just want you to understand how much he loves you, selflessly loves you. He would gladly rip himself to shreds just to patch those parts of you that he broke. Just like what you went through for him, to get him back."

Her words, and their meaning, ring true. I love him fiercely, I always will. I just needed time to work through the hurt.

"I know, lass. I know," she says, seeming to read my mind. She pulls me into a tight hug, helping to hold me together as my heart breaks again. I probably just ruined any chance at reconciliation with him, the man I love most in the world, with the way I just acted; he didn't deserve that. And now I don't know if I ever deserved him.

Chapter 22

My whole body is trembling as I storm through the castle towards the council rooms the next morning. I was yanked from sleep by my phone ringing off the hook, only to be met with a frantic, sobbing Natalie upon answering.

Maddox and the other changelings' voices sound through the hallway as I reach the door, discussing tactics on finding the missing villagers. They all turn, shocked at my sudden entrance. Maddox jumps from his seat and starts towards me, but thinks better of it and stops short, instead taking in my wide-eyed state from across the room. "What's wrong?"

"People from my hometown are going missing too." I glance between everyone in the room, "They began vanishing the day we left for California. One every day since then, and now, Natalie's little brother has been taken." My heart clenches as I say the words. The young boy, Owen, is like a sibling to me.

"Just last night?" Fin asks.

I shake my head, "Only a few hours ago. It's still night there."

The mood in the room immediately shifts, everyone wracking their brains for solutions.

"That isn't all," I add, turning the group from their thoughts and back to me. "There was a message left for me where Nat's brother was supposed to be." Pulling my phone from my pocket, I lay it on the table for everyone to see and open the newly received e-mail containing a photo of the note:

You made your choice, and I don't like to lose. You could've prevented this. You can have them back when you accept my offer.

My heart skips a beat entirely. I know that handwriting, that paper. It's the same ancient looking scrap of paper that was stuffed inside the drawer of my bedside table for so long. Everything finally clicks into place; there's only one who could be responsible for it. I don't know why it didn't dawn on me before. "It's Finnbhear," I breath out, pushing my hair out of my face, palm planted on my head as if I can stop my brain from imploding.

I can feel Maddox go dangerously still at my side. "What offer is he talking about?" His voice is full of dangerous calm. The kind of quiet, seething anger that sends a shiver up your spine.

Realizing that he is in the dark about the first message, I quickly fill him in, only stealing quick glances at his face, feeling the weight of guilt even though I can't help Finnbhear's infatuation. But the heavy feeling is quickly overcome by indignation. How *dare* Finnbhear try to spin this into being my fault? How *dare* he try and hurt people that

I love, in order to quell me into submission? Without a word, I turn on my heel and head for the front doors.

I've made it up the castle drive and into the road before anyone catches up with me, my anger spurring me on swiftly.

"What are you doing?" Fenrir's voice sounds in my ear, his hand on my arm spins me around to face him abruptly. He's taken aback for a moment by the fire in my eyes, but recovers quickly.

"I am not just going to sit idly by while he *blackmails* me and hurts innocent people because he didn't get what he wanted," I spit, flinging my finger in the direction I'm headed, the Seelie Court.

Maddox catches up to us now, hearing my words to Fin. A flash of something akin to jealousy shines in his eyes as they dart curiously between the Viking and I with Fin's hand still on my arm, but it's gone as quickly as it came. His eyes lock onto mine, "You can't just go waltzing into Finnbhear's throne room like that."

Reflexively, my chin shoots up in defiance as I look at him, "Watch me." Pulling my arm out of Fenrir's grasp, I start for my destination with renewed determination, spurred on by sheer stubbornness now. I don't look back, but I know the two of them are hot on my trail. They'd never let me walk into something like this alone, no matter how stupid it is.

This time, I don't even notice the curious little creatures peering at me from their hiding places as I enter the Faerie Realm. No, my sights are set on that great tree as if I can see straight through to the king sitting there on his throne. And I'm not stopping until I get there.

Ignoring the fatigue beginning to set in, I push myself up the many flights of stairs to the doors that are closed this time, all the while Maddox and Fin are protesting a few feet behind me.

"Wait!" Maddox breaths out, but I don't listen. I stop only long enough to brace a hand on each of the heavy wooden doors. Pushing with every ounce of rage within me, I manage to burst through them.

The room is filled with faerie courtiers, dignitaries, guards, and just as I suspected, Finnbhear sitting upon his grand throne. Their heads all turn at the commotion and surprisingly, their bodies part slightly to let me through, my eyes never leaving the faerie king.

Before I even make it to the front of the room, my arm shoots out to point an accusatory finger at the auburn-haired faerie. "*Give. Them. Back.*" I spit, stopping just in front of his dais, as far as his guards will let me get, leaving me to just stand there and seethe.

King Finnbhear runs his assessing gaze over me slowly. Only then do I vaguely realize that I'm wearing the tight black leggings and tank top that I usually train in, having slipped them on quickly this morning after talking to Natalie. The barely contained desire in his eyes only serves to fuel my anger. A leering smile plays on the edge of his lips as he slowly brings his eyes back up to my face. "You're at least going to bow, *girl*." His voice is contemptuous, nothing like the benevolent king I had met a year ago as he levels his hard eyes at me.

I hesitate for a moment, feeling the eyes of the entire room boring into me. For the first time since I left the castle, I feel uncertain of my actions, my breath hitching slightly. It's then that I feel the comfort of a familiar, steady presence at my side.

"She bows to no one." Maddox levels a challenging stare at the king; that quiet, dangerous fury seeming to come off him in waves, Fenrir just as fierce behind him.

Finnbhear drags his eyes over to Maddox, his face flat. "Come now," the faerie's baritone voice is patronizing, "you don't actually think we would let you all go without replacing you." It's unsurprising that he knows exactly why we're here.

I cock my head at him, "We?"

He huffs a single deep laugh at me, looking pointedly to the warriors behind me. "Yes, *we*. Mab, Áed, and myself. We gave up some of our best assets when we let your friends go." He leans back in his throne as if he's tired of the conversation already.

"What does that have to do with targeting people close to me? Where's Owen?" I demand.

Finnbhear waves lazily to the doors just beside the dais, silently beckoning someone forward. My indignation is ripped from me just as fast as the breath in my lungs when I see who it is he has called forward.

I can only blink for a moment, thinking that what I'm seeing must be a trick. Only, no matter how hard I blink, the person standing there beside the faerie king's throne doesn't vanish. Breaking through the fog of shock, I finally muster up enough strength inside me to speak. "Natalie?"

My best friend is standing there beside Finnbhear looking, strangely, quite proud of herself.

"Nat, what is happening? Where's your brother?" The uncertainty in my voice paints a satisfied look over the king's face.

Thankfully, Natalie has enough awareness to look ashamed when she quietly answers, "He's not here."

I can only stand there, my face twisted, confusion rendering me speechless.

"He was never here," the auburn-haired king laughs quietly as he shrugs, his lithe shoulders rising and falling gracefully. "I saw a chance to draw you here and get what I wanted..." Finnbhear shifts his eyes, indicating me, before staring challengingly back at the dark-haired prince at my side. "And your little friend here was all too willing to help me do just that."

"You think that snatching people from their families, their very lives, would make me come to you? And taking my oldest friend?" I sneer at him.

Finnbhear's face is full of self-satisfaction, "It got you here, didn't it?"

I can feel Maddox trembling with rage next to me, "You faeries are all the same: coveting pretty things and taking them as if they're already rightfully yours, using them until they're no longer shiny and new. Do you really think I'd *let* you take her, only to discard her the moment she's not of interest to you anymore?" He seethes, "I'll gladly die before I let that happen."

"The last time I checked, *boy*," Finnbhear grins cruelly, knowing his next words are a low blow for Maddox, "she's no longer yours to fight for."

Instead of backing down, a fire is lit within the warrior's striking eyes. "I'll always fight for her." His words are full of truth, and I know they were meant more for me than the faerie king before us. They strike a chord in my heart that hasn't been touched in so long. I truly don't deserve him, but I will never be more thankful for his unconditional love. Before I can dwell on it any longer, Finnbhear's voice cuts through the silence.

"But anyway, you misunderstood what I told you before," the Seelie King drawls, bored of us all. "I didn't snatch your friend away. *She* came to *me*."

My head jerks to Natalie, trying to meet my friend's down-turned eyes, the sting of betrayal making me almost breathless.

"Is that true?"

She shrugs off some of the shame causing her to hide her face, finally looking at me from under her lashes. "I just want to be a queen too," her voice trembles as her admittance tumbles out. "It's not fair that *you* get to be somebody, and I don't."

I start to take a step toward her, but Maddox's strong hand holds me in place beside him. "What are you talking about, Nat? You've been my best friend for years. I had no idea you felt that way." I gesture toward our little group which has grown in the last few minutes with the arrival of the other changelings, "You *need* to get out of here. Just come with us and we can work everything out."

She's crying into her hands now, not willing to look at anyone. For a split second I think it's from shame, but when she finally brings her head up to stare at me, her face is twisted with rage. "It's *not fair* that you get to be loved by him and you didn't even have to try!" She throws a hand out to indicate Maddox, her words spilling out as quickly as her angry tears. "I had to sit through *months and months* of you going on and on about him, even though he had left you. Only to find out that he loved you enough to go through literal hell for you?"

The hatred in her confession hits like a physical blow, making me take a step back into Maddox. His steady, comforting hand is on the small of my back in an instant, our closeness seeming to fuel Natalie's jealousy even more.

"*I* was always the one that was desired, not you; you were a nobody. But you get to leave for one random trip and come back having lived through an actual fairytale. All while I was stuck in our crap hole of a town, doing anything to get a guy's attention, and still not being enough to warrant a second phone call," she sobs out, taking a breath to compose herself before starting her attack again. "But you got your real-life fairytale, your happy ending, and you didn't even have to try. Well, now I get one too, my own king and my own fairytale."

Despite all she has just hurled at me, despite the hurt I feel after her outburst, I mostly feel pity for her. I never knew she thought so little of herself, always acting like the confident, outgoing one; but it was a façade, and Finnbhear saw straight through it, playing on her weakness. She was spun a gilded tale, not knowing the darkness behind it all. No one deserves to be trapped in something so wicked.

"Natalie, listen to me. You're playing at something that you don't understand," my voice is soft as I speak to her, like I'm speaking to a wounded animal. "Whatever he's promised you isn't true. I know he's told you a pretty tale, but it will turn into a nightmare so very quickly. Please, just leave with us before you do something you can't reverse."

A single, humorless laugh from Finnbhear cuts in, "Oh, it's too late for that."

We all go silent waiting on his next words, but they never come. Instead, from somewhere behind the grand throne, Áed emerges, coming to a halt to lurk just behind Natalie. I can feel all the blood drain from my face as I watch the wicked king's hand come up to caress her hair. She jerks violently away from him and toward Finnbhear, only to be stopped by Áed's hand wrapping around her arm. He clicks his tongue at her, "No, no darling. You belong to me now."

She strangles out a sob, her face agape, looking between Finnbhear and Áed in horror. Then her eyes turn to us, full of pleading. "What's happening? What's going on?" She's frantically trying to get out of Áed's hard grasp.

Finnbhear's dark laugh echoing through the room sends chills down my spine. "I promised you'd be with a king if you got your friend here...I never said which one."

Chapter 23

As Natalie starts to plead with the cruel kings, I feel the cold hilt of a blade being pressed into my hand. My head snaps up to Maddox, questioning his actions.

He leans down to come inches from my face, his hands making sure the dagger is secured tightly in my grip. "You need to leave, now. I'm going to get Natalie and be right behind you." He turns quickly to Fin and the rest of his friends, gesturing back to me, "Make sure she gets out of here safely." He pushes me back toward the Viking with one hand, drawing his sword with the other, only a breath before he brings the blade up through the torso of one of Finnbhear's men.

He had been sneaking up behind me, ready to seize me for his king. My heart is in my throat; I would've never noticed him. I was too distracted, which is exactly what they had wanted. There is no time to dwell on it as the room erupts, guards and courtiers alike drawing hidden weapons.

My throat feels like it has closed up completely. This is all my fault. I had stupidly walked right into Finnbhear's trap, making all of my friends follow me into it, and now it's only the few of us against an entire mob. If one of us doesn't make it out of this, it'll all be because of me.

Fin is pulling me through the melee with one hand, all while clearing our way through with an axe in the other, but in the middle of all the chaos we get separated. Fear grips me for a split second when I realize I'm alone in the middle of the fight, but I tamp it down. Letting fear take over is a sure-fire way to die in this situation. My lack of training is quickly apparent and I silently curse myself for not keeping up with it. I barely manage to even sloppily dodge or fight off the creatures around me. I've finally started inching closer to the door, breathing a short sigh of relief when I see a path through, but my body goes cold when a roar of pain erupts from somewhere behind me through the sharp clang of steel. I turn on my heel just in time to see Maddox go down, disappearing into the mob of otherworldly creatures surrounding him.

I'm able to take one running step towards him before being met with a solid body, scooping me up and hauling me over a shoulder. Fin's strong arms hold me firmly in place as he carries me toward the doors leading out of the throne room.

"No!" I use all my strength to wrestle against his hold. "We can't leave him; we have to go back for him!" My voice breaks with the last few screeched words.

The Viking adjusts his grip on my fighting form. "I have to get you out of here. I promised him." His voice is as gentle as he can make it over the clamor in the room. "He wouldn't want your life in danger just to save his."

My heart nearly sputters to a stop altogether as Fin's words cement my worst fears, making my thoughts spiral. He can't be gone. My mind immediately replays the harsh words I'd said to him just last night, and he had still been here to save me. Guilt at how I'd treated him settles over me like a heavy shroud. I never got the chance to fix things with him. We still hadn't set things right between us, and now we never would. I think I'm still sobbing, at least as much as I can tell over the ringing in my ears, as we pass through the trees and back into our world. Fin only stops when we make it inside Mairead's fence line.

It feels as though I've been drugged, my tears coming slowly but steadily now, as I stare blankly into the space around me.

"If I let go of you, are you going to stay here?" Fin asks gently, but the command laced in his question is clear. I nod silently, not caring that he can't see, only just noticing that it's night in our world now. I hadn't even been aware of the sudden change from sunlight to darkness as we'd passed through the Otherworld's entrance. I hadn't noticed much of anything as I'd cried and fought, all while Fin raced us out through the crowd of fair folk that had gathered outside, curious of the commotion. He had carried me out past them all, never stopping, not chancing any of them catching on and stopping us themselves.

He sets me down softly on the cool grass of Mairead's lawn. His eyes watch me carefully, ready to grab me again if I make any move for the forest.

"Please go back for him," I choke out the words, looking up at the Viking.

He looks deflated as he answers me, "I have to get you back to the castle, I'm not going to leave you here alone. I made a promise to keep you safe."

"Fin, *please*." I beg him, barely able to get the words out as another sob wracks me. "I promise, I won't move. Please, you can't just leave him there." The pit in my stomach threatens to swallow me whole at the thought of Maddox, his body, being stuck there. Someone so selfless and beautiful and good, never leaving that awful, ugly place.

Fin's resolve is beginning to crumble when we hear rustling in the trees. I'm on my feet and Fin is on his guard in an instant. We stand there, waiting and watching, our shallow breathing the only sound coming from us. What seems like an eternity later, Theo, Thomas, and Kellan emerge from the dark woods. My knees almost buckle at the sight of a lifeless form being carried between the three of them.

"Maddox," I whisper, taking a step towards them, but Fin pushes me back, brandishing his axes and storms for someone emerging from the trees just a few feet behind them.

Thomas shoots his free hand out to stop the blonde warrior, earning a confused look from the both of us. Thomas shakes his head at his friend, "He helped us. He watched our backs so we could get Maddox out," he says breathlessly. "We'll talk more later. First, we need to get Maddox help. *Quickly*."

I swallow back a protest as the young man following them comes fully into view. Liam. I bite back the harsh words that threaten to leave my mouth, the man being carried between the warriors is more pressing. When I make it to the group in the road, none of them want to fully meet my eyes and see the torment on my face.

"He's alive?" My throat feels as if it's on fire, my voice sounds like it too.

It seems like it takes all of Kellan's strength to keep his eyes locked on mine as he speaks, "Barely."

Fin pulls me to him as they carry Maddox past us and into Mairead's cottage. We follow just behind, coming through the door as they lay him on the old couch. A gasp escapes my lips, new tears starting as I see him clearly. He's wounded *everywhere*, but the worst of it is a gaping slash spanning the length of his entire torso, like he's been torn open down to the muscle from shoulder to hip. What manner of clawed creature did this, I don't know, but I've never seen anything so gruesome. It's nothing short of miraculous that the cut isn't deeper, thankfully missing any vital organs. But he's still bleeding out and there's no way he can last much longer like this.

Kellan steps over to me, planting himself directly in my line of sight, "You don't need to see this." He grips my shoulders, trying to turn me back toward the door.

My eyes are wild as I look up at him, "You can't kick me out of here." I dig my heels in as much as I can against the strength of the warrior, "*Please* Kellan, I need to be with him. You can't keep me from that."

He places his firm hands on either side of my face, locking my eyes with his, "Trust me, Carlin, you don't want to see this. We need to help him, and I need you to get Mairead. Can you do that for me?" His gentle, probing voice pulls me out of the desperate panic threatening to take hold of me. "Carlin? Can you do that for me? You need to go now, get to the castle as fast as you can."

I nod wordlessly up at him. Without another word, he lets me go to head out the front door and into the road. I steal a glance back toward the forest, a fleeting worry of what will happen next with Finnbhear and the others crosses my mind. But that can wait. For now I have to get to Mairead. I push the thought of those terrible creatures in the forest out of my mind as I break into a sprint for the castle.

Chapter 24

I burst through the doors of the castle, panting wildly but not slowing until I nearly run square into Claire and Mairead in one of the long hallways, finally skidding to a stop. They obviously know something is wrong given the state of my entrance.

"What is it? What's wrong lass?" The old faerie holds me firmly in place with her hands as Claire places a calming hand on my shoulder, worry written in the lines of both their faces.

"Maddox," I pant, my words coming out frantic. "We need you at the cottage now. It's an emergency, Mairead. We have to go now!"

Her kindly face is wrinkled even more with confusion, "Slow down, dear. Just tell me what's happening."

New tears start to spill, replacing the ones that had dried on my face in the wind as I ran here. I croak out the words, "He's dying."

Claire pulls me to her, trying to give any form of comfort, leaving Mairead gaping at me for a moment. She gathers herself after a breath, calling urgently for the pixies to show themselves. In a blink the little creatures are there in the hallway with us and she tells them to get to the cottage to help Maddox immediately and wait for her there.

I take a step to follow her, heading for a car in order to get back to the injured prince as quickly as possible, but my steps falter and I nearly lose my footing when my knees give out. Both Mairead and Claire manage to grab me before I fall completely.

Mairead gives me an assessing look, "You're bleeding."

"Your stitches!" Claire gasps.

I look down at my black shirt, now wet with blood across my abdomen. In the midst of the chaos following the battle in the Seelie Court, I hadn't even felt my sutures rip. I'd noticed I was jittery and lightheaded, but had chalked it up to an adrenaline rush.

"You need to take care of that before you faint completely," Mairead commands, her voice leaving no room for argument. "I will go to the village to get the doctor and then to the cottage. Claire, you stay here, help get her patched up and keep her calm." With that, she leaves to get to Maddox, moving faster than I've ever seen her move.

The redhead ushers me through the castle and into my rooms, only letting me stop once we're in the bathroom. She swallows hard, preparing herself to look at my stomach before tentatively lifting the soaked fabric from my skin, examining the wound. The stitches that Fin had sewn in had popped at some point, leaving my still-fresh injury open and steadily bleeding. Claire fills the sink with warm water and soap, and we both get to work cleaning the blood and the cut.

"There has to be a first-aid kit in here somewhere," I say to her. "We'll have to close it back up or it'll keep bleeding."

She blows her hair out of her face as she stoops to rummage through the cabinets and drawers, finally coming up victorious with a little red box in her hand. "Found it! But I have to admit, I failed home-ec in school, so I don't know how good I'll be at stitching anything." She gives me a sheepish look, "But I can try."

I take the box from her, looking through the contents, thankfully finding a package of zip-stitches. I wave the package in the air triumphantly, "Good thing we don't have to find out."

She breathes a sigh of relief along with me as she takes the package from my hand. "Oh thank God," she says, opening the plastic and getting to work at pulling my skin together with the zip-tie style bandage. "I mean, I would've done it, because you're my friend. but I was already getting sick just thinking about it." We share a much-needed laugh at that, both of us greatly relieved that she wasn't going to be the one sewing me up.

"That will have to do for now, but I'll probably need actual stitches as soon as someone can do it," I tell her as she finishes closing the wound.

She dusts her hands off, trying her best to be comical and lighten the mood hanging in the air, but it's too heavy to shake off that easily. "Now, let's go sit down and you can tell me what in the world has happened," she says over her shoulder as we walk back into my bedroom.

I've just finished telling her the story when we hear urgent footsteps down the hall. Jumping from my seat, I yank my door open to meet whoever it is, Claire just a step behind me. The group of changelings disappear into Maddox's room across the long hallway, Theo staying behind to come to us.

My friends seem to forget everything for a moment when they see each other, embracing sweetly, then parting to let Claire check him over for any injuries. I look away, partly out of politeness, partly from the way it makes my heart clench. Theo apparently notices over Claire's head and clears his throat, turning my friend's attention to me. Her smile is apologetic, but I wave off her unwarranted guilt, instead looking to Theo.

The question in my eyes must've been enough for him, because before I even open my mouth he speaks, "He's stable for now. Mairead and the pixies did everything they could to patch him back together enough for the doctor to have *something* to work with."

I push out a breath I didn't realize I was holding.

"But it's still up in the air. All we can do now is wait and pray," he tells us.

We all turn when the door to Maddox's room opens, Fin stepping out quietly.

I stride toward him, "Can I go in now? I need to see him."

He nods, putting his arm around me as he leads me into the room where Thomas and Kellan are standing next to the bed. They step back, letting me through to see the handsome warrior lying there, unconscious. It doesn't feel real, seeing him like this. I thought the sight of him in Áed's domain was gut-wrenching, but there are no words for the sight before me. He looks as if he's sleeping, but the binding wrapped around his blood-stained torso quickly shatters that illusion.

Sitting gently on the edge of the bed, I run my fingers through the thick, dark curls starting to form in his hair, letting my hand trace down the side of his face, following the path of the cuts and bruises marring his elegant features. I look to the group standing behind me, "What happened?"

Thomas speaks softly to me, his usually stony face wrinkled ever so slightly with worry. "We don't know. We were separated when we heard him scream, then we all headed straight for him. Liam was actually there before any of us, keeping Finnbhear's people away from him." It's a shock to hear of Liam's help, given everyone's history with him.

"And that brings us to what we are going to do about him," Kellan says, looking around at everyone there. "He's waiting downstairs with Mairead."

A single incredulous laugh escapes my lips, "I'm surprised *she* hasn't thrown him out yet."

Fin takes a seat in the nearest armchair, addressing the room, "He's pretty much begged to be allowed to stay here. He knows if he goes back after what he did in that throne room, they'll kill him."

"I want to object, especially after all of the things he's done and how horrible he's been to everyone here," I answer him. "But I can't, and it seems as if you four have already come to a conclusion also."

The disgusted scoff that comes from Claire's mouth surprises us all. "How can you all agree just like that to let him stay here, when we all know how awful he is?"

Fin looks to her, understanding her apprehension. "He might've done some questionable things, to put it nicely, but when you grow up like we did," he gestures to all his friends around the room, "yearning for affection and love from creatures that aren't capable of anything like it...you'll do more and more to try and win them over, but it's never enough."

The room is silent for a while, everyone lost in their own memories and thoughts.

Fin's statement makes me feel a bit of compassion for Liam. "If everyone's in agreement, then I think it's settled," I tell them. "He'll stay."

Everyone nods solemnly, except Claire, who looks as if she's fighting hard to swallow back a protest. Theo raises a steadying hand, assuring her, "This doesn't mean he has our trust yet. We'll keep a close eye on him, and if he does anything to give us question about his motives, he's gone."

The majority of the next two weeks are spent with each of us taking turns sitting by Maddox's side, sprinkled with discussions of Finnbhear and his inevitable retaliation, leaving us questioning when the faerie royals might make their move. The injured warrior hasn't seemed to make any progress, and it has been eerily quiet when it comes to the Otherworld, setting the whole castle on edge.

I feel as if I haven't slept in years when I finally lay down this time, but I refuse to get more than a handful of hours, not wanting to be away from Maddox any longer than I have to be. Even though I could've sworn I'd just closed my eyes, it's morning when I'm jolted awake by tiny hands pulling and prodding at me, along with tiny voices calling my name. I sit straight up in bed, looking around at the diminutive beings before my eyes focus on Flynn and Bramble who are jumping up and down excitedly.

"He's awake, he's awake!" Brambles high voice squeals, "He's awake and asking for you!"

She barely has time to finish speaking the words before I'm flinging open the door and rushing down the hall. His door opens when I'm only a few feet away, the sight of him standing there on the threshold driving me to move even faster. I crash into him, almost knocking us both to the floor, my arms wrapping around him, the joy at seeing him awake and upright making me forget that he's still hurt.

He lets out a small groan of pain as my body meets his. Immediately I try to pull away, but his strong arms wrap around me tightly, not letting me go. He shushes my protests as he picks me up, pulling me closer to him. Crying into the crook of his neck, I allow the emotions built up over the last few weeks to spill over.

"I am *so sorry*, Maddox," I rasp. "I was cruel to you when you only acted out of selfless love for me, and I held it against you. I almost lost you and I would've never been able to set things right. I hope you can forgive me, but I understand if you can't." My confession of guilt, the worry and fear of losing him, the regret for not forgiving him sooner, and the relief at seeing him alive all comes out in sobs against his skin, his hand running soothingly along my back, calming my tears.

"My love for you is no fickle thing, Mo Chuisle." His soft words coupled with the timbre of his voice are like a balm to my soul. "Forget it all. It's done and over and we never have to go back to it again." He sets me down gently in front of him to look me in the eyes, wiping the tears away as he takes me in, just before his lips meet mine. The way he kisses me clears away all the guilt and sadness in my heart, leaving only room for him. He pulls away, leaving his forehead pressed to mine for a moment, breathing me in, before straightening fully to lock his breathtaking eyes with mine. "I am completely and fiercely in love with you," he assures me, "and that is all you need to hold on to. *I* am sorry that I ever made you question it."

Reaching up to settle my hand on his face, my thumb traces a few of the cuts still healing there; both of us unwilling to part with this moment. "You should be resting." My voice is gentle as I reprimand him, "You're still in no shape to be up and about like this."

He gestures to his biggest wound, "I'm better than you think, I promise." At my questioning expression he explains, "Mairead and the pixies have been coming in every night while the rest of you slept to patch me up little by little."

The brownie's kind voice sounds from behind us, "We didn't want to say anything until we knew that we could do it. We didn't want to give anyone false hope. He's still healing, but is nowhere near as bad as he was."

Turning to her, I pull her into a tight hug, letting my gratefulness be known through it, unable to find adequate words.

Before long the others have found us, all ready to see and speak to their friend. The other warriors take a moment to tell him about Liam, when Maddox notices him standing, self-consciously, just behind everyone. Maddox makes his way over to him, thanking Liam for his help. The rest of us begin conversations amongst ourselves, trying to make it less awkward for the newcomer.

After giving them some time, I make my way over to the two of them, still deep in conversation. Liam stops when he sees my approach, inclining his head to me. "Thank you for letting me stay here. I know it wasn't an easy decision for any of you."

"Everyone deserves a chance at forgiveness, Liam." I mean the words I say to him. "If it weren't for you, Maddox would've never made it out of that throne room."

He doesn't reply, but the gratefulness and relief written all over his face is evident.

"Why did you do it?" I ask finally, my curiosity peaking.

He's silent for a thoughtful moment before answering, the look in his eyes making me feel for him, for what he'd gone through. "I never thought there would be a way out, never dared hope for it." He waves his hand, indicating the group of changelings, "I grew up hearing this lot talk about some *One True King*. Then you come along, and I thought you were all crazy. Or maybe I was a little bitter, there was no way someone like that could ever exist, especially after all that we had lived through." He laughs a bit to himself, "But that was just it, we'd lived through it all. No matter how bad it was, we always made it through, and that couldn't have been pure luck. Then I saw everything that had happened between you two. Not only the curse broken, but the goodness and pure love there between all of you and living long enough to see other changelings being set free...It planted a seed inside that made me start thinking."

He huffs a laugh again, but this time I think it's to mask the wavering in his voice. "So I thought, 'Alright, *Great King*. If You *truly* exist. if You really can hear me...give me a clear way out.' And the next day, here you lot come waltzing as pretty as you please into Finnbhear's throne room, and I knew that was it."

Trying not to cry myself, I give him a kind smile, grateful that we were able to show him the light and be a part of the chain of events that changed his heart. The look on his face seems to be a mix of happiness and embarrassment at opening up so much to us. So I decide to lighten the mood a bit, shooting him a sheepish grin. "While we're at it...I'm sorry I stabbed you."

He laughs outright at that, shrugging playfully, "I've had worse, but I hear you have one to match now."

Everyone is still happily congregating in the hallway until Mairead, barely containing her joy at having all of us together again, ushers us all downstairs for breakfast, making us promise to wait about jumping into solving the next problem until we've at least spent some time just enjoying each other.

Chapter 25

A s I let out a quaking breath, Claire catches my shoulders with her hands, smiling sweetly at me. "You look beautiful, and he is completely and utterly in love with you. There's no need to be nervous."

"Now go out there and get your prince," Mairead says as she adjusts my crown of baby's-breath before nudging me gently, the pride she feels evident in her face and voice.

Taking one more steeling breath, I step out into the castle gardens, everything lit by the blue ethereal glow of thousands of sprites, with my simple white gown flowing gracefully behind me.

I round the corner of the hedges and he is there, more handsome than I've ever seen him, standing under the trees at the edge of the garden with the local minister. The second our eyes lock onto each other, my nerves vanish. My steps can't carry me fast enough, everything seems to be moving in slow motion. I can barely keep myself from running to him.

He's only been awake and healing for a couple of days at most, but after what happened in the Seelie Court, after I'd almost lost him, we knew we couldn't be apart any longer. Our friends helped us throw these plans together as quickly as possible.

Finally, I make it to Maddox. His eyes are alight as he takes me in, enveloping my hands in his as he begins his vows to me. "Of all the things I've had the privilege of doing in my lifetime, the greatest thing I'll ever get to do is love you. When you're lost, I promise to be the one to find you. When you're afraid, I'll fight for you, and when you're weak, I will carry you."

Maddox's voice behind me pulls me from the memories of earlier in the night as I stare up at the full moon, his arms wrapping around me. "You should be sleeping." His voice is soft in my ear, the lilt of his accent never ceasing to thrill me. "And you don't need to be out here in this, you'll get too cold." He pulls gently at the white fabric of his shirt, hanging loosely around my form.

I lean into his bare chest, resting all of my weight on him, "I'm completely fine. I just couldn't sleep; the excitement hasn't quite worn off." I crane my neck to smile up at him.

"You could've woken me, you know."

"You were sleeping too well, and you need the rest. You aren't completely healed yet, in case you've forgotten." I shrug as I continue, "I haven't been out here long, I just wanted to see the lake without having my life in danger."

We both laugh as I settle even more deeply into his arms, looking out over the moonlit loch. After our small, simple wedding ceremony, Mairead and Claire had surprised us by leading us to the lake house which they had managed to fix up these last few days, insisting that we needed to have a place for just the two of us. We had gladly accepted and spent our first night as husband and wife here together.

The tiny stone house looks proudly out onto the water with it's one massive cathedral-style window. When I couldn't sleep, I could see the white orb of the moon reflecting off the surface of the water and decided to get some fresh air. It hadn't taken Maddox long to notice my absence. I had only just stopped at the edge of the shore when I heard his approach behind me.

"Besides, it looks like a storm is coming. I wouldn't have been out here long." I stare up at the pitch-black clouds just starting to move in over the horizon, the look of them reminding me of billowing smoke.

Maddox's arms go slack around me, startling me from my thoughts. My head snaps up to look into his face as he stares up at the sky.

"That's no storm."

"What is it then?" I ask, the urgency in his voice making my heart sputter.

He pulls me back into the lake house as he speaks, already headed back toward the door to leave. "Stay here, I have to go get the others. This house is heavily warded, do not step foot outside until I come back to get you."

I round on him, "*What is it*, Maddox? At least tell me what it is I'm hiding from!"

He only pauses long enough for his eyes to meet mine, silently pleading for me to stay put. "It's the Wild Hunt." And with that, he disappears out into the night, running for the castle and the other warriors sleeping there, leaving me to feel like I'd just been hit with a ton of bricks. Of course they hadn't forgotten, they were just waiting for us to be distracted.

Moments later I am pulled out of my pacing by a familiar, horrible braying. Stopping at the large window to listen, I notice fingers of black clouds have started to creep over the moon now. The hounds are coming, the harbingers of the Wild Hunt, and it sounds as if they're moving toward the sleeping village, getting closer with every passing second. All those people, completely unaware of the horror about to strike.

I know he told me to stay here, but Maddox still hasn't returned. It's taking too long, and I can't just sit here and cower while the village is being overtaken. My mind is made up in an instant, flinging me into action. I throw on the pants from the new fighting leathers the boys had commissioned for Claire and me, not even bothering to take off Maddox's billowing shirt before pulling them on. Sparing no time, I slide on my boots and run into the blackening night, grabbing the leather string usually hanging around Maddox's neck, before I cross the threshold.

It seems to take me no time to get to the quiet village, adrenaline spurring me on swiftly. Nothing is stirring, it's eerily still. Not a single noise sounds over the bellowing of the hounds moving in, like the very land around me is holding its breath, waiting for what's to come.

I breathe a small sigh of relief that there aren't any villagers out and about, thankfully all tucked safely inside their homes. Knowing that something had to be coming, and to keep any more innocent people from being taken, we had given them any and every protection against the faeries we could find. Rowan berries, iron, ash, and a whole host of other charms and wards to keep their homes, and whatever is inside them, safe. The fact that they'd seemed to listen to us willingly takes a bit of the edge off my nerves.

When I make it to the village center, the noise of the black dogs is joined by a cacophony of other noises within the growing black cloud that has now snuffed out the whole of the sky on the horizon. A stampede of hoofbeats and the squeals of horses, paired with the wild shrieking of the ghostly hunters riding them, are all growing closer and closer, and there is still no sign of Maddox or the others. It isn't long before the writhing blackness is close enough that it starts to blanket the ground around me like a thick rolling fog, making way for a group of obsidian hounds to emerge just across the square from me.

Spindly fingers of fear start to creep slowly up my spine at their guttural growls and depthless red eyes, but I'm all that stands between these nightmares and innocent people. I refuse to back down. Keeping my eyes on the creatures, I pull Maddox's leather necklace from around my neck and hope that it will work, even if it's not the warrior wielding the enchanted sword.

Saying a quick but urgent prayer, I utter the word needed and wait for the tiny sword to grow, "Fás." It does, and the relief washing over me helps to fight back the ever-growing fear in my gut.

The terrible hounds stalk slowly toward me, seeming to enjoy the tension building between them and their prey. But I know they're waiting for their masters, who are growing ever closer inside the wall of black clouds taking over the land. They'll be emerging any second now.

Planting my feet firmly, I fix the weighty sword in my hands, readying for the onslaught. The pack of terrible hounds springs into action, their Alpha taking the lead and the rest following a few feet behind him. I know there is no way I can best all of them, but I cannot give any ground in this fight. If I go down, I will go down swinging.

The Alpha is upon me in a breath. Due to no small miracle, I bring Maddox's sword up into the thick, shadowy body just as it lunges into the air, jaws readied to take me down. Righting myself from the effort of the strike, I notice that the other hounds have formed a wall behind me. Gnashing jaws inch closer and closer, blocking any way out, just as a member of the Wild Hunt emerges at a gallop from the wall of black clouds at my other side.

Shadows and darkness ripple off his body in waves as he raises his sword, readying his strike. I make the split-second decision to go after the hounds first, praying with everything within me that I can take them out before the ghostly hunter reaches me. Either way, I know I am on the losing end without any help.

I swing with all my might, sinking the steel into the head of another hound. That was a mistake. By some miracle or mishap, I managed to swing hard enough that the blade is stuck fast in its skull and I can't get it out. The shadowy rider is almost upon me and I have no way left to fight.

I can hear the hooves of the crazed mare growing closer with every breath and a heavy wave of panic crashes over me. The hunter is close now. I didn't realize just how close until I turn to face him, my body instinctively tensing for the blow that is only another breath away.

His black sword comes down hard. But instead of meeting my body, steel sings as Maddox meets the blow with his own sword, pulled from the skull of the hound not a moment too soon.

My knees nearly buckle with relief as I realize what's happening. The warriors, along with Claire and Liam, have finally made it and are taking on the rest of the hounds behind me.

Maddox swiftly defeats his opponent before turning to give me another sword, keeping his own for himself. "What were you doing out here alone? I thought I told you to stay put," he demands, quickly looking me over for injuries.

There isn't much time to speak before the rest of the Hunt will emerge from the shadows. "I knew they would get to the town before any of you could've made it. I couldn't just sit in that house, hiding, and watch it happen."

Before he has a chance to answer me, we're jolted by the sounds of familiar voices coming from the wall of shadows. It's everyone who has been taken in the last few weeks and more. All of their voices, Natalie's among them, seem to echo from within the shadows, all pleading for help.

Fin and the others, having quickly overcome the hounds, stop to listen also. I take a step toward the dark clouds, but Maddox's strong arm on my torso stops me abruptly. I glance to him, ready to protest, but his pointed look stops me. The rest of the stampede of hunters burst from the twisting wall of shadow, never slowing, and headed straight for us.

My head snaps to my husband beside me for a moment before turning back to face the onslaught. "If there is a way to get those people out, we *have* to try."

Maddox steals quick, questioning glances at his friends behind us before turning back to me, locking his eyes with mine. "We can get you and Claire there. but you have to be on your guard. I don't know what lies within that darkness."

I nod to him breathlessly, knowing my redheaded friend is doing the same beside me as he and the other changelings step up, creating a formidable wall between the Wild Hunt and the two of us.

Fin's voice rings out in front of Claire and I, never taking his eyes from the fight surging toward him, "We will clear the way, but as soon as you two see a path, take it. No hesitation, just go."

I look to my friend smiling weakly at me, knowing fear is gripping her as strongly as it is me. We squeeze each other's hand once, each trying to reassure the other, as the first sounds of steel upon steel ring out into the night.

They all effortlessly strike down their enemies, never showing any signs of hesitation or fear, only focus. For a fleeting moment I'm stunned at the warriors' fierceness. I've seen them fight before, but never like this, never this intense; it's magnificent. It hasn't ever been a mystery that they were highly skilled, but it's never been more evident than tonight.

I have to pull myself out of the trance of watching their every move when I see a pathway through the melee. Claire and I break into a sprint, taking the chance they've given us to get to the other side of the square where the shadows are surging. We've nearly made it there when a phantom horseman steps into our path, spear raised high above his head and aimed to strike.

Fin's battle axe splits the air between us, along with the head of the phantom, and the shadowy mare is taken down in an instant by Maddox's great sword. But Claire and I have gotten separated, each taking a different direction to get around the danger in front of us. I reach the wall first, the curling fingers of darkness seeming to reach out at me, swallowing up any light left around them. I hesitate for a moment, unsure and frightened of what may come, but I hear a voice from behind me.

"Go!" Maddox's clear voice eases my fear as he speaks to me between strikes, "I will find you." His steady eyes meet mine as I smile softly at him, taking a steadying breath before I turn and step into the blackness.

Chapter 26

I am enveloped in a darkness so deep I can't see my hands in front of me. It's an utter shock to my system. There is no light here at all, no sound at all, despite the screams we heard from outside and the clash of noises just beyond the shadows. The only sound now is my own heartbeat, loud in my ears as I blindly take a step forward, slowly making my way further into the blackness.

The very air hangs heavy with dread and fear. The writhing shadows seem to coat my skin with it. My head whips around, my heart leaping into my throat as the screaming suddenly starts again. At first it's sporadic, then it comes in every possible direction. I don't even know which way to turn. Terror threatens to freeze me to my spot.

"Please, is anyone there? I don't want to be here anymore." The sobbing voice of my childhood friend sounds from somewhere nearby.

I turn in the direction I think it's coming from, my voice barely a whisper when I speak, "Natalie?"

"Carlin?" she answers warily, the sound of her voice getting closer. "Carlin? Is that really you?" Her voice is a rasp.

"Natalie, keep talking. I hear you and I can get to you."

She starts to cry again. "You can't. I'm lost and I can't find my way," she whispers through her sobbing.

"Nat, yes I can. I'm getting closer; I can tell. Just keep talking to me and I'll find you." I push down the quaking fear in my voice, trying to reassure her.

"I can't leave," she rasps to me. "He says I'll never get out, there's no way out after what I've done."

The indignation in my voice seems to echo off the shadows around me, "Who says?"

"Me."

I hear Áed's poisonous voice right in my ear, seeming to come from everywhere and nowhere all at once.

"She knows all is lost, she'll never leave. You can't get to her, and you'll never lead her out." The voice of the wicked king is akin to the hissing of a snake, his words causing my friend to weep even harder. I can hear him laugh at her before he speaks from the shadows again, this time only to me, "She's keeping herself here, really. All the guilt she feels chains her here. She knows she'll never be forgiven, knows she's undeserving of it. All that she's done is trapping her here, I don't have to."

The self-satisfaction in his voice enrages me, but I take a steadying breath. I know a better way. "Listen to me, Natalie," I call out to my friend. "All is not lost. I forgive you."

Her weeping lessens as I speak to her through the blackness and shadows slowly begin to dissipate around my body with every word spoken. I can see her crumpled form starting to appear the smallest bit through the darkness.

"I hold nothing against you," my voice quivers with emotion as I continue. "No matter what you've done, no one deserves to be trapped in darkness like this. But Nat, there is a better way, and there comes a time where we *all* have to make that choice. I can stay here with you, trying to lead you out forever and it won't do any good. Ultimately, *you* are the only one who can make that decision. There is someone out there who is greater than all of this, just waiting for you."

I've made it to her now. The blackness has cleared from around me and she's knelt there on the ground in front of me, head in her hands as she sobs. I kneel down with her, making her look me in the eyes. "You need to choose, Natalie, for yourself. Even when we're out of here, you can't keep straddling that line between light and dark. If you do, just know that you've made your choice, and it won't be the right one. Do you want to live in the light or darkness like this forever?"

Her eyes are clear as she looks at me, my words taking root in her heart. But as she opens her mouth, she disappears from the shadows, even before she has a chance to utter a word.

"Who are you to think you can overcome us?" The seething voice isn't only Áed's, but some twisted version of the three Otherworldly rulers. It sounds as if it's coming from just behind me, so I swing for it, but my blade meets nothing.

"It doesn't matter who I am! I know what you are, and I am not afraid of you. You only have a foothold here because we humans gave you that power, not realizing the wickedness that lies underneath the beautiful masks. You're just gilded, wicked creatures seeking nothing but to deceive and destroy. You will be defeated one way or another." My voice echoes into the blackness.

Their voices keep taunting, coming from every angle, causing me to swing in whatever direction I think it's coming from. Fighting a battle with an invisible foe wears me down quickly and my strength is waning.

"One light," Áed's voice makes me turn again, striking for nothing. "One *little* light, alone, in all this darkness. You're doomed to be snuffed out, devoured."

A heartbeat of silence passes as I look around. I'm knocked onto my back swiftly, the maw of some dark creature snapping inches from my face. It's Áed, I realize as he taunts again, the shadows taking the form of a great beast around him.

He's right. I'm completely alone here.

Fear takes hold then, causing me to shrink into myself, the shadowy jaws snapping just inches from my face so close I think I can almost feel breath coming from the horrible maw. Even if the little bit of darkness around me is at bay, there is still so much more to go. And for a moment, I'm truly fearful. I'm lost and alone in the rage of this terrible wicked storm, and I've let him wear me down to my last shred of strength.

"Don't let him fool you. Help is coming," a still, small voice sounds in my mind.

From somewhere within the shadows, I hear Maddox's voice then. "I see you Carlin. I'm almost there."

"Just hold on, Carlin! Help is here," Claire's frantic voice is close too.

"Get up," says the voice again, calming my fears. "Take a stand."

I push myself off the ground, rising up to face the darkness again.

"You're alone, caught in my web. Your help isn't here." Áed comes into view just in front of me this time, his voice dripping with hate and wickedness.

"She is not alone." Claire's voice sounds just beside me now, full of defiance.

"Where is your help? Your Great King?" Áed taunts again, "I don't see him."

"He sent me." Maddox's voice sounds from behind the wicked king, just before his sword severs the head from his shoulders.

The shadows begin to clear then, shrinking back toward the foul place they came from. We're finally out of that horrid darkness and relief washes over me, tears beginning to fall.

"You're alright, Mo Chuisle." Maddox pulls me tightly to his chest. "It's finished, they're all gone. It's done."

As quickly as it started, it's over and a strange stillness has settled over everything. I look around, in shock or awe I'm not quite sure. We made it. The darkness is gone and so are all the evil and vile things that came with it: Áed, Mab and Finnbhear among them. The Otherworldly Rulers were taken out by the very warriors they had trained to fight their kind.

All my friends are standing there, Natalie included, unharmed and speechless as we take in the now peaceful night around us. Villagers emerge from their homes to look around, wide-eyed after what they'd awakened from their sleep to witness.

"Is it over? Are they gone?" one of the villagers asks hesitantly.

"Their rulers are," Fin says quietly, still breathless from the fight. "And I wouldn't expect the creatures that came with them to show themselves for a while."

A few of the murmurs from the crowd catch my attention. A small group of villagers who had been still on the fence about giving Maddox their trust as a leader are fully behind him now. Their doubts have been soothed by what he, and the rest of us, have done to protect the villagers tonight.

I feel Maddox take in a deep breath behind me before he speaks, addressing the people who are obviously waiting for something to be said. "For too long we have allowed evil to have a foothold here, some out of ignorance, and others out of denial. But there is no room for either anymore. No more will I allow any of you to be deceived and ensnared, becoming slaves to that darkness. It ended tonight. If you knowingly choose to walk down that path, so be it, but no one will ever be pulled in by deceit again."

He continues addressing the crowd drinking in his words, every bit the gracious ruler. "And please know, even though I will hold the title of *king* here, there is only One True King, and I am just an ambassador of His kingdom." He gestures to the whole of our group standing behind him, "We all are."

Epilogue

"**C**an I open my eyes yet?"

        I laugh as Maddox leads me somewhere within the castle, my golden coronation gown swishing quietly around my feet as we walk. We have a quick stolen moment alone after the event and he, apparently, has a surprise for me.

It's been a few weeks since that final battle with the horrors of the Otherworld, and people who had been lost for years began emerging from the tunnels of the Underworld, no one being left to hold them there any longer. The villagers, still overwhelmingly grateful for our actions, decided to formally recognize us as their leaders and not just the rulers of the Otherworldly creatures on this side of the gate.

The preparations began immediately for a coronation ceremony, with Mairead at the helm, but Maddox has also had something up his sleeve, not allowing me anywhere near the ballroom, which is where I suspect we are headed now.

My heart is still swollen with pride at the memory of my view from the old thrones at the head of the local chapel, filled to the brim with the people most important to us. Our friends and family had all beamed with pride as we took our vows to protect this realm from the remaining evils of the Otherworld.

A knowing smile had grown on my lips as my eyes settled on Natalie and Liam together, a sweet bond forming between the two of them, both feeling like they'd been through something only the other could understand.

"Open your eyes, Mhuirnín."

I look to Maddox, so handsome standing there in his crown, eyes alight with love and excitement as he glances pointedly up at the ceiling. My gaze follows his and the sight before me takes my breath away. The tiles depicting the story of the stolen prince have been moved around and even added to.

"It's the story of us," he says softly in my ear.

And it is. The céili, the night of the ball, my fight in the Underworld for him, all the way to that final battle and, ultimately, our coronation.

Turning slowly, I take in every detail of the beautiful artwork. The feel of his eyes on me is palpable.

"I wanted to thank you, for loving me when I was nothing." He speaks into my ear as I wrap my arms around him, unable to find adequate words for what I'm feeling.

Pulling back, I lock my gaze with his, "You were never nothing."

The well of emotions behind his striking eyes is impossible to miss as he bows gracefully, kissing my hand. "Would you allow me the pleasure of a dance?"

I feign shock, placing my hand over my heart, taking pains to make sure my own dainty crown doesn't slip. "I seem to recall being told something like, *Maddox doesn't dance.*"

The playful sparkle in his eyes makes my heart sputter as he takes me into his arms, spinning me into a graceful waltz around the empty ballroom. "With you I do."

Pronunciation Guide

Ceíli – Kay-lee
Mairead – May-reed
Mhuirnín – Voor-neen
Mo Chuisle – Mow Kooshla
Tír na nÓg – Teer-na-nog
Finnbhear – Fin-a-var
Áed – Aid

Acknowledgments

First and foremost, I want to thank God. Thank you, Lord, for allowing me to write this book, for giving me the ideas, means and courage to see it to completion. There were many times I felt like throwing in the towel but that still, small voice wouldn't stop urging me to keep going.

Now, onto my family: Eric, Isaac, Momma & Shane, Grandma & Poppa, Marlene and many more. There aren't enough words to express how grateful I am for the encouragement, the support, and the help each and every one of you gave. You all will never know just how much you each helped to keep me motivated. Whether it was a quick question about the progress of my manuscript, listening to me gush about my characters or offering financial help, you all had a part in making sure this story went farther than my own computer. I love you all!

I would also like to thank my editors, Arielle Bailey and Miriam Ellis. You two were the best a newbie writer could ask for. Thank you both for being patient with me, my many questions and mistakes. Thank you for being kind and helpful with your critiques and edits and not crushing a novice writer's dreams.

To fellow author Morgan G. Farris, thank you for being a friend and mentor through this process, even from the very start. You were always open and welcomed my many questions along the way and I am very thankful for that.

A huge thank you to David Gardias from bestselling-covers.com for making my vision come to life with your amazing work on the beautiful cover art and also for being patient and kind while I struggled to figure things out on my own.

Alex Robertson Cash at Moments by, Alex, thank you for the beautiful and professional author headshots! You helped to make my book a finished product.

And lastly, thank you to everyone who has picked up this book and given it a chance, you all are playing a part in making my dreams come true. I hope and pray that this book will not only be a source of enjoyment but encouragement to you.

About the Author

Kelsey Chapman spent most of her life living in daydreams before finally taking the leap to put them to paper. Dreamt up to get through hard times as a teenager her debut novel, Unmasked, is one such story. Born and raised in Northeast Alabama, she now lives there with her husband and son, enjoying reading, writing, baking and spending time with family.

Printed by BoD¨in Norderstedt, Germany

9 798988 257714